GIAN

THE TRASSATO CRIME FAMILY, Book #1

BY LISA CARDIFF

GIAN

Limitless Publishing, LLC
Kailua, HI 96734
www.limitlesspublishing.com

Formatting: Limitless Publishing

ISBN-13: 978-1-68058-693-0
ISBN-10: 1-68058-693-9

CHAPTER ONE

Evangeline

I hate silk boxers.

Oddly, this thought floated through my mind as I threw Kevin's last pair of silky blue boxers out the front window onto the tree-lined street. You'd think when his clothes, shoes, and other personal effects tumbled out the window of the brownstone, somebody would stop and ask me what the hell I was doing. That's what would have happened in my hometown—except I lived in Brooklyn now, and nobody cared enough to pull their ear away from their cell phone long enough to question me.

I sat down on the couch and lifted the last sip of Bordeaux to my lips. Drunk, and vindictively happy, I had polished off two bottles of Kevin's precious 2009 Chateau Lafite-Rothschild. I think it retailed for around two thousand dollars, and it probably wasn't meant to be inhaled by one person over the span of an hour, but fuck it. I didn't give a shit. When faced with the decision to throw them

1

out with the rest of his crap or drink two bottles, I decided somebody might as well enjoy them. I had. There's nothing like four thousand dollars of liquid courage to make me realize my seriously sad excuse for a life had to change.

Picking up my phone, I contemplated Kevin's tenth text message in the last two hours. The first one made me cry. This one made me giggle hysterically. It was the kind of laugh that could only be found at the bottom of a bottle of wine…or two.

Kevin: *Evie, please forgive me. It will never happen again. I love you, only you. Nobody can replace you. You're my everything.*

I guess I preferred it to his initial excuse, when he tried to convince me the sex meant nothing, that it had been part of the creative process. Seriously, did he really think I was an idiot? Yes, he did, and I didn't disagree. Somehow, over the last year, he had sucked the life out of me until I transformed into someone I didn't recognize, a shell of my former self.

With the last of my tears drying on my face, I considered throwing my phone out the window with the rest of his stuff. After all, he'd paid for the phone, the brownstone, my car, my clothes, my shoes, and my entire fucking life. Not one thing in this entire apartment belonged to me. I should probably throw myself out the window and leave the rest of the shit here because other than me, every last item belonged to him.

I picked up one of his shiny white marble

coasters, sitting on his perfectly polished espresso-stained coffee table. I rolled it between my fingers, contemplating my life. A few seconds later, I tossed it at the original artwork of Ana Ivanka, his latest conquest in the art world. Foolishly, I believed his little protégés were learning the ropes from the incredibly talented and renowned Kevin Ryder. Apparently, I had missed the mark by a cornfield-wide margin. Now I understood it clearly. For Kevin, the ropes meant painting and fucking. Mostly fucking.

Dumb, right? No wonder none of his protégés were men. He claimed it had something to do with the creative synergies between men and women, which in reflection, really meant, "I like fucking random artists on the side."

Granted, I missed plenty of clues over the last year. No, missed didn't adequately describe my behavior.

Dismissed.

Rationalized.

Ignored.

Overlooked.

All four words more accurately described my behavior when the truth flashed in front of my face like a neon sign on a daily basis.

While I could attribute my behavior to many things, it all came down to one defining event. Exactly one year ago, I'd ruptured my Achilles tendon while auditioning for what could have been my third role on Broadway. At the time, reviewers heralded me as the next big star. I was a shoo-in for a lead part, or so all my friends in the know told me.

Regrettably, like all good things, my life had been ripped apart in a matter of seconds. One minute I leaped into the air, the next I landed and rolled my ankle. I heard a snap, and flames shot up my leg. I didn't need to see a doctor to know it was more than a sprain.

Unable to work and lacking resources, I desperately clung to all the remaining pieces of my life. At the time, that meant investing my energy in my relationship with Kevin. In retrospect, I should have packed my meager belongings and caught the first flight home.

Now, I found myself in the same situation, only amplified one hundred times. I didn't have any money, aside from the three hundred dollars in my wallet and the joint bank account I shared with Kevin, which I refused to touch. I hadn't contributed any money to the account.

Dropping my head into my lap, I screamed a slightly unhinged and utterly unbalanced cry. It didn't begin to relieve the stress building inside of me with every passing second. What could I do? I was jobless, moneyless, and homeless, or would be when I rallied enough courage to walk out the door.

When I left my mom's house two and a half years ago, she warned me New York would eat at my soul until I became a hollow shell. I laughed in her face because I didn't think history would repeat itself. Unlike her, I wouldn't settle for being a second-rate dance and acting teacher in a little-known town in Nebraska. I refused to give up until I had the world in the palm of my hand.

In my mind, I had more discipline and talent than

my mom, and that was all I needed. Unfortunately, neither of those things meant much in New York. It might open a door or two, but to keep that door open, I needed connections, lots of connections, more than a girl from Nebraska could ever dream of having, and a really good string of luck.

The buzzer rang. I opened the door to find Carmela Trassato's hopefully cautious face on the other side. I'd met Carmela in a coffee shop a few days after I moved to New York. Hopelessly lost, I'd asked her for directions to an audition, and she'd escorted me there. We exchanged phone numbers, and slowly, she became a permanent fixture in my life.

"Hi, Evie."

"Hey, Carmela," I responded, opening the door wider, welcoming her into my soon-to-be ex-apartment owned by my soon-to-be ex-fiancé.

"I guess I'm a little late to stop the shit storm." Carmela pushed her not quite black hair away from her face as she looked around my normally meticulous apartment.

"Yep, and I already drank his precious bottles of Bordeaux, so I can't even offer you a really good glass of wine." I kicked the door shut with my foot, enjoying the black smudge my lace-up pale pink flats made on the pristine white paint. Kevin would freak when he saw it.

Carmela flopped down on the sofa, propping her feet on the coffee table, another thing that would drive Kevin crazy. He never liked Carmela. He said she was too aggressive. Most likely, because she always called him on his lies and pretentious behavior. She saw through everyone. She had to. She came from a huge Italian family that I suspected had more than a few unsavory connections. She never admitted anything, and anytime I questioned her, she changed the subject so skillfully I barely noticed until a few hours later.

"Do you think he'll let you stay here when he sees the debacle on the sidewalk?" Carmela picked up the empty bottle of wine and inspected the label.

"He says it won't happen again."

"And you believe him?" Carmela asked, raising her beautifully sculpted eyebrows, the kind you can only find in a salon.

I sighed. "No. I'm not that dumb."

"Thank God." She raised one hand into the air. "Finally. You've seen the light. Are you telling me I won't have to endure another moment in his company?" She never referred to Kevin by his name. She called him the prick, the art douche, or *scecco*, which I think loosely translated to jackass.

I shoved her shoulder lightly. "About time, huh?"

"No comment." She tossed the empty wine bottle on the floor. A few deep burgundy drops splattered on the white and black cowhide rug. "So what's the plan?"

"I don't have one. I'm done with Kevin, though."

A disbelieving look flashed across Carmela's face, and while I hated that she doubted my conviction, I understood. I had overlooked so much of Kevin's crap in the past six months that I barely believed myself.

"For good this time. I promise."

Carmela shifted toward me and pointed at my ankle. "How's physical therapy going? Do you think you can start auditioning again?"

My stomach bottomed out, mirroring the trajectory of my life. My gaze bouncing around the room, I considered my words. I settled on the truth. "I've been lying to you. I haven't gone in a really long time."

Her almond eyes narrowed. "What qualifies as a really long time?"

I rubbed my tear-stained face. "I haven't been to rehab in nine and a half months. I haven't tried to dance since the day I fell." My voice wavered, and I wondered when Evie from Nebraska disappeared and this weak, pathetic girl hijacked her soul. If someone told me I would be in this position after living in New York for a little over two years, I wouldn't have believed it. I was better than this. A better dancer. A better actress.

Somehow, after I met Kevin, my life fell apart. First my career, then my ambition, and slowly my friends disappeared one by one, except Carmela. Now, I only had a worthless ex-fiancé to show for my life.

"Do you still want to act on Broadway?"

"I do, except every time I think about what the doctor said, I want to curl into a ball and die."

The corners of her lips tugged down into a frown. "The doctor said if you finished rehab, you could dance again."

I rubbed my hands along my thighs. "Not exactly. He said I *might* be able to dance again, but

7

that he couldn't guarantee anything." I lowered my voice. "A ruptured Achilles tendon can be a career-ending injury for a dancer."

"So you gave up without knowing for sure."

"I was busy," I lied. In actuality, the thought of packing up my bags and crawling back to Nebraska scared me to death. When Kevin proposed, I seized the opportunity to focus on something other than the end of my childhood dreams. I put my career on hold and micromanaged every detail of our wedding plans.

Carmela jumped up and clapped her hands together. "Well, let's pack your stuff and get you out of here before Kevin shows up. I'm not sure you're strong enough to face him yet."

I didn't bother arguing with her. "Where to? I don't have money to rent my own place."

Carmela looked pointedly at my finger, where I still wore my two-carat custom-designed wedding ring. "Pawn your engagement ring. It will pay for a few months of your living expenses and physical therapy, and you always have your credit card. In the meantime, you have me, and that means you can stay at my place until you figure out how to put the pieces together."

Exhaling loudly, I twisted the ring on my finger, contemplating pawning it for cash. I'd never liked it. I told Kevin I wanted a sapphire, not a diamond, and something rough-cut, not refined and uptight like the ring he'd designed for me. He never listened to me. Everything revolved around him and what he wanted.

When Kevin had to work late, I convinced

myself he had to finish a few commissioned paintings. When I saw a red lipstick stain on his collar, I attributed it to paint. When he spent an entire party introducing his protégée to all of his friends and ignoring me, I called him a good mentor.

"Don't you think I should give it back?"

Carmela's eyebrows shot up. "No. You caught him screwing another woman in his art studio. Consider it your severance package."

"Yuck."

"Which part?" she questioned.

"Both." I took off the ring and stuffed it into my pocket. It didn't mean anything, and all things considered, it never had. "I feel so dumb," I mumbled.

"Why? He took advantage of you. *He* should feel dumb. You, on the other hand, should feel lucky you found out before you married him."

I shoved my tangled strawberry blonde hair away from my face. "Not about the cheating—although, that is embarrassing enough. After we'd been dating for a month, I asked him what color my eyes were."

"And?" she said, planting her hands on the sides of her hips.

"He said blue. Can you imagine? My eyes aren't even close to blue. What a fucking loser. He could have said brown or hazel. He said blue. Even though I knew better, I stayed with him because I wanted the fairytale." I tipped my head to the ceiling. "Now look at me."

"You're right where you're supposed to be."

I scoffed. "Broken, depressed, and

unemployable?"

"No, you're smarter and more worldly. Every girl needs a reality check now and then, and now that you've had yours, you'll be smarter next time."

My phone vibrated on the coffee table again. "He's getting impatient," I commented, watching the phone skip across the slick, dust-free surface.

"Then let's move."

CHAPTER TWO

Gian

"No way, Carmela. I won't consider it." I picked up a towel, wrapped it around the back of my neck, and I walked out of the home gym and into my adjacent bedroom. "Stop asking."

"Gian, you need a personal assistant, someone to stock your kitchen, water your plants, go to the dry cleaners, and stop by the house when you're out of town," she called after me. Her four-inch red heels clicked against the wood floors with every step. "You're rarely home between running the nightclub and your social life. What's the big deal? You'll barely see her."

I halted mid-stride and swung around, glaring at my twin sister. "The big deal is that I don't want a fucking assistant. I don't need anyone nosing around in my business, especially someone who's not family. I can't have random people in my space. You know that. Besides, I don't need anyone else when I have you."

11

Carmela folded her arms across her chest. "Evie isn't random. She's my friend, and I don't have time to do any of that stuff for you. I have a life too, you know."

"I don't want a stranger in my home."

Carmela huffed. "Fine. Can you find a position for her at the club? She could do inventory or bartend."

"Does she have any experience?"

She shrugged. "What's so hard about counting bottles or pouring a drink?"

"It's a lot harder than it looks." I rubbed the towel down the side of my face.

She smiled and batted her eyelashes. "Please, Gianluca. I need you," she said, drawing out my full name. I hated that name. Nobody called me Gianluca except our dad and strangers.

"You're not going to let this go, are you?"

"No, and you're going to help me."

"What makes you think that?"

"Because you're my favorite brother, and you're always there when I need you. Right now, my really good friend needs you, which by extension, means me."

"I don't have any openings."

She clipped the back of my head with her open palm like my mom had when I was a kid. I fucking hated it. "Well then, make one."

"Easy, Carmela. No need to get violent. I'll find something." I leaned my hip against the wall, placing myself out of striking distance. "Tell me about this friend."

"What do you want to know?"

"For starters, what's her name?"

"Evie Jeffers."

"Am I supposed to know the name or something?"

Carmela shrugged. "Maybe. Maybe not."

"Great." I rolled my eyes. "Tell me what makes Evie Jeffers so special."

"Like I said, she's a close friend of mine, and she's had a string of bad luck. She needs a break."

"What kind of bad luck?"

"She's an actress and—"

I held up a hand. I didn't need to hear one more word. I'd dated an aspiring actress last year for three months. She'd tried to sell a sex tape of us to a few websites, thinking it would give her the exposure she needed to land a breakout role. I shoved my foot so far up the website owner's ass as soon as I got wind of it. Luckily, it never saw the light of day, and I learned my lesson. I'd had enough of fame whores to last me a lifetime. Besides, I needed to keep a low profile.

I'd been promoted from soldier to capo six months ago when our dad's health had deteriorated to the point where he couldn't work. At twenty-seven, I became the youngest capo in the Trassato crime family. If everything went my way, I'd be promoted to underboss or consigliere by the time I reached thirty-five. As for Dominick, the boss and my uncle, I wanted to position myself so I was on the short list to be his replacement when the time came.

Without question, my promotion had pissed off a few people, and I couldn't risk adding fuel to the fire. My dad only agreed to step down if I succeeded him. Some of the older soldiers didn't like it, especially Carlo, but he could go fuck himself. Everyone knew he had the tendency to disappear when it came time to do the "heavy lifting." He'd always make up some pathetic excuse about being sick or not knowing how to find the person.

While I may not have been around as long as Carlo, I'd earned the promotion. I'd been doing my dad's job plus mine for a solid year after my dad was diagnosed with cancer. Dominick didn't fight my dad, which didn't surprise me. He encouraged made men to nominate their sons for membership, believing it incentivized the members to keep the omertà or the oath of silence.

However, Dominick didn't play games. If he thought someone had been taking unnecessary risks and endangering the family, or by extension him, he considered it a direct show of disrespect, and there'd be severe consequences.

I sliced my hand through the air. "You can stop right there. I'm not interested."

"You haven't heard her story, Gian. How do you know?"

"I can't have a personal assistant or someone working in my bar who will call attention to me or my business."

Carmela shook her head. "Evie isn't like Becca. She wouldn't do that. She's not looking for instant fame. She's a hard worker. She's landed a few big roles on Broadway, and her prospects were really promising until she hurt her ankle last year. She needs a steady income for a couple of months while she gets back in shape. When she's not working for you, she'll be at rehab and in the dance studio. She doesn't have time for anything else."

"She hurt her ankle a year ago?"

"Yeah? So?"

"Why is she still in rehab?" I'd fractured my wrist in a bar fight when I was twenty-one. I had a cast for six weeks, and I had to do a shit load of physical therapy for the next few months, but it sure as hell didn't interfere with my life for an entire year.

Carmela fiddled with the cuffs of the white shirt peeking out of the sleeves of her bright red power suit. "She had some other things going on that diverted her attention."

I pinched the bridge of my nose. "Like what?"

"She got engaged and moved in with her fiancé. She put off her rehabilitation to plan the wedding."

I raised one eyebrow. "Uh-huh, and where's the fiancé now?"

"She broke off the engagement."

"Why?"

"It's none of your business." Carmela lifted her chin and squared her shoulders. I knew that look. I had seen it countless times when she faced off with our mom. I wouldn't get much else out of her. Her stubbornness drove our parents crazy.

"Is the ex going to be a problem?"

"No," she answered without hesitation.

"Will I be dealing with a blubbering mess every day?"

"Absolutely not. Evie is a strong person with a

good head on her shoulders, and she's really talented. She just needs a little help right now."

"So let her stay with you until she's back on her feet."

"She has been. She doesn't want to be dependent on me financially until she starts making money. She wants a job, but if she finds a normal job, she won't have enough time to train or go to auditions. If you hire her, she'll have flexibility and a place to stay."

My brows snapped together. "A place to stay?"

She shifted on her feet. "Well, yeah. I thought she could stay where you take your...your whatever." She waved her hand. "You know what I'm talking about. The apartment above your club."

I chuckled. "What are you, in kindergarten? You can't say it."

She cocked her hip to the side. "Screw you, Gian. The last thing I want to talk about is my twin brother hooking up with all those random..." She shivered. "You know."

"You've got a point." I chuckled. "I'm not sure I'm the person to help your friend."

"Interview her, and if you like her, offer her a two-week trial period. That's all I'm asking."

Though my mind scrambled for a way to sidestep her request, in the end, I caved. I'd hire her for a trial period and terminate her when it was over. It'd be easy enough to scare her away.

"Bring her by the club tonight, and I'll interview her. That's all I can promise you."

She pressed a kiss to my cheek. "I knew you'd help."

"I have a feeling I'm going to regret this," I grumbled. "Now get out of here. I need to shower."

She held up her hand. "One more thing."

"What's that?"

"Don't hit on my friend. She doesn't need another asshole in her life."

"Got it. I'll keep my hands and mouth far away from her."

She narrowed her eyes. "And every other body part."

"Have a little faith in me. I'm not that bad."

"No, you're worse, and we both know it."

CHAPTER THREE

Evangeline

After crashing on Carmela's couch for a week and submitting job applications everywhere and anywhere, I didn't have a single viable job prospect. Well, I had one. Carmela's twin brother had agreed to interview me for a position at his club tonight. My stomach churned at the thought of working for Gianluca Trassato. I hadn't met him. I didn't know much about him except the little gossip I overheard from some of my actor friends when I introduced them to Carmela. Basically, they said he was a man-whore with connections to the mafia.

Common sense told me to stay far away from him. Unfortunately, I didn't have any other options except going home or running back to Kevin, neither of which I wanted to consider. Kevin had asked me to give him back the engagement ring, which I planned to pawn to fund my life. I hadn't decided what I should do.

I climbed out of the taxi and stood on the street

with my hands parked on the waistline of my skirt, watching the scene in front of me. Laughter floated through the air, and bits and pieces of conversations filtered into my ears. The line to the club snaked around the block.

Nightclubs weren't my scene. I'd successfully avoided them since I moved to New York City a couple of years ago. Initially, I worked too much to do anything other than meet friends for dinner. After I met Kevin, we went to art galleries and charity fundraisers.

Though Carmela had told me my name would be on the bouncer's VIP list, I fleetingly considered abandoning this whole adventure and going back to her apartment.

I can do this.

I need this.

I swallowed the lump in my throat and marched forward, weaving through the throngs of people to the front of the line. Holding my head high, I ignored every groan and unflattering comment aimed at me.

After giving the bouncer my name, I stepped through the open doors, pausing for a second to allow my eyes to adjust. The club was dimly lit with flashing lights. Music pounded from the speakers, vibrating my bones and muddling my thoughts. Writhing bodies moved on the dance floor, on the balcony, and in front of the bar. Thousands of teardrop-shaped crystals hung from the ceiling, reflecting the light and swaying with the music. It felt like I was underwater or in a cave.

I pushed, elbowed, and shoved my way to the

bar, ignoring three inappropriate touches in the process. Scanning the shadows, I didn't see Carmela anywhere. Just my luck, she was late.

"Excuse me!" I shouted, fighting to get the bartender's attention. Technically, I shouldn't order a drink. I was here for an interview, not a night of debauchery, but I needed something to settle my nerves. I made the mistake of answering a call from Kevin today, and he'd done his best to convince me to give him another shot. To my disgust, I briefly considered meeting him for dinner—then, I heard Ana's voice in the background, and I lost my shit.

Waving my hand, I leaned forward, resting one elbow on the counter. "Hello?"

"Hey, beautiful. Let me help you out. What are you drinking tonight?" a deep voice rumbled next to my ear.

Eyes narrowed, I glanced to the side, ready to shoot down the offer. Then, I froze when my gaze landed on Michelangelo's David in the flesh. Wavy dark hair neatly styled. A long, angular nose. Heavy-lidded, almond-shaped eyes. Sinful lips curled upward at the corners in a perpetual smirk. Expensive suit. Broad shoulders nearly twice the width of mine. Narrow waist. Thighs that...*oh shit*.

I lifted my head, meeting his topaz-colored eyes. The lopsided grin on his face told me my not so subtle perusal hadn't escaped his attention. Jittering my ankle in circles, I licked my lips. His eyes locked on the motion like a predator zeroing in on his prey.

"No, thanks. I'm good," I blurted out, desperate to end the encounter. Accepting a drink from him wouldn't kill me—though after the fallout with Kevin, I'd sworn off men for the foreseeable future. I needed to get my career back on track and concentrate on my goals, and only then could I consider inviting another man into my life, even for one night.

"It's only a drink. One drink." He grinned, his eyes somehow managing to look like fire and ice at the same time. "Unless you want it to be more."

My stomach jumped, and for a second, I couldn't breathe. "I'm sure you're busy with whatever guys like you do in places like this."

"No, I'm really not." He chuckled, and the sound went straight to my heart like someone injected me with a shot of adrenaline.

"Maybe later." I glanced over my shoulder, desperately looking for Carmela. "I'm waiting for someone."

My phone buzzed in my purse. I flipped open the flap of my clutch and read the text.

Carmela: Something came up. I'll be there in an hour. Don't you dare leave before I get there.

I groaned.

"Did you change your mind about the drink?" the man pressed.

My shoulders slouched, and I sighed. "I'd love one."

He rapped his knuckles on the counter, and the bartender magically appeared in front of us. "Marc, I'd like a Maker's Mark on the rocks, and lady would like…?" He directed the full force of his attention to me, looking at me questioningly.

"The same," I said weakly.

His eyebrows lifted. "A whiskey drinker, huh?"

"No." I exhaled shakily. "But I could use something to take the edge off."

He cocked one eyebrow. "Bad day?"

"More like a bad year."

"Do you want to talk about it?" He bent to the side and said something to the man sitting next to me, who immediately vacated his seat.

"No." I laughed. "And you don't need to pretend you want to hear my sob story either."

The bartender placed two lowball glasses on the bar top filled with a golden-tan liquid. I tossed back half of it in one giant gulp. Fire spread through my stomach, and the hair on my arms stood on end.

"Come on. I'm a good listener," the man prodded. He swirled the brown liquid in his glass, revealing two tiny red buttons on the cuff of his white dress shirt.

"Are you serious?" I said, studying the sharp, yet appealing, angles of his face and the strong column of this throat. His dark hair nearly brushed the collar of his shirt. I folded my arms across my waist, battling the urge to reach out and touch it. This was not good. I couldn't remember the last time a guy affected me like this. Despite all his practiced charm, Kevin never caused my heart to riot in my chest.

"Absolutely. That's what strangers are for." He slid his forearm along the counter and pitched his torso closer to mine, ignoring his drink.

Ignoring the bodies brushing against us.

Ignoring strobe lights flashing on the dance floor.

Ignoring everything aside from me.

Unwanted desire hummed through me so powerfully—I couldn't take my eyes off him. I was intensely aware of every pesky inch separating us.

"Fine." Crinkling my nose, I tossed back the rest of my whiskey and puckered my lips. "I'll give you the quick version. I caught my fiancé cheating on me one month before our wedding. I broke off our engagement."

"Ahh," he said, his grin widening. "This calls for a celebration." He raised his hand, summoning the bartender again. The soft weave of his dark suit brushed against my arm, and a shiver darted down my spine. "A refill for…?"

"Evangeline."

He edged closer to me. "Another drink for Evangeline," he said to the bartender, without breaking eye contact with me.

Electricity zipped through my nerve endings, and my stomach fluttered with anticipation. I blinked, unable to comprehend how such an insignificant touch could do so many crazy things to me. "And you are?" I asked, mentally cursing the throaty sound of my voice.

"Gian." He lifted his glass. "To a fresh start, new friends, and new adventures."

I clinked my glass against his and took a sip, mindful of the fact that I had an interview in an hour or so.

"You're rather innocent looking. You don't

come to places like this often, do you?"

Nervous laughter bubbled from my lips. "Just because I don't like clubs doesn't mean I'm innocent."

The corners of his lips twitched. "Then why are you here?"

I raised and then dropped one shoulder lazily, the whiskey warming me from the inside out. "Like I said earlier, I'm meeting someone here." I brought the glass to my lips again.

"Is that your way of telling me you're not leaving here with me tonight?"

"Um…" I choked mid-swallow.

I wiped my mouth with the back of my hand, training my gaze anywhere other than on him, and that's when I spotted Kevin. He pushed Ana's white-blonde hair away from her face, leaned in, and kissed her. My stomach plummeted to the floor, and my vision blurred at the edges. While I didn't want him back, I couldn't pretend seeing them together didn't hurt. He had texted and called me every day this week trying to get back together. What a piece of shit.

"Hey, look at me," Gian coaxed, his warm breath tickling my ear.

Hostility and remorse clogged my throat, nearly suffocating me. I couldn't believe I pushed my career to the back burner while I wasted a year of my life on him. Kevin caught me staring, and he flashed me a condescending smirk. I wanted to throw my drink at his head. Rather than cause a scene, I swirled around, facing my back to Kevin and Ana, and mentally kicked him in the balls.

"I'm sorry. I need to get out of here," I rasped, iciness seeping through my veins.

With the pad of his thumb and forefinger, he angled my head toward him. "What's wrong?"

I opened my mouth, fully intending to lie, only it didn't happen that way. "My ex is here."

"Where?" he asked softly without releasing his hold on my chin.

"Behind us. Two tables to the right."

He dropped his hand and quickly glanced to the side. "The man sitting across from the blonde-haired woman wearing the red dress?" he asked, flashing me a heart-warming smile that was a little bit playful and a whole lot wicked.

I nodded, smoothing my hands over the folds of my short A-line skirt that suddenly seemed hopelessly frumpy in comparison to Ana's flamboyant red dress with symmetrical waist cutouts.

"That's good," he murmured. He clamped his hands around my hips and scooted me closer to him. So close, I saw every inky spike of his eyelashes. He smelled of soap and a faint hint of spicy aftershave, and my eyes fluttered in response.

"Why's that?"

"Because he's watching us right now."

Alarm shot down my spine. "Are you serious?" When I twisted to catch a glimpse of Kevin, Gian's hand framed one side of my face, forcing all of my attention on him.

His thumb brushed over my bottom lip, and the air buzzed with tension. "Shh," he whispered, bringing his lips within striking distance of mine.

Butterflies exploded inside of my stomach. I begged my body to move away. It wouldn't listen.

I sucked in a breath. "What are you doing?"

"This," he answered, feathering his perfect lips across mine. "And this." He tugged me flush against him. "Put your arms around me, and give your ex a good show," he uttered against my lips.

I hesitated for a fraction of a second, then a rush of memories flooded my brain.

All the nights I had waited for Kevin and eaten dinner by myself.

How I put my life on hold to build a future with him.

The sounds echoing through his art studio when I caught him fucking Ana.

The countless times I suspected Kevin of cheating and I looked the other way.

I couldn't help wanting to hurt Kevin and show him I wasn't some pathetic clinger without options. I curled my fingers around Gian's neck and pulled him closer to me. His hand slid up my thigh, not far from the hem of my skirt.

"Is this good?" I whispered. His golden eyes held me hostage, and my pulse skyrocketed.

"Close." His lips crashed against mine. They were smooth and firm, and he tasted like whiskey—sweet with a hint of caramel and vanilla. I opened my mouth and let him inside. His tongue stroked mine, deep and unrelenting, devouring me until sparks of desire fired in me. Within seconds, I didn't care why he was kissing me. I wanted to wrap myself around him and lick every inch of his olive skin. My hand slid down to his chest and snuck between the buttons of his starched white shirt. My fingers toyed with the contours of his chest.

A moan rumbled from his mouth, and just like that, I was insanely turned on. Warm goose bumps showered my arms, and I buried one of my hands in his raven hair. I couldn't remember the last time I'd been so needy for a man. I clung to this stranger like I needed him more than my next breath. Maybe I did. Maybe he'd help me forget. Maybe he was the key to starting over.

He leaned back, severing contact, his lips swollen and his pupils dilated. "Not here."

"What?" I said, breathlessly unable to think clearly.

"Let's go somewhere more private. Follow me."

He threaded his fingers through mine, guiding us through the crowds of people. When we reached the rear of the bar, he pushed a door open marked No Admittance and led me down a darkened hallway. My heels clacked against the concrete floors, and my heart thrashed against my ribcage.

At the end of the hall, there were three doors. The one directly in front of us was closed. The one on the right had a lit exit sign above it, and the one on the left was open. He pulled me into the room with the open door and closed and locked it behind us.

"What is this place? Are we going to get in trouble?"

"No." He backed me into the wall, fusing our bodies together again. "Nobody will bother us." He swept my hair over my shoulder and buried his lips in the crook of my neck, tasting, biting, and sucking. God, he smelled good. Too bad I couldn't relax. My muscles tensed, and my stomach knotted. What the hell was I doing? I didn't know this guy. Carmela could be looking for me.

"Relax, Evangeline." His hands slipped beneath the hem of my cropped top, watching me with his eyebrows raised expectantly. "You can stop this whenever you want. We're just having a little fun, and I'd prefer it happened without an audience. Wouldn't you?"

The idea of hooking up with a stranger in the back room of a bar scared me—though not enough to convince me to stop—and he was right. I wanted to have a little fun. I wanted to feel the excitement of touching and kissing someone new. I wanted to do something different. Be someone different.

Nodding, the air whooshed out of my lungs. "Okay."

CHAPTER FOUR

Gian

The second she conceded, I snagged her clutch purse out of her hand and tossed it on the sofa to the right of us. If she were smart, she wouldn't believe a word out of my mouth, and she'd stay far away from me. Unfortunately for her, I was too much of a bastard to send her away. One taste wasn't close to enough.

With her pale, flawless skin and lithe dancer's body, she wasn't the type of woman who normally drew my attention. But *marone*, when she leaned over the bar to order a drink and her skirt lifted, flashing the sinful curves of the backs of her thighs, I had to talk to her. I'd never felt an affinity for a woman's legs in my life. I was more of a breast man, but one look at her legs, and I became a convert.

Conflicted vibes radiated off her, and part of me knew I should leave her alone, especially after the story of her ex-fiancé. I didn't want anything to do

29

with a woman still pining after another guy, not even for one night. That changed the instant her ex looked at her like he owned her. I took what I wanted, what she needed, and I had every intention of taking this as far as she'd let me tonight.

I twisted my fingers in her strawberry blonde hair, angling her head so I could see her entire face. Her wide brown eyes peeked at me from beneath her lashes, her gaze roving all over me, my skin blazing with heat. She swallowed back her uncertainty, her long, elegant throat flexing. A smattering of freckles dusted the bridge of her nose like stardust. I'd give my left arm to make her smile.

"Fuck, you're beautiful," I growled against her lips. A moan tumbled from her mouth. It had to be one of the sexiest sounds I'd ever heard. My tongue slipped between her lips, and within seconds, the kiss spiraled into something primal and untamed. Her teeth grazed my lower lip, and my hands were everywhere and nowhere all at once.

I slipped my fingers under the hem of her skirt, and her skin was every bit as soft as I had imagined. She intoxicated me with her smell—jasmine mixed with soap. Her hands skated down my chest, and she palmed the front of my pants. Sparks ignited under my skin, and I wanted to throw her down on the floor, sofa, anywhere. I needed my pants down and her clothes gone.

A sharp thud echoed against the wood door. "Go away. I'm busy," I barked, slipping my hand inside her damp panties. I wanted to fuck her so hard she'd forget her pansy-ass ex and any other guy who came before me.

Something slammed against the door. "Open the door, Gian. You're supposed to interview Evie tonight."

Evangeline's muscles tensed under my fingertips, and I groaned. "Sorry," I whispered next to her ear. "It's my sister. Give me five minutes to get rid of her."

She dug her fingers into my biceps, and her face drained of color. "Oh crap. You're Carmela's brother."

I raised my eyebrows. "You know my sister?"

"Gianluca, open this door right now!" my sister yelled. Evangeline shoved me away from her, and I stumbled back a few steps, reeling from the revelation that she knew Carmela.

"I'm Evie," she hissed. "The person you're supposed to interview right now."

I raked my hands through my hair. "Oh fuck."

"My thoughts exactly." She smoothed the front of her skirt and tucked her hair behind her ears. "Carmela, it's Evie. We're nearly done." She sat down on the sofa and crossed her long legs then snapped her fingers. "Stop ogling me and open the door."

I buttoned my suit jacket and rubbed the back of my neck in frustrated resignation. After a deep breath, I opened the door. "Hey, sis."

"What's going on?" Carmela asked. Her gaze ping-ponged between Evangeline and me.

I shrugged. "Nothing. I ran into your friend at the bar, and we decided to start without you."

She rocked back on her heels and pinned her

friend with her stare. "Are you already done?"

"Actually," Evangeline said, coming to her feet, "we decided it wasn't a good fit for either of us."

"What?" Carmela yelled, her eyes shooting daggers at me. "Did you do something to her?"

I held up my hands. "What the hell, Carmela?"

My sister aimed her finger at me. "You said you'd help."

"It's fine, Carmela. He said he'd make some calls for other jobs." A wobbly smile pulled at the corners her mouth. "I'm going to take off. I've had a headache all day."

Carmela squeezed her friend's hand. "What happened?"

Evangeline rolled her eyes. "I ran into Kevin, and I think he's still here, which means I want to be anywhere other than here."

"Okay. I'll see you at home in an hour."

"Nice meeting you, Evie," I said as she stepped into the hall.

She glanced over her shoulder. "Likewise."

"I'll be in touch to finish our...conversation." My gaze dropped to the back of her long, toned legs. I had no intention of letting her walk out of my life like the last twenty minutes hadn't happened. In fact, I wouldn't be satisfied until I had her naked beneath me more than once.

She paused, and her back stiffened. "Yeah, let Carmela know if you hear of another job."

After she left, her scent lingered in the air of my office. Fortunately, my sister didn't say anything until the hall door slammed. It gave me some time to clear her from my thoughts.

32

"So what really happened?" she asked, her hands on her hips.

"Nothing. We had a drink. We talked. You knocked on the door." I crossed the room and sat down behind my desk. "I think she changed her mind about working here when she saw her ex."

"Yeah, that makes sense. Do you think you can help her find something else?"

"I'll make some calls tomorrow," I said, scrolling through my missed texts. Dominick prohibited us from using cell phones for business unless we used coded text messages.

"That doesn't sound promising."

I read the message from Tony Red one more time. Tony Red had been nicknamed for his penchant for fast red cars and violence. Once, he drove a pickaxe through a man's stomach with so much force, he ripped up the floorboard when he pulled it out.

Tony Red: Meet you at the bar in thirty minutes. Have a Tom Collins ready for me.

To most people, it sounded like he needed a drink. I knew better. Tony Red and I had created our own language when I started working with my dad five years ago. The text referenced one of my soldiers, Tommy Calvo. Everyone knew he had a drug problem. To date, Dominick hadn't done anything about it. That was about to change. I received a tip that he'd been skimming money from deadbeats when we sent him to collect. He'd gone missing seven days ago. Apparently, Tony Red had found him, and they were headed here.

"Sorry, Carmela, I can't talk now."

She pursed her lips. "What's going on?"

"Something came up," I answered without looking at her.

"That sounds like code for get the hell out of here."

I chuckled. "It's nothing major, just a little meeting. I'll call you later."

She hesitated near the open door for a second and then she glanced over her shoulder. "Thanks for meeting with Evie. It's been hard watching her ex be such an ass to her over the last year. She deserves better. She's a sweet person."

My gut twisted. She'd kill me if she knew what actually happened with Evie. "Yeah, sure. I'll make sure she lands on her feet," I said, squeezing her shoulders.

She pecked me on the cheek. "Good, because I owe her. She stuck by me when Rocco died, and I want to return the favor now."

CHAPTER FIVE

Evangeline

"Oh shit. Oh shit," I repeatedly mumbled as I half-ran, half-walked through the bar. I didn't think my luck could get any worse.

My ankle.

My disaster engagement.

Running into Kevin tonight.

Throwing myself at Carmela's brother.

Now, I was back to square one because there was no way I'd work for Gian after hooking up with him. I couldn't believe I didn't recognize his name. Granted, Carmela always called him Gianluca and he introduced himself Gian, which sounded a lot like John. Once I saw them side by side, I couldn't believe I missed the similarities between the two of them. They had identical light brown eyes and the same glossy, dark hair.

I needed to forget how incredible it had felt to be in his arms, his mouth moving against mine. Or how close I was to begging him to strip off my clothes. Or how disappointed I felt when Carmela interrupted us.

My stomach heaved, and I covered my mouth. Oh my God, I hooked up with the male version of my best friend. With my hands trembling, I stepped into the street, frantically flagging down any taxi in the proximity.

I climbed inside the first one that stopped, and I finally felt like I could breathe normally. I gave the driver Carmela's address, laid my head back, and closed my eyes. Lately, my life had been one mistake after another. Tears snuck out of the corners of my eyes, and I wanted to slap myself. I was so sick of crying.

The taxi stopped moving, and I discreetly wiped my face with the back of my hand.

"It'll be twenty-five bucks," the driver said.

I reached for my purse—then, I remembered I had left it on the sofa in Gian's office. "Shit." I threaded my fingers through my hair. "I'm sorry. I left my purse at the bar. Would you mind driving back?"

The driver glanced over his shoulder. "Do you have money in your house? I can wait."

"I don't have a key. It's in my purse."

The driver rubbed a hand down the side of his face. "Are you serious? Your purse might not be there anymore."

I swallowed back the sobs edging up the walls of my throat. "I left it in the owner's office. Nobody will take it, and you can double the fare."

"The owner?" he said, his voice softer than a few seconds ago.

"Yes. I'm friends with the owner and his sister."

He pulled away from the curb. "I'll take you back. Don't worry about doubling the fare. I'm happy to help out a friend of the Trassatos."

Contemplating his swift mood change, my eyes narrowed for second. Maybe what my friends whispered about the Trassato family was true. I tugged on the hem of my shirt then decided it didn't matter either way. I had kissed Gianluca Trassato. So what? It wasn't a big deal. If the rumors about him were true, Gian had plenty of women coming and going in his life. In all likelihood, he had dismissed me from his thoughts the minute I exited his office. I'd be smart to do the same.

"That'd be great. Thanks for your help," I replied, already feeling better.

Fifteen minutes later, the driver pulled up in front of Gian's nightclub. "I'll be right back," I said.

"Don't worry. Take your time."

I headed directly to the bouncer at the front door, circumventing the line to get in the bar. It hadn't decreased much since I went in the first time. After a quick explanation to the bouncer, he unhooked the red velvet rope and let me inside again. Not stopping to look for Kevin, Carmela, Gian, or anyone else I might know, I darted through the crowds of people to the back area of the bar leading to Gian's office.

Unlike when I had followed Gian through the No Admittance doorway, a large man now stood in front of the door. He wore a black suit, an impeccably starched white shirt, and a dark tie.

"I need to get back there," I blurted out.

37

Folding his bulky arms across his chest, he glanced at me, a frown on his face and his dark eyes narrowed. A wave of cold rushed through me. Something about him made me grateful I hadn't run into him in a dark alley.

"No."

"I left my purse in Gian's office. I had a meeting with him earlier."

He pursed his lips, a dubious look on his face. "The answer is still no. He's busy right now. Come back in an hour."

I heaved a worn out sigh. "I need to pay the taxi outside, and I don't have any money."

He shrugged. "Find someone who cares."

"Can you go back there and get it for me?" I asked impatiently. "I left it on the sofa in his office. It's a black clutch purse."

"No. No one is allowed back there right now. Including me."

"What the hell am I supposed to do?"

He arched one messy eyebrow. "I don't care. Just find somewhere else to do it."

"Are you fucking kidding me right now?"

His dark eyes jerked to mine. "Look, lady, you can either come back in an hour, or I'll have someone escort you out of here."

"Thanks for your time." I spun on my heel. "Asshole," I said, flipping him off without turning around.

Admittedly, it was childish, but I'd gotten sick of men pushing me around. Gian had probably already moved on to some other woman for the night, and this time he added security so they wouldn't be interrupted. Well, he and his goons could go fuck themselves. If that man refused to let me get my purse or go back there to get it for me, I'd try the exit door I saw earlier.

CHAPTER SIX

Gian

Tony Red and Sal escorted Tommy Calvo into my office with a gun pointed at his head. His stringy dark hair stuck out in every direction, and blood dripped from his nose. Carlo followed them inside, his hands shoved deep in his pockets.

"Shut the fucking door!" I yelled at Carlo. I didn't know why Tony Red had recruited him tonight, especially when I was one second away from putting a bullet in Carlo's head. Some of the guys told me Carlo had attempted to persuade Dominick to take me out based on fabricated charges. If he didn't watch himself, I'd punch his ticket and worry about the implications later.

I dragged a wooden chair to the middle of my office and pointed to Tommy. "Have a seat."

Tommy shrugged and rolled his eyes. "Don't mind if I do."

I circled his chair with my hands behind my back. "Do you know why you're here?"

"I don't have a fucking clue," Tommy snarled, his nostrils flared and his eyes narrowed. "You better have a damn good reason because Tony Red yanked me out of The Smoking Gun in the middle of a lap dance."

"Where have you been for the past week?"

He stretched his legs out in front of him, his eyes fixed on the ceiling. "Taking care of my nonna. She's been sick."

"Don't fucking lie to me."

"I'm not."

I slammed my fists into his face. First, an uppercut to his jaw. Then, a left hook to his right cheek. And finally, one more punch to his nose.

A sickening crack echoed through the room, and his nose bent sideways. He slumped forward in his chair, cupping his face. Blood seeped between his fingers, dripping onto his shirt and pants.

I pulled a gun out of the waistband of my pants. "I strongly advise you to start showing me some respect, or you won't like the consequences. And yes, this came from him." I brushed my hand along my jaw to indicate I meant Dominick. To avoid being caught on a wiretap fingering Dominick for a crime, we weren't allowed to say his name out loud in circumstances like this, so we touched or pointed to our jaw.

Tommy dropped his hands, his eyes wild. "I'm sorry, Gian. I had some shit come up this week. It won't happen again."

"By shit coming up, do you mean skimming money from deadbeats to feed your drug habit?" I asked.

41

"I don't do drugs, and I would never steal money from the family."

I released the slide of my gun. "Is that right?"

He held up his hands in surrender. "I borrowed some here and there, but I'll pay you back."

"When?"

Tommy swallowed hard and then grabbed a white handkerchief out of his pocket and wiped his face. "Tonight. I can borrow the money from my brother." His brother wasn't part of the Trassato family. He owned a deli in Bensonhurst.

I pointed at Tony Red. "Check his pockets."

Tony Red grabbed Tommy by his collar and wrenched him to his feet. He pulled a roll of cash out of one pocket and a bag of white powder out of the other. He handed them both to me and shoved Tommy back into the chair.

I stuffed the roll of cash in my pocket. "How much is here?"

Tommy licked his lips. "Two grand."

"You owe me ten grand more."

Tommy nodded without giving me eye contact. "Okay. I can get it tonight."

"What about this?" I asked, holding up the plastic bag filled with white powder.

He rubbed his hands up and down his thighs. "Somebody gave it to me at the club. I wasn't going to touch it."

I threw the bag at his face. "Look at me when I'm talking to you." He glanced at me then looked away. His eyes were red and dilated. "You're a soldier. You're a member of this family, and you're walking around high as a fucking kite. People see you shoving drugs up your nose. You're making a fool of yourself, and you're making the family look incompetent."

"I don't do drugs," he said, shaking his head furiously.

"So you're telling me if I had you pee in a cup, it'd come back clean?"

"Fuck you." He jumped to his feet, and the chair fell backward, clacking against the floor. Contempt slithered across his face. "What I do in my free time is none of your business. If I want to do a few lines or get drunk, I'll do it. The family doesn't own me. You don't own me, and Dominick sure as hell doesn't own me."

In a matter of seconds, Tony Red had his gun out. I held up my hand to stop him, but he didn't bother looking at me for approval. He pulled the trigger.

Tommy tumbled to the ground with a loud thud. His head bounced on the floor like a ball. Blood stained the front of his white shirt. His dark eyes stared sightlessly at the ceiling.

I wiped a splatter of blood on my cheek with the back of my hand. "Tony, what the hell? Do you realize what you did? We weren't supposed to kill him."

Tony shoved his gun into the holster hidden inside of his suit. "I couldn't take his shit anymore. He mentioned him, he disrespected you, he skimmed money, and I was sick of him talking to us like we're a bunch of jerk-offs. If you get in trouble from the higher ups, you can pin this on me. I don't care. He deserved to die."

I ran my hands through my hair, my mind searching for a way out of this mess. Dominick wouldn't like that Tommy ended up dead. If we explained the situation, he'd probably think Tony was justified, but it reflected poorly on me that I couldn't control my soldiers. "Carlo, go out the side door, and pull the car around. Tony will carry out the body."

"What are we going to do with him?" Carlo asked. I threw the plastic bag of cocaine on top of Tommy's lifeless form.

"Dump his body along with the drugs on the street in the Bronx. Make the police believe it was a drug deal gone bad."

Carlo folded his arms across his chest. "What are you going to do?"

"Clean up this fucking mess." I gestured to the door. "Now move, before this blows up in our face."

CHAPTER SEVEN

Evangeline

Exhausted, cold, and beyond pissed off were the only words to describe how I felt when I yanked on the exit door to Gian's nightclub, and it didn't budge. I wandered to the corner of the building and watched the people laughing, talking, hugging, and stumbling as they left the nightclub.

Leaning against the brick wall, I brushed strands of my hair away from my face and tipped my head to the sky. Things like this only happened to me. I must have done some seriously bad stuff in my previous life to deserve my nonstop run of back luck, or maybe it meant I needed to suck it up, pack my bags, and move home.

Resigned to waiting until the full hour expired to go back inside, I closed my eyes. An air conditioning unit thrummed somewhere in the shadows. I shivered. The early summer air had grown damp and clammy since I'd sent the taxi driver away after exchanging phone numbers. He'd been surprisingly accommodating.

Less than thirty seconds later, the side door swooshed open. A dark-haired man in a pinstriped suit kicked a wooden wedge under the bottom of the door and jogged down the street.

I didn't waste a second. When he disappeared around the corner, I shimmied through the opening, careful not to disturb the wedge. I slipped off my heels so I wouldn't make any noise and tiptoed across the hall, the cold concrete stinging my bare feet. The door to Gian's office was cracked. I paused by the entrance, listening for voices. First came the low rumble of Gian's voice followed by a muffled voice I didn't recognize.

With one hand balanced on the doorjamb, I leaned forward and peeked inside. Unlike the bright overhead fluorescent lights in the hallway, Gian's office was dimly lit. When my eyes adjusted to the light, I saw a man with his arms and his legs spread wide on the floor, a dark liquid staining the front of his shirt. I leaned forward another inch. The man looked vacant, pale, and his eyes were fixed and unblinking. Then reality slapped me in the face. He was dead.

An involuntary gasp skipped from my mouth. My heart exploded in my chest, and my knees buckled. I reached for the wall to stop my fall, and my shoes slipped out of my grasp, clattering onto the floor.

My head jerked up, and my gaze collided with Gian's. His golden eyes looked like the fires of Hell, his face a blank mask. Long seconds ticked by. I rolled my neck, trying to clear my foggy brain and backpedaled a few steps. "I'm sorry. I didn't mean to intrude. I forgot my purse. I'll come back later."

"Evangeline, come in here. We need to talk," he said, his voice hard and forceful.

I swallowed the lump lodged in my throat. "I have to go."

He lunged forward, and I ran. Less than six steps later, his arms closed around my waist. My muscles tensed, and adrenaline surged through me. My heart drummed erratically inside my chest. My arms flailed wildly through the air like a wounded animal. I donkey-kicked backward, and he grunted. Within seconds, he whirled me around and pinned me to the wall. The bass from the music in the club vibrated the drywall, shaking my bones.

"Let go of me," I hissed through gritted teeth, ignoring the stomach-churning cocktail of anger and fear swirling inside of me.

"Listen," he hissed. "You need to shut the fuck up and do everything I say, or you will end up at the bottom of the Hudson River. Got it?"

I sucked in a breath. "My friends know I'm here. They're waiting right outside for me. They'll call the cops if I don't come out in a few minutes."

"You're lying."

I stared at the floor so he couldn't see my eyes. "You don't know that."

His frame curved over mine, his dark eyes imprisoning me, and my shoulders slumped. "I won't hurt you," he whispered, his lips brushing against my earlobe. I squeezed my eyes, hating the equal measures of lust and terror whirling inside my gut like a tornado. "But I can't promise my associates won't unless you play along right now."

Tears swelled in the corners of my eyes. "How? What do you want me to do?"

His thumb brushed over my lower lip, and I struggled to take a breath. "You can start by painting a smile on your face and acting like you're not afraid of me."

Every instinct told me to fight. My mind circled through a dozen or more escape plans, all with equally horrific endings. "How do I know I can trust you?" I said softly.

"You don't have a choice. You don't have any bargaining power right now."

"I won't tell anyone about this, not even Carmela. Let me go, and we'll never see each other again."

His mouth flattened. "No."

The pads of his fingers brushed over my nipples, and pleasure zigzagged through my nerve endings. Damn my body.

"I hate you," I whispered, glaring daggers at him.

"Get over it." A click sounded behind us.

"Put down the fucking gun, Tony. You're not killing my fiancée tonight," Gian said.

My eyes widened, and he captured my ear between his teeth. "Follow my lead." He spun around and enveloped me in a one-armed embrace.

Gian's friend silently inspected me like a wad of gum on the bottom of his shoe. "This chick is really your fiancée?"

"Yes. Why the fuck would I lie?"

Whistling, the man slipped his gun back inside

his jacket. "Fuck, Gian. When the hell did this happen? Why didn't you tell anyone?"

"Evangeline is a friend of Carmela's." Gian smirked. "You know how she is. She'd kick my ass if she thought I came within a mile of any of her friends."

"Yeah, you're right about that. Carmela is a firecracker." With a smoky chuckle, he held out his hand. "I'm Tony."

I didn't make a move to shake his hand—then, Gian squeezed my shoulder and gave me a minute shake of his head. I caved.

"Nice to meet you," I said, my voice as weak as my handshake.

"What the fuck is going on?" a man shouted behind us. "Who the hell is she?"

The man who propped open the door charged down the hall with his gun drawn. Gian shoved me behind him.

"Carlo," Gian said through clenched teeth. "Don't point a gun at my fiancée."

Carlo's eyebrows snapped together. "Why is she back here?"

"The door was propped open," I muttered.

"You left the door open?" Gian's body vibrated with barely restrained rage.

Carlo shrugged, his heated stare roving down to my thighs and back up. "I didn't think anyone would be dumb enough to sneak inside."

"Exactly," Gian countered, his voice icy. "You didn't *think*. Carlo, help Tony and Sal wrap up the body, and get it out of here. I have shit to do."

"We're ready to go, and Sal cleaned up your

office," Tony answered.

"Call me when it's done." Gian guided me into his office. "Sit," he said, gesturing to the sofa.

I plopped down and buried my head in my hands. "What do we do now?"

"We go to Carmela's house and pack your bags. You're moving in with me."

I lifted my head. "No fucking way. I don't know you, and based on what I witnessed a few minutes ago, I don't *want* to know you."

"Sorry, sweetheart." He twisted my hair around his finger and I shivered. "Until I know I can trust you, and I can convince everyone else to trust you, you're going to be living with me as my fiancée. It's the only way to keep you safe."

Sweetheart? What decade is this? And why do I like him calling me that? What is wrong with me?

I wouldn't call myself a feminist or anything. I liked a man who opened an occasional door for me and picked up the tab after a nice meal. Lord knew, I wished Kevin had done more of those things when we were together rather than acting like a self-absorbed asshole.

I lowered my lashes and tugged on the hem of my skirt. My nerves were fraught, and I couldn't speak, so I stared unblinking for a prolonged beat. "How does pretending I'm your fiancée do anything?"

"That's the way things work in my world. As long as you're my fiancée, no one will touch you. When things calm down, we can both get back to our lives, and this will all be forgotten."

I bit my lower lip to stop myself from crying. "I

don't get it. Why are you doing this? Why do you care what happens to me?"

Exhaling, he scrubbed his hand down his face. His eyes darkened like a storm was brewing inside of him, but the emotion disappeared nearly as quickly as it materialized. "Because you're important to my sister."

I picked at tiny threads in my skirt, trying to comprehend everything that had happened. "What are we going to tell Carmela?"

He loosened his tie and opened the top two buttons on his shirt. Reaching out, he gently brushed his fingertips along my cheek. "That it was love at first sight or that we've been seeing each other secretly for a while."

My face heated. "She won't believe us."

He managed a faint smile that failed to reach his eyes. I couldn't get a good read on this man. "It's your job to make her believe, sweetheart."

"Fine. I'll do my best." I squared my shoulders, desperately trying to suppress the dread and hopelessness raging through me. I needed to find a way out of this mess.

He tossed my purse in my lap. "Let's get out of here. We'll be lucky to catch Carmela while she's still awake if we wait much longer."

I rose to my feet, fleetingly wishing I had the power to transport myself back in time to the moment before I injured my ankle. I would have marched off the stage before I jumped, I would have broken up with Kevin, and I would have stayed far away from Gianluca Trassato. Too bad wishing and hoping were useless.

I followed Gian out of the building, feeling more alone than ever.

CHAPTER EIGHT

Gian

Evie stared at the door to the apartment she shared with my sister, her eyes shuttered and her mouth pinched.

I threaded my fingers between hers and tilted my head toward the door. "Do you have keys?"

She dropped her head and swayed into me. For a split second, I thought her knees would buckle under the weight of what we needed to do. I coiled my arm around her waist, drinking in the sweet scent of her strawberry-colored hair. Having her in my life and home would be a disaster, but I had made my choice, and I wouldn't back down after I gave my word. She needed my protection.

She cleared her throat and wiggled out of my hold, her sharp elbow wedging beneath my ribs like a dagger.

"Don't touch me." Her hand dove into a tiny clutch purse, and she pulled out a keychain with a lone key dangling from a pair of gold ballet

53

slippers.

"Get over yourself. You were about to fall."

Her eyes hardened. "I was not." Her shoulders snapped back, and like magic, the hesitation and powerlessness rolling off her disappeared.

I snatched the key out of her hand and unlocked and opened the door in a matter of seconds. Evie stepped in front of me, her head held high and her hands wrapped around her purse like it was a shield.

Carmela sat on the sofa, fiddling with her iPod. She caught my gaze, and her brows snapped together. "Hey, guys." She slipped off her headphones and rested them around her neck. "What's going on? Did you give Evie a ride?"

I glanced at Evie. She stood frozen, her muscles tensed, and her eyes wide like she didn't know what to say. "Um," she muttered. What was her problem? Either she sure was a piss poor actress or Carmela had lied to me.

I settled into the gray and white chevron patterned club chair. "Listen, Evie is going to move into my place."

My sister shook her head slowly like she didn't understand what I had said. "You mean at the apartment above your bar? I thought Evie decided she didn't want to work there."

I rubbed my hand over my lips. As much as I hated lying to my sister, I didn't have a choice. While our dad always did his best to protect her from the ugly side of being affiliated with the Trassato Crime Family, and I intended to do the same, that didn't mean she was in the dark. She'd seen enough over the years to know our family was about more than love, loyalty, and tradition. And if she didn't get the full picture as a kid, she sure as hell understood when her fiancé was rushed to the hospital with four bullet holes in his chest after a shootout with the DiTonnos.

"No. She's going to move into my home with me."

"What?" She jumped to her feet with her hands curled into tight balls next to her black lounge pants. "Why the hell would she do that?"

"Carmela," Evie said, her hand dropping onto the top of my shoulder. "Gian and I..." She paused, visibly swallowed, and plastered a megawatt smile on her face. "We're dating."

Carmela's attention locked on me like a sharp shooter. "Dating? You broke up with the art douche last week, and my brother doesn't date. He...he..." she flicked her wrist in my direction, "has meaningless flings that last hours, not days or months."

Coming to my feet, I slipped an arm around Evie's waist, acutely aware of the way her body stiffened under my hand. Carmela needed to shut the hell up so Evie didn't end up more suspicious of my motives and me than she already was. I needed her compliant and trusting if our ruse had any chance of succeeding.

"That stopped the minute I met Evie," I said.

Carmela's eyebrows shot up. "Are you seriously trying to convince me you are a changed man as of..." she glanced at the clock on the wall above her long rectangular fireplace with zen-like black rocks lining the bottom "...three hours ago?"

Evie leaned her head against my shoulder, strands of her silken hair tangling in my whiskers. "Carmela, we met a few months ago. We were friendly in the beginning, but it recently evolved into more."

"Wait. I don't get it." Carmela frowned. "Why didn't you mention you knew my brother?"

I squeezed Evie's waist, signaling her to let me answer. "I asked her not to. I know how protective you are of your friends, and I thought it'd be better to keep it quiet until her ex was out of the picture and she was ready to commit to a real relationship. We both knew we couldn't keep you in the dark much longer when you asked me to hire her."

"Are you serious, Evie?" Carmela asked, her voice climbing higher with every syllable. "You just got out of one fucked up relationship, and now you're moving in with my brother? My fucking *brother*? Do you realize how crazy this sounds?" She pinched the bridge of her nose. "Tell me you guys are only messing with me because this is absolutely insane."

I kissed the side of Evie's head. "Go get your things. Let me talk to my sister alone."

She leaned into me, her lips brushing against the rim of my ear. "I can't stand you. You know that, right?"

Ice seeped deep inside of my core, and my fingers dug into her waist. Even though this arrangement was a necessary hoax, she needed to remember her place. "You only wish you did, sweetheart, but don't worry. I won't hold it against you."

56

Evie's heels clacked over the honeyed hardwood floors, and a door slammed. I had saved her ass for reasons that were becoming increasingly unclear. She was going to fuck this up if she didn't reel in her emotions. Part of me wanted to follow her down the hall and rip into her for being ungrateful. If she barged in on any other capo, she'd be at the bottom of the Hudson River by now.

"Gian—" Carmela wagged a red-tipped finger at me "—tell me the truth. What's really going on?"

"There's nothing to share."

"You seriously want me to accept the fairytale you've tried to spin? I know you, and I know Evie. I don't believe for one second that you've changed your ways or that she would jump into another relationship. She planned to marry that pathetic excuse for a man until a week ago because she thought she loved him. She would never be interested in someone like you. Don't take this the wrong way, but you aren't boyfriend material, and up until right now, you've never pretended to be."

I shrugged, ignoring her attempt to bait me. "Maybe you don't know either of us as well as you thought."

She shoved her hair away from her face. "She doesn't keep secrets."

I glanced down the hall. What was taking her so long? "Everyone has secrets."

She sucked her lower lip into her mouth and grasped my hand. "Please don't push this relationship. Evie doesn't need someone in her life who thinks being faithful is optional."

I hesitated, a toxic cocktail of guilt, anger, and

regret sloshing around in my gut. "Trust me. I won't hurt her. I asked her to marry me."

She gasped. "What?"

I tugged on the collar of my shirt. Why the fuck did it suddenly feel like it was a hundred degrees in here? "We're engaged."

She studied me like she had suddenly acquired a superpower designed to ferret out lies. After a beat, her shoulders sagged, and she leaned against the flared arm of the sofa. "Please tell me this is a joke."

"It's not." I shifted my feet. "I wanted her to know I was serious about her, and I am. This is what I want, what we both want. Don't worry, though. We're not rushing to set a wedding date or anything. We'll take our time."

"You're not going to back off no matter what I say. Are you?"

I didn't respond for a split second, the echo of her frustration and defeat swirling around us. "No, and I'd appreciate if you didn't meddle in our relationship. We've got enough to work through without adding your opinions into the mix."

She squeezed her eyes closed. "Fine, I'll reserve judgment for now, but if I suspect you of cheating on her or playing games with her, all bets are off."

"Thanks." I kissed the top of her head.

"Is everything okay?" Evie said, pausing at the end of the hallway, a suitcase in one hand and an oversized purse in the other.

"Yeah." Carmela crossed the room and wrapped her arms around Evie. "Let me know if you need anything."

"I'll be okay. Don't worry about me."

I collected the suitcase from Evie's hand. "Did you get everything?"

"I think so." She made eye contact with my sister. "Thanks for everything, Carmela. The apartment, the pep talks, your advice. Everything. So much."

"Of course." My sister looked like she was going to cry. We needed to get the hell out of here because I wasn't entirely sure Evie wouldn't blurt out the truth if pushed.

I laced my fingers through Evie's and led her out of the apartment. The minute the door closed behind us, Evie yanked her hand from mine and wiped it on her skirt.

"Do you think she believed us?" she asked.

I took a deep breath. "For your sake, I hope so."

CHAPTER NINE

Evangeline

Footsteps echoed on the hardwood floors.
Clack.
Shuffle.
Tap.
I looked up from the half-eaten food, my hungry gaze landing on Gian. I shamelessly drank in the angles of his face, so bronzed in comparison to his white collared shirt.
A week.
Seven Days.
One hundred sixty-eight hours.
That's how long had passed since I made a deal with Gianluca Trassato.
For the most part, we communicated on an as-needed basis, and we barely spent any time in each other's presence. All told, I'd only seen Gian four times, this moment included. I was starting to think he didn't come home most nights, which should have made me happy, except it didn't. I was lonely.

My life had imploded, and I didn't have anyone to confide in anymore.

"Oh. I didn't know you were here," I said around a mouthful of food. "Lucky me," I mumbled under my breath.

He paused, his spine snapping straight. His dark stare raked up my seated form, finally settling on the wall above my head. "I came home to change." He tugged his shirtsleeves, and the light glinted off his mother of pearl cufflinks.

"Fabulous." I dragged my fork through my rice, now less appealing than it was seconds ago. "Well, now you can be on your way."

Five fluid strides and he bridged the distance between us. "What's wrong with you?"

I raised my brows, a closed-lipped smirk on my face. "Nothing. I'm perfect. My life has never been better. I must admit I underestimated the appeal of being under house arrest. It certainly has it charms."

He leaned his hip against the kitchen counter and folded his arms across his chest. The way his well-honed muscles pulled and stretched the fabric of his suit didn't escape my attention. In fact, I was pretty sure a demon butterfly took flight inside my stomach every time I looked at him. *Dammit.* I hated him. I hated this whole situation. He was bad for me. Sadly, certain turncoat parts of my body apparently failed to receive the message.

"I haven't stopped you from doing anything."

I tossed my fork on the countertop. It slid across the slick surface and tumbled to the floor with a loud clank. "You have someone following me." I waved my hand cheekily. "Why don't you strap a tracking bracelet around my ankle and get over it?"

Gian had Tony follow me everywhere like a living, breathing fucking shadow. It wouldn't have been so bad if he talked to me, but conversations with him were nonexistent. He didn't resemble the guy I met the night this whole thing started. He rarely made eye contact, evidently preferring to pretend I didn't exist. I couldn't blame him. He was only following his boss' lead.

Gian rubbed his fingers over his lips. Those same lips that were perpetually lifted at the corners like he was the keeper of all my dirty secrets, amusement shining in his amber-colored eyes. "You know, now that you mention it, that's not such a bad idea."

I yanked on the soft fabric of my favorite pair of boyfriend jeans and kicked out my leg. "Go ahead. You might as well."

His fingertips brushed over my ankle, and a jolt of uninvited heat surged through me. I jerked my leg away from him, and he sighed.

"This isn't a game, Evie. I'm doing this for you."

"Yeah, whatever. Just go."

He stared at me for a prolonged beat then closed his eyes, his nostrils flaring. "Are you going anywhere tonight?"

"Nope. If you haven't noticed, I don't have much of a life anymore."

His jaw fixed in a stubborn line. "You go to physical therapy and train every day. You don't have any expenses. I feed you. I house you. You don't have to work. Sounds ideal if you ask me. What more do you need?"

I threw up my hands. "I don't know. Maybe some human interaction. Maybe some freedom. Both of those would be a good start."

"I can't talk about this right now. I have a meeting at the club."

"Of course you do."

He raked his hands through his wavy hair, his eyes flashing with annoyance. "I'll get Tony. He'll be here all night if you need anything."

I didn't answer him. There wasn't anything to say. Living here was like living with ghosts. Tony rarely talked to me. Gian avoided me. I was sick of it. I was sick of everything. Everyone. I had spent the last year being Kevin's puppet, feigning interest in his art world, ready to sacrifice my dreams on the altar of marital bliss. Though Gian made the pretense of giving me the means to achieve my goals, I didn't have anything else. No life, no love, no friends. And for the life of me, I didn't know which was worse. Self-pity swelled inside my chest, which only made me more frustrated with myself.

He headed to the door without giving me another look, much less another thought.

I flinched when the door slammed. A couple of minutes later, Tony entered the house and sat in a chair inside the front door.

Everything inside of me ached with sorrow, regret, and a hundred things I couldn't name, and I didn't have anyone to blame except myself.

I tossed my half-eaten box of Chinese takeout into the trash and tucked my purse under my arm. "I'll be back in a couple of hours." Tony stood up, and I waved him away. "You don't need to come with me."

Tony's hand curled around my shoulder. "You can't go anywhere alone. Gian won't like it."

I whirled around and cocked one eyebrow. "I don't care what Gian does or doesn't like. I don't work for him. He doesn't need to keep tabs on me."

I was suffocating on my loneliness. A few more days of this and I'd start talking to random people on the street or myself. I'd walked away from Kevin's cheating ass, and nothing had improved. Now, I'd become Gian's pseudo fiancée, which in his world was code for prisoner. I couldn't eat, breathe, or sleep without an escort.

Tony sucked in his lips, making his beak-like nose more prominent. "You told him you were in for the night."

I shrugged. "So? What's your point? It's not like he's rushing home to hang out with me."

"He's busy," he growled.

"Whatever. If it's a problem, call Gian and tell him I'm going out again."

His eyes narrowed. "Even if he agrees, you still can't go anywhere by yourself."

"Right. I forgot. I'm a prisoner." I rolled my eyes. "Why don't you call your boss while I go to the bathroom and get ready?"

Not waiting for a response, I rushed to the bathroom and locked the door behind me.

Unlike the place where I lived with Kevin, Gian's three-story brownstone hadn't been chopped up into multiple residences. The main floor consisted of a living room, dining room, kitchen, study, and a powder room. The second floor had two bedrooms and a bathroom. The third floor was one large master suite inhabited by Gian, or at least, that was what he told me during my five-minute tour the night I moved into his house. I'd never seen it. He also had a coveted two-car garage on the garden level.

Five monster steps on the striated porcelain tile and I stood in front of the double-hung window. I pried it open, climbed onto the top of the toilet, and stuck one boot-clad foot out the window and then the other. I dangled from the sill for a moment, the pulse in my neck pumping hard, the suede toes of my boots scraping against the weatherworn brick. I closed my eyes, counted to three, and uncurled my fingers. Three feet felt like ten as I whooshed through the air, landing ungracefully on the bluestone patio. A lightning fast jab shot up my weak ankle.

"Fucking hell," I muttered.

I scrambled to my feet. The wind howled in my ears, and my hair lashed the sides of my face. A red candy bar wrapper tumbled over the tips of my shoes. I scanned the shadows, searching for any witnesses, and listening for footsteps or voices. I didn't see or hear anyone.

With my back pressed to the building, I crept around the corner, my hair snagging on the roughened brick. The second I reached the tree-lined street, I took off in a full-blown sprint.

One block.

My ankle burned.

Two blocks.

The narrow buildings blurred into a kaleidoscope

of brick, surprised faces, and gleaming yellow lights. I collided with elbows, shoulders, purses, and chests, not bothering to make any apologies. I just kept running. Needing space. Needing freedom.

Three blocks.

My feet pounded on a metal sidewalk cellar door, and mini-booms echoed through my ears.

Four blocks.

My lungs burned like I'd swallowed a mouthful of lava. I couldn't remember the last time I'd been so out of shape. For as long as I could remember, I spent every waking hour dancing. A year of doing nothing had changed me into a wind-sucking weakling.

Five blocks.

My purse pounded against my back.

Six blocks.

I couldn't take another step.

I paused, my chest heaving like a faulty life vest with a gaping hole. *Screw this.* I ripped the phone from the side pocket inside my purse, pulled up my Uber app, and summoned the first available car. In less than a minute, a black town car pulled up to the curb, and I slid inside. My damp shirt mimicked Velcro when I settled into leather back seat.

"Where to?" the driver asked, lowering the volume of his radio.

"Um…" In truth, I didn't have anywhere to go. Carmela, who'd been my only outlet for escape and commiseration for over year, was no longer an option.

My two conversations with her had been strained. While she hadn't said or done anything blatantly hurtful, she'd acted distant. Without her, I didn't have anyone. I had no intention of calling my mother. I refused to sit through another hour of my life listening to her chastise me for making bad decisions. She made it clear she thought I should have moved home after I broke off my engagement with Kevin, and in retrospect, I couldn't disagree.

The driver swiveled in his seat, his left hand tapping an imaginary beat on the steering wheel. "Well? Where do you want to go?"

I rubbed my temples, my mind wildly grasping for any plausible destination. "What's the nearest hotel?"

"I don't know." His nearly black eyes narrowed, and then he nodded. "I think there's a Marriott near the Brooklyn Bridge."

I leaned forward, a small burst of excitement rushing through me. "Perfect. Take me there."

"You got it."

Rubbing the frayed hem of my shirt, I stared at the parade of people, all faceless and nameless. A few stared at their phones, some chatted with their companions, and others walked with purpose as though their whole life depended on them making it to their destination.

Meanwhile, I sat in frozen horror while my actions caught up with me. Gian wasn't Kevin. He wouldn't accept my defiance with nothing more than a few well-aimed barbs calculated to trash my self-esteem. The dead guy on the floor of his office said enough about his capacity for violence to have me regretting my impulsive actions.

Gian, for some unknown reason, had decided to

protect me when he should have put a bullet in my head and dumped me in the nearest body of water. My finger hovered over my phone as I considered calling Carmela for the hundredth time in the past week to spill the truth. I didn't know if she could protect me from her brother—though, if anyone could, it'd be her. Then again, maybe I didn't know her as well as I thought I did. She couldn't have grown up with Gian and remained blind to the reality of who he really was. Who her family really was.

The driver cleared his throat. "We're here."

"Right." Nodding absently, I opened the door. The brisk wind whipped around me, transforming my shirt into a billowing sail. "Thanks. Have a good night."

I jogged into the two-story lobby and stepped onto the escalator, my heart still beating erratically from both my run and the fear building inside of my chest with every additional inch of distance between Gian's home and me.

Standing in front of the honey-colored wood check-in desk I typed a text to Gian.

I'm fine. I needed some space. I'll be back in a few days.

My shaky index finger hovered over the send button, debating the pros and cons of contacting Gian. A woman interrupted my musings, and I shoved my phone back into my pocket without sending the text.

"Can I help you?" she asked, a practiced look of

interest on her face.

"Yes." I dug my driver's license and credit card out of my wallet and slid them across the speckled solid countertop. "I need a room. Only for a night or two. Anything will work. It's just me."

"Let me see," she answered, her hands flying over the keyboard. A minute later, her eyebrows raised expectantly. "We have a standard room or a suite. Do you have a preference?"

I tapped my chipped pale pink fingernails on the counter and blew out a strangled breath. "The standard room will work fine."

I pulled out my phone and deleted the unsent text. Gian could wait.

CHAPTER TEN

Gian

"What the fuck do you mean 'she's gone'?" I growled, my impatience multiplying with every passing second.

Tony interlaced his fingers and inverted them, the cracking noise booming in the tight hallway of my house. "I don't know, G. She told me she wanted to go out. Then she got mad that I was going with her, and she went to the bathroom. When she didn't come out after twenty minutes, I knocked on the door. She didn't answer, and I kicked it open." He lifted and dropped one of his gorilla shoulders. "She was gone."

"Obviously." I glared at the still open window, the white shade flapping in the breeze. "What time did she go into the bathroom?"

"Around 9:30."

I glanced at my watch. "That was an hour ago. She could be anywhere by now."

He frowned. "She's your fiancée. What's the big

fucking deal? She'll be back. I think she's got her panties in a bunch because you've been ignoring her."

I clenched my teeth. "I'm not ignoring her. I've been busy. We have a lot of shit going on right now no thanks to you and your trigger happy finger."

Dominick had lost his mind when Tommy Calvo turned up dead. As I suspected, the whole thing fell on my head despite the fact Tony had pulled the trigger. Of course, Carlo had been whispering in Dominick's ear for the past three days, feeding him a pile of half-truths meant to take me down a notch.

He smirked. "Yeah, I've heard exactly how busy you've been with that new bartender at the club. Carlo told me she's been glued to your dick for days."

I rolled my shoulders, tamping down my anger. Tony needed to back the hell off. "I'm training her."

"Right," he scoffed, waggling his eyebrows like a circus clown. "Training her to suck your dick. I heard you took her back to—"

Hooking my fingers into the collar of his shirt, I yanked him closer to me. "What I do or don't do is none of your business." I pulled him fractionally closer to me, my nose not quite touching his. "Got it?"

I hadn't done much of anything with the new bartender, Angela, and not for a lack of trying. She was exactly my type before I met Evangeline. Long blondish hair, curvy as sin, and a bubbly personality that promised straightforward, uncomplicated fun. I even dug the way her cute ass swayed from side to side when she strutted around the bar.

However, every time I tried to seal the deal, I couldn't do it. My fucking fake fiancée popped in my head, and guilt twisted in my gut. I couldn't explain it if I wanted to, and I didn't—especially not to Tony.

Three nights ago, I invited Angela up to the apartment above the club for a drink. After a taking a few shots, she peeled off her dress and sprawled out the kitchen table. On autopilot, I wrapped her legs around my waist and crashed my lips against hers. And all I could think about was Evie.

It stopped me in my tracks for few seconds. Once I mentally shoved her image away, I spent two minutes groping, touching, and all around pretending, and for the first time in my life, I didn't feel a thing. Not even a micro-twitch in my dick.

She tasted wrong. She smelled wrong. Her rock-hard hairsprayed hair felt wrong. Everything about her was wrong because she wasn't Evie—the one woman who would never be mine. Disgusted with her and myself, I asked her to leave, and I'd been avoiding her like a communicable disease ever since.

Without question, the whole thing was stupid, and I hadn't been thinking clearly. If word trickled back to Carmela that I touched Angela, no matter how fleeting, she'd likely rip my dick off.

The night in my office with Evie haunted me. Her scent. Her strawberry hair that looked like flames when the light hit it. Her long, toned legs. Her pouty lips.

And so much more.

All of it made me desperate to get Evie out of my

head. Allowing our relationship to become intimate would be a huge misstep. I had been dodging my parents' calls for days. They heard I was in a serious relationship, and my mom was over the moon. Generally, she never expressed much interest in my love life, which meant this thing with Evie could quickly spiral out of control, and I'd find myself exchanging vows with a woman I didn't know anything about solely to keep my parents happy.

Tony raised his hand in surrender. "I'm not passing judgment. You can do whatever you want. I don't understand why you're so set on marrying this chick when you're still playing the field."

Feeling deflated, I shoved him away from me. "Yeah, well, I have my reasons."

He looped his thumbs over his leather black belt with a shiny gold buckle. "I gotta admit your relationship doesn't make sense. You're still young, and it's not like your old man is pushing you to get married." He paused. "Or is he? I heard his treatment isn't going well."

I swallowed over the boulder-sized lump in my throat. My dad looked worse every day. He'd lost too much weight, and he spent most of his time in bed. While he claimed it was the chemo, I knew he didn't have much time left.

I stuffed my hands into my pockets. "My dad doesn't have anything to do with it. He's got enough on his plate without worrying about my love life."

"Yeah, I know." He glanced to the side and cleared his throat. "I walked the block, and I didn't see any trace of her."

"Did you track her phone?"

He blinked. "Her phone?"

What an idiot. "Remember I installed that cell phone tracking app on her phone? As long as she doesn't shut it off, we can tell where she is."

He ruffled his hand through his hair. "I didn't pay attention when you were explaining it. I didn't get why you'd need to keep tabs on your fiancée. Most women don't try to evade their soon-to-be husband."

"Yeah, well, Evangeline isn't most women, ya' know?" I mumbled, padding down the hall to the study.

He snickered. "I see that now."

I logged onto my laptop and pulled up the tracking program. A few taps on the keyboard and I had an address. I typed it into Google.

"She's at the Marriott." I pulled my car keys from my pocket. "I'll be back within the hour."

"What are you going to do? Break into her room and demand she comes back here with you?"

I shrugged. "If I have to."

He folded his arms across his chest. "What's really going on with this chick? You've barely given her a second thought all week. She looks like she sucked on a lemon every time I mention your name. You don't sleep in the same bedroom. And now, she jumps out of the window and flees in the middle of the night. That's not normal behavior for a couple in love." He angled his head to the side. "Hell, that's not normal behavior for a couple in *like*."

"It's complicated." I scrubbed my hand down the side of my face, inhaling a deep breath through my nose, frustration coursing through me. Evie's actions made it difficult to keep her safe. Tony's suspicion didn't bode well for my charade to keep Evie out of harm's way. It was only a matter of time before everything blew up in my face.

"Complicated, how?"

My mind raced for a simple explanation for the treacherous game we were playing. The temptation to tell the truth weighed heavy in my thoughts. The minute I opened my mouth to confide in Tony, I stopped. If my father taught me anything over the years, it was that I couldn't trust anyone, especially with my words and thoughts. According to him, they could become my worst enemy, and right now, I understood exactly what he meant. I made my bed, and I needed to keep my mouth shut and stay the course.

If I confessed to lying about my relationship with Evie, Dominick would lose it. Except now Evie wouldn't be the only one with her ass on the line. Dominick would consider my lie a betrayal of the family, and in a matter of days, we'd both find ourselves on the Trassato hit list. My position, my dad, Dominick being my uncle—none of it would matter.

"We got in a fight. There's nothing to tell."

"A fight about what?"

"Nothing. Everything. I don't know. Since when do I have to answer to you?" I opened the front door. "*Fatt' i cazzi tuoi*. Now get out of here. I don't need you anymore tonight."

75

His dark brows snapped together. "I thought you still needed to take care of some stuff at the club."

"Yeah, well, plans change." I pinched the bridge of my nose. "In fact, it's the weekend. Go do whatever you need to do for a couple of days. I need some time alone with Evie."

"Well, you watch yourself, got it? We don't need any trouble with Carlo breathing down our necks." He jerked up his chin and slapped my shoulder. "Let me know if you need anything, eh?"

CHAPTER ELEVEN

Evangeline

My eyes fluttered open, and I blinked a few times, struggling to adjust to the inky darkness of the room. After checking into the hotel, I stripped off my shoes and my jeans and climbed into the bed in a long-sleeve shirt. Worrying had kept me from sleeping soundly for days, so it didn't surprise me when I feel asleep almost immediately.

I glanced at the clock.

12:58 a.m. and I was fully awake.

Sighing, I moved to switch on the lamp on the nightstand. Mid-reach, the shadows shifted, and I realized what had woken me. A man stood at the side of my bed.

My heart banged against my ribcage with enough force that I was surprised I didn't hear a bone crack. A scream burst from my lips, but like lightning, a hand covered my mouth. I dug my fingernails into the man's hands, thrashing, my hair curtaining my face.

"Jesus, Evie. Relax. It's me."

I froze, and my vision focused on the man looming over me, his features hidden in the shadows.

"Gian?" I whispered when he lifted his hand. "What are you doing here?"

He flipped on the light next to the bed. "What do you think I'm doing here?" he asked, his quiet response laced with enough displeasure to make my stomach to flip over.

I scrambled to sit up, my back pressed against the wooden headboard, clutching the starched white sheet to my chest. "I...I..." I swallowed over the emotion stuck in my throat. "I don't know."

Pacing along the side of the bed, he pointed his finger at me, his eyes heavy-lidded. "You think I should ignore the fact that my fiancée climbed out of my bathroom window and checked into a hotel across town? You think I should go on with my life and pretend you didn't make me into some fucking joke and put both of us in danger with your half-assed plan to escape? You think that's reasonable? You think that sounds like something I would do?"

I curled my fingers a little tighter around the sheet. "Fake fiancée," I said through gritted teeth.

He halted. "What the fuck does that have to do with anything?"

"Everything." I tossed the sheet off my legs and jumped out of the bed. I wouldn't get anywhere, cowering under the covers like a frightened child. I hadn't done anything wrong. I planted my palm against the center of his chest, ignoring the wall of muscles underneath the pads of my fingers.

"Nothing I do is your business. Not where I go. Not who I talk to. Hell, if I wanted to go out and fuck strangers at the bar night after night, you couldn't say a damn thing because we have a fake relationship. You get that? Fake. Let me spell it for you in case you didn't catch what I said: F. A. K. E."

His hand clamped around the back of my neck, pulling me closer to him. I could see every tiny fleck of green and gold in his volatile eyes. "You're wrong. As long as you're under my protection, you will do everything I tell you. If I say jump, you jump. If I ask you to demonstrate a pirouette or whatever the hell you dancers do, you'll do ten. And if you so much as look at another—"

My heart rate skyrocketed, and my vision dwindled to a pinprick. I couldn't hear over the rage swirling inside of my head.

"No," I said without thinking about the consequences of my answer. I knew better than to taunt this man.

His eyes darkened. "No?" The single word floated from his lips in slow motion. He released my hand, and I stumbled backward, the backs of my thighs colliding with the edge of the mattress. "Let me be clear. If you so much as feign interest in another man, I will destroy him."

"What's that supposed to mean?" I asked, my eyes flaring.

His temple ticked hard. "Exactly what you think it means. In my world, a man who can't keep his fiancée in line loses respect. He isn't a real fucking man."

Smoke-like tendrils of defeat coiled around my chest, and I plopped down on the bed, burying my face in my hands. "Why are you doing this? I just want out. I don't get it. I'll sign a blood oath, pledge my first-born, or get lobotomy. Whatever you want. Name it, and end this farce."

The bed dipped next to me, and we sat side-by-side in silence. My skin prickled with awareness. The suffocating weight of my predicament flooded the air, making me feel more claustrophobic than I'd ever divulge out loud. Although I wanted to ask him to go, I knew the request would be in vain.

He pried my hands away from my face and pinned them to my sides. "I'm trying to protect you, Evangeline, I really am. You need to stop fighting me every step of the way. Play by my rules for a little longer, and you'll get your life back."

I twisted my torso to face him. "I will?"

He tucked a strand of hair behind my ear, and the pads of his fingers tarried along the side of my neck. I could only describe the look in his eyes as torn and adoring. My pulse raced under his fingertips. "You will."

I swayed toward him, and his arm circled my shoulders, pulling me next to him. "You promise?"

"Yeah," he whispered, his warm breath ruffling the top of my hair. "You need to stop fighting me, though. Tony is already suspicious, and while I trust him with my life, he could say something to someone who wants to take me down."

"Like who?"

"All you need to know is that the threat is real. These people kill first and ask questions later. What you saw that night at my club is nothing. They don't give second chances."

"You did," I said.

"Yeah, well, I don't know why I did it. I shouldn't have. It's probably going bite me in the ass." He pinched his eyes closed for a second, and I missed the attention. The heat. Something warm and welcoming swirled inside of me whenever he focused on me. "Now we're stuck."

I brushed my hand down the side of his face, and his stubble pricked at my fingertips. "I know. I'm sorry. I just..." I didn't know what to say. In retrospect, my actions were selfish. I'd snapped under the pressure that had been building long before I met him. "I hate being alone all the time."

"What about Carmela?" he murmured, staring down at me through hooded lids.

I paused long enough to take a few stuttering breaths. "What about her?"

He ran a callused thumb across my lips, and my heart squeezed. Damn him. I didn't want to feel anything around him. All week, I had tried without much success to wipe the memory of our kiss from my brain. Late at night, when I couldn't sleep, my thoughts would inevitably circle back to him.

The feel of his hands against my skin, his taste, his scent.

And then I couldn't sleep because I'd spend hours analyzing why I couldn't stop thinking about him when he hadn't shown me a flicker of interest in days. Until now...

His hand tightened on my shoulder, bringing my thoughts back to this moment.

"Why don't you give her a call? I'm sure she'd be happy to hang out with you."

I swallowed back the pain inching up the walls of my throat. I needed Carmela, more now than ever. I couldn't do this without her. Over the last year, she'd had my back through every up and down. Now it looked as though I had used up all of her patience. "She's pissed at me. She hates me. She doesn't want anything to do with me."

His brows crinkled together. "That doesn't make sense. Of course she doesn't hate you."

I swiped the back of my hand across my eyes, attempting to erase the tears leaking out of the corner of my eyes. Stupid tears. Stupid me. Could I be any more pathetic?

"She really does. I called her a couple of times this week, and I might as well have been talking to a wall. She's pissed about us. She thinks I've been lying to her for months. She thinks I was cheating on Kevin with you."

His lips thinned. "Did she say that?"

"No, but I know her. She *thinks* it."

"I'll talk to her."

My hand curled into the lapel of his jacket. "What are you going to say?"

The corners of mouth lips twitched, and he braced his forehead against mine. "I'll think of something."

"Maybe we should—"

He cut me off by kissing me, except it wasn't any old, forgettable kiss. His mouth consumed mine, stealing the words I needed to say. Stealing the thoughts I wanted to hide. He lingered, taking his time as if nothing mattered except his lips against mine.

I lit up one nerve ending at a time like a choreographed firework display.

Boom. Pop. Crash.

With every explosion, another chink in my armor dissolved. Armor I desperately needed to get out of this mess with my heart, soul, and career intact.

Unbidden, a moan slipped out of my mouth.

"You like that?" he said, his voice scratchy. His eyes were hypnotic, his lips curled up in invitation. He was intoxicating. Addictive.

He was going to be my downfall.

Motionless, I stared at him, acutely aware that we sat on a bed in a hotel room alone. Picturing him running those calloused hands all over me should have made me nauseous. For some reason, it didn't. Images of twisted sheets, the hot slide of skin against skin, and his naked frame above me flashed through my mind.

My eyes popped wide with panic, and I scrambled to my feet, needing to sever the hold he had on me. He shot me a cocky grin that managed to simultaneously irritate me and make me want the wrong things. Things that would only muddle our situation. Things that would only send more mixed signals. Both of us knew the end game, and it wasn't a happily-ever-after. I didn't need to invest time in another tragic love story. Been there, done that. Got the visual of my ex screwing someone else tattooed on my brain.

I cleared my throat and waved my hand between us. "Why did you do that?"

He stood and buttoned the top button of his suit jacket, and I saw the gun tucked in a holster near his hip. A shiver ghosted down my spine.

"Because I wanted to," he replied. "Are you ready to go?"

I frowned. "Where?"

"Home." His gaze roamed down my bare legs and back up again, taking so much time to complete the action that goose bumps actually showered my skin. "I already settled your bill. We need to go. I can't have my guys thinking I'm a pussy who doesn't know how to handle his fiancée."

I yanked on the hem of my shirt, feeling exposed. "I don't want to waste your money. I'll leave in the morning."

"Sorry, sweetheart." He snagged my purse from the top of the dresser and slung the heavy leather hobo bag over his shoulder. "That's not happening. You can either come willingly, or I'll throw you over my shoulder and carry you out." He shrugged. "I pride myself on how reasonable I've been to date, but there's only so much I can take. Consider this decision a red line you don't want to cross."

I jutted my hip to the side, our gazes locked in a silent battle. The only sounds were the faint ding of the elevator and the revving of cars on the busy Brooklyn street outside the window.

He flexed his hands, the lone tell in his otherwise calm demeanor. "Don't test me, Evie. I'm not in the mood. I will ground your ass, and you can kiss your physical therapy and training goodbye. You won't be able to leave my house for any reason until this is over."

I plucked my jeans off the arm of an electric blue club chair and shoved my legs into them. "Fine. You don't have to threaten me. I get it." My voice was a vacant, unattractive rasp that mirrored how I felt inside.

CHAPTER TWELVE

Gian

"Fuck my life." I disconnected the phone and tossed it on the desk in my home office.

In the last twenty-four hours, Evie and I had managed to establish a fragile truce of sorts. We stopped avoiding each other. We weren't fighting. I convinced myself the kiss in the hotel room was an error in judgment, and I successfully ignored every last urge to push the relationship into something we'd both regret.

Now my mom and Carmela had come up with some half-assed plan to convert the family Sunday dinner into a fucking engagement party. I tried to talk my mom out of it. I told her I had to work. I told her Evie had a cold. I told her the timing wasn't right, and Evie and I wanted to wait a couple of months prior to making any sort of formal announcement. I told her Evie would want to invite her out-of-town family. None of my excuses mattered the minute she pulled the trump card. She said she wanted to have the engagement party while my dad was still healthy enough to enjoy it.

I couldn't blame her. If our engagement were real, I'd be insisting my mom threw an engagement party. Hell, I'd fast-track everything. The engagement party, the bridal shower, the wedding. It'd be a done deal in thirty days, maybe less. However, nothing about our relationship was real, except the chemistry between us that I couldn't smother regardless of how hard I tried.

I opened the door to the office and spied Evie resting on the sofa with her legs curled into her chest. Aiming the remote at the television, she clicked through channel after channel, never stopping long enough to hear more than a word or two.

"Hey." I crossed the room and leaned my hip into the arm of the sofa. "Are you busy? Can we talk?"

She raised her eyebrows, keeping her gaze glued to the flickering flat screen. "Go ahead."

"My mom has a family dinner at her house every other Sunday."

Her thumb paused mid-click. "Uh-huh."

"Tomorrow is one of those Sundays."

"That's fine." She shrugged, and her white shirt slid down, revealing the top of her creamy shoulder. "I'm okay hanging out here by myself. I won't run off anywhere if that's what you're worried about."

I stretched out my legs and crossed my ankles. She wasn't going to like this. "Actually, my mom invited you. She decided to make Sunday dinner an engagement party for us."

Her head whipped toward me, and she muted the volume of the T.V., blanketing us in silence. "What?" she finally said, her voice hardly a whisper. "Are you serious?"

"Yeah." I nodded, avoiding making eye contact like a damn pussy. I hadn't felt this pathetic this since I was a kid and my mom yanked me into the house by ear for peeling the bark off the neighbor's tree. "It won't be that big of a deal. Carmela will be there, and she invited a few other family members."

My mom claimed she had only invited a few people, but a few people to my mom might mean anywhere from ten to thirty. This was bad on so many levels. I didn't know where to start. Pulling Evie further into my life made it harder to extract her when the time came. She'd hear things she shouldn't, see things that couldn't be unseen. From there, she could infer a whole lot of stuff better left in the shadows. When the idea flashed through my mind and I claimed we were engaged, I never considered how quickly the fiction would snowball into more.

"I don't think this is a good idea. Once you introduce me to your parents, there are going to be expectations, and it'll only drag this out longer." She picked at the hem of her white shirt. "I want my life back, and I don't see how perpetuating this lie is going to do that."

"You're probably right, but I already agreed. I can't back out now. She's probably started prepping the food and calling our relatives. I can't let her down."

"And you think celebrating a fake engagement is

somehow the lesser of two evils? That she'll somehow be proud you created this illusion only to tear it down in a month or two?"

I focused on the silent sitcom playing on the television screen. The actors patted each other's backs and tossed their heads back in laughter. They lifted their drinks and toasted some unknown occasion, accomplishment, or anniversary.

"Gian," Evie barked. "Are you listening to me?"

She slammed the remote onto the black coffee table Carmela had selected along with most of the other furniture. I didn't care enough to make the effort. For the last few years, I split my time between here and the apartment over the club, but neither of the places felt like home. They were places to sleep. The last time I had a real home was when I lived with my parents.

I jumped up and headed to the kitchen. I needed a drink.

"Did Carmela tell you what's going on with my dad?" I asked without turning around.

"No." She followed me down the hall, the soft shuffle of her bare feet unnaturally loud in the confined space. "She changes the subject every time I ask her about anyone in her family." A regret-laden chuckle escaped her mouth. "If she said more, I might've recognized you that night at the bar, and this whole mess would've been avoided."

"Maybe," I answered noncommittally. I grabbed a beer out of the refrigerator and held it up. "Do you want one?"

"No. Alcohol was one of the things I gave up this week. I need to get back in shape if want to land a role anytime in the near future."

"Right." I cracked open the top, and a hissing sound filled the air. "How's physical therapy and training?"

"It's fine so far." She folded her arms across her waist. "Tell me about your dad."

I took a large pull of my beer. "He was diagnosed with cancer two years ago. The treatment was working until six months ago, when things took a turn for the worse. He doesn't have much longer."

She dipped her head, her coppery hair catching the light, making it look like flames dancing around her flawless face. God, she was fucking beautiful. Even the tiny bump on the bridge of her nose somehow added rather than detracted from her looks. Maybe it gave her character or personality. I couldn't put my finger on it.

"You don't know that."

I tapped the can of beer against my leg. "He refused to do any more treatment. The chemo and radiation were making him too sick to do anything other than lay in bed. He said he would rather have three or four quality months than a year of hell."

She bowed her head and licked her lips, sadness etched into the planes her face. "I'm sorry to hear that, Gian. That sucks." She paused, and for a second, I didn't think she'd say anything else. "Carmela never breathed a word."

"Yeah, she doesn't confide in many people. She holds in her emotions and pretends everything is fine."

She stared sightlessly at the wall over my head. "Huh. I guess that makes me a shitty friend. I complained to her nonstop about my pathetic excuse for a fiancé. She always listened without complaint when she had real problems." She rolled her head like she was attempting to unscramble her thoughts. "I suck. No wonder she doesn't want to talk to me anymore. I'm the worst kind of friend: a self-absorbed asshole."

I set my beer on top of the counter. "Hey. That's not true."

"No. I really am."

"Come here." I threaded my fingers through hers and pulled her closer to me until our shoulders made contact. "She told me you helped her after her fiancé, Rocco, died. She said she would've never gotten through it without you. That's what a real friend does. She won't forget that simply because she's pissed about us. She'll get over it."

"Maybe." She tipped up her head, her brown eyes glossy. "She really said that?"

"Yes." I tapped the tip of her scrunched up nose. "So she repaid the favor by helping you with Kevin."

Her attention drifted to the side, and she squared her shoulders. "What does your dad have to do with this engagement party?"

"Nothing. Everything. I don't know." I despised talking about my dad dying. I spent the first thirteen years of my life both hating and fearing him. That all changed when he opened his world to me. Hate and fear shifted into love and respect. Rather than wanting to run away from him the minute I turned eighteen, I wanted to stay and prove my worth to him. Make him proud of me. That was probably what made him a great capo. Nobody wanted to let him down. I was still trying to earn everyone's respect, but I'd get there.

"Is it because he's dying?" she whispered so low I nearly missed her words.

"Yeah, I guess so. I want to make him happy. I want to make my mom happy, and if having a stupid engagement party makes them happy if only for a couple hours, I'll do it."

Her too-knowing gaze collided with mine, and then her eyebrows raised. "All right. I'll do it. But if you get a wild hair up your ass and decide to get married for the same reason, I'm not doing it. I narrowly escaped one disastrous marriage, and I will not consider jumping into another to grant your dad's dying wish to see you married. With my track record, I'd pick cement boots and a swim in the Hudson over a white dress and stroll down the aisle without batting an eye."

An involuntary chuckle burst between my lips. "Wow. Okay. Good to know. Death is better than marrying me. If I didn't have a healthy ego, I'd be crushed right now."

She rolled her eyes. "If the gossip about you is any indication, you'll recover." She flipped her messy braid over her shoulder. "In fact, if what I've heard about you is close to truth, I think you'd pick death over marriage."

My lips kicked up at the corners a notch, and I pressed a kiss to her temple. "Don't believe everything you hear." I snagged my beer from the counter. "Be ready at four-thirty tomorrow."

She dragged her perfect white teeth over her

92

lower lip. "What should I wear?"

I took in her black yoga pants and loose white cropped top that had wreaked havoc on my senses since the minute I found her curled up on my sofa. It'd been damn hard to ignore the game of peak-a-boo her shirt played with her belly button while we were talking. "Anything you want."

"That's helpful."

"It's the truth. You look good in everything." I paused, enjoying the way a pink blush spread up her pale cheeks. "I'd probably avoid sweats, swimwear, and ball gowns just to be safe."

"Ugh. You're such a jerk."

She punched my shoulder, and I laughed. I fucking *laughed*, and not the hollow laughter elicited by a dumb joke. It was the kind you felt deep in the pit of your gut. What was this woman doing to me? Where had the hard-as-nails Gian gone? I'd been an immovable brick with singular focus since my dad introduced me to dark side of Trassato family at age thirteen. All that changed the moment I laid eyes on Evangeline. I'd caved and caved and then caved some more.

CHAPTER THIRTEEN

Evangeline

As the sun slipped below the horizon, Gian and I climbed the front steps of his childhood home. A two-story brick house with a black lacquered door loomed in front of us. The more I tried to convince myself meeting his family and representing we were engaged meant nothing, the more slippery the thought became.

I backpedaled a few steps, intuitively sensing if I breached the threshold of the Trassatos' home, there was no going back.

Gian wrapped his arm around my shoulder. "You'll be fine. Do your best to look excited, make small talk, and we'll be free to leave in two or three hours."

I rubbed my lips together, probably hopelessly smearing my peach-hued lipstick. "That's a long time to act like we're madly in love and engaged."

He pressed the doorbell. "We're not on a stage or anything. There will be plenty going on other than the two of us. Use those acting skills Carmela raved about, and it shouldn't be a problem."

Acting seemed like a cakewalk in comparison. Nobody got hurt. I wasn't lying; I was working. Telling a story. Sharing my love of the theater with the world. Right now, I was about to strut into someone's home and lie to everyone, including my best friend. The thought made my stomach flip. I didn't like lying, and I didn't like playing games. Yet somehow, I had managed to put myself in a situation that necessitated doing both.

"I thought you'd never show up," said a dark-haired woman with eyes so similar to Gian's I knew she had to be his mother. She wore an elegant light blue suit that did little to tame her abundant curves that wavered somewhere between sultry and matronly.

"Mom, you said to be here at five." Gian glanced at his wristwatch. "And it's five."

"Hmm. I thought I said four-thirty. Everyone is already here. How's my *bambino?*" She pulled him into a one-armed hug and kissed both of his cheeks, leaving smudges of red.

Gian mumbled something under his breath that I couldn't understand.

"And you must be Evangeline. I'm Helena." She took both of my hands, her eyes crinkling at the corners, a broad smile on her face. "Look at that hair, your dimples, and that skin...it's so pale. No wonder Gianluca is so taken with you. You're beautiful."

"Thank you." I grinned so hard I thought my cheeks would crack. For some stupid reason, I imagined the action would somehow magically tame the disquiet circling in my gut like a swarm of bees. "I can't believe we haven't met before."

She nodded and clasped her hands in front of her chest. "I'll have to show her how to cook your favorites. I'm sure she doesn't know how to make to real Italian food. She'll probably open a jar of canned sauce and pour it over plastic noodles."

My mouth hinged open, and Gian slotted his fingers through mine. Granted, I *didn't* cook much. Raw vegetables and canned soup were what I lived off when I moved to New York, which meant I only needed a refrigerator and a microwave to stay alive. My eating habits hadn't changed when I moved in with Kevin either. He worked late most nights, and when he came home at a normal hour, we went out to eat or ordered delivery. Gian's mom would probably freak if she knew how limited my skills really were.

"I don't know, Mom." He pulled me inside the house, his mouth tight. "Evangeline is really busy for the next month with her job. Maybe after things slow down."

Helena nodded. "Of course, of course. After the wedding, things will probably calm down. She'll have plenty of time then. I'm sure you'll both want to start having babies real soon."

My stomach knotted. I didn't know how to respond. I never thought about having kids. I'd spent most of my life singularly focused on my career. When I got hurt, I threw everything I had into planning a wedding I didn't care about. At the time, I would never have admitted it, but I didn't think I would've made it down the aisle with my ex even if I hadn't barged in on him and his current protégé in flagrante delicto.

"Yeah, maybe. We'll see. That's a long way down the road," Gian answered, his voice as deflated as I felt.

A two-story foyer with a sweeping staircase greeted us. Laughter, shouting, and the hum of steady conversation echoed off the white and black marbled floor. *Shit.* This was a full-blown party, not an intimate gathering of a few family members. My insides quivered like jelly, and I stopped walking.

Gian squeezed my hand. "You'll be fine."

"You lied," I said, dropping my voice an octave.

He glanced at me, the ruthless determination in his eyes making them darker. Harder. "I know. I didn't have a choice. You wouldn't have agreed if I told you the truth, and when my mom says a few people, it could mean anywhere from two to fifty."

I wrenched my hand out of his, my heart rate increasing with every passing second. "Gian, I'm really freaking our right now. I don't think I can do this."

He pushed my hair away from my face, and a shiver danced down my spine. "I won't leave you alone. We're a team."

"Is it too late to feign sickness? I'm pretty sure I could enact a catastrophic fall or projectile vomit on demand or some combination thereof if I concentrated really hard." I pointed at my four-inch putty-colored heels. "A fall would be convincing with these stupid shoes."

"Is something wrong?" Helena whirled around,

her gaze swinging between Gian and me.

"Go ahead, Mom," Gian said. "Evangeline is nervous about meeting the whole family. You know how that goes. She's worried about making a good impression. Give us a minute."

"Sure." She flashed a close-lipped smile. "Don't be too long. Your dad is tired today. He had a bad night. I don't think he'll stay awake much longer." With that parting shot, she plodded down the hall, her low nude-colored heels clicking over the tiled floors.

"What the hell, Gian?" I stabbed my finger in the center of his chest. "I didn't sign up for this."

"Relax, sweetheart. We've got this under control." He shoved his hands in the pockets of his black trousers, the corner of his lips twitching like I amused him. Like this whole thing amused him. "This is about doing what we have to do. I want both of us to have a long life, and that means doing whatever it takes to walk away from this without raising anyone's hackles."

I closed my eyes for a splintered second, fear and sadness creating a toxic brew in my gut. I sucked in a deep breath and dragged my fingers over the emerald necklace my brother gave me for my sixteenth birthday. I wore it everywhere. It reminded me of who I was and where I came from, and that I had family who cared about me no matter how far we drifted apart.

"I know. I get it." I flung my arm toward the flurry of noise filtering from the back half of the house. "Lead the way, but do us both a favor and tell the truth next time. I don't like being blindsided."

"I love it when you're reasonable, sweetheart." He kissed the top of my head. I curled into him, inhaling his scent and running my hands up and down the tight weave of his suit jacket. His hand slid under the fall of my hair, and a thread of longing wove around me, which proved absolutely nothing except that chemistry between two people could defy logic. Or at least, that's what I told myself.

With that thought, I shifted away from him, but I didn't get far. His hand rounded my waist like an iron shackle, keeping me glued to him with little effort. Heat crackled from the roughened pads of his fingers, and the skin beneath my thin silk dress tingled, rendering my clothing nearly worthless.

The minute we entered the great room, loud applause mixed with a few whistles thundered through the air. I relied on my acting skills and channeled the feelings I'd be experiencing if this moment were real.

Carmela kissed Gian and then me. She was the first of a long line of people congratulating us with hugs and kisses—so many kisses, my cheeks were probably a kaleidoscope of reds, pinks, and peaches. Tony was there, along with a few other faces I recognized from the night my life imploded in the back of Gian's club.

When the crowd of people showering us with well wishes finally dissipated, the distinct pop of champagne bottles opening reverberated through the room like a gong announcing the beginning of the ceremonies. Carmela and Helena filled glasses with pale yellow, bubbly liquid. My stomach sunk like I swallowed a boulder. Blood pumped through my veins loud enough to drown out the roar of celebration.

"Smile," Gian whispered next to my ear. "You look like you're going to be sick."

"I *feel* like I'm going to be sick," I muttered.

Carmela held up two flutes with our names etched into the glass. "Gian. Evie."

I accepted the glass from her, and yeah, it was awkward. I did my best to avoid direct eye contact with her and anyone else in the room. Unfortunately, a man with his forearm resting on the fireplace mantel had a different agenda. His cold, dark, glittering eyes zeroed in on me like a bird of prey, calculating my weaknesses and extracting my secrets. The heat of his stare burned through me like the fire of a thousand suns. Goose bumps spiraled down my arms.

He cleared his throat. "As the head of this family, I'd like to make a toast."

Almost as if this man were Moses parting the Red Sea, a hush fell over the room, and everyone lined up like good little toy soldiers.

I leaned into Gian. "Is that your dad?"

"No. My uncle, Dominick. Why?"

"Just wondering, because that man sure as hell doesn't look sick." His arms and shoulders, although bulky, didn't disguise the muscles straining and pulling against the seams of his custom-tailored suit. He had the right amount of gray to achieve a distinguished salt and pepper look. While he was shorter than Gian, he didn't need height to make an impression. His eyes alone would scare the shit out of anyone—maybe even Lucifer.

"Gianluca, I've told you this many times, and I'll repeat it again now. I am proud to call you my nephew and my godson. You know I'd do anything for you. Anything. Now that you're taking the next step in your life, I have every faith that you've chosen well. I have a few words of counsel for you and the lovely Evangeline." He rotated his square chin to the side, his lips flat and lifeless. "You earn respect from your spouse with actions, not words. Always respect and listen to her because a real man takes care of his family. Be careful of lines crossed that can never be uncrossed. Every betrayal starts with trust. Every enemy starts as a friend. Every lie has a grain of truth. Behind every sin is a sinner." He lifted his glass, and the entire room followed like minions eager to implement their evil leader's plan. "May your days be numerous and your troubles trivial. *Famigila per cent'anni!*"

Dominick's stare never wavered from mine as his rubbery lips engulfed the rim of his glass. Then he laughed—though, he hadn't said anything funny. I forced myself to meet his deadened gaze, trying to bury my fear. Like a snake preparing to strike, his lips curled upward, and he made a slashing motion with his hand across his neck. The air went from festive to heavy with tension. I couldn't get enough oxygen in my lungs.

Oh my God.

Oh my God.

What the hell am I doing? This is insane. These people are certifiably crazy.

Gian kissed my temple and tapped his glass against mine. "Drink, sweetheart, or you'll insult my uncle."

With more than a little tremor in my hand, I raised the glass to my lips and took a giant sip of the champagne, craving immediate anesthetization. I didn't taste anything. It could have been a glass of arsenic, and I wouldn't have noticed.

The sugary bubbles clung to the walls of my throat, suffocating me. My eyes flared, and for a second, I seriously thought the drink would make a less than graceful reappearance on the spotless ivory Aubusson rug beneath my feet.

My emotions seesawed from breakdown to out of control laughter and back again with alarming frequency. Frost coated the walls of my veins, only to be replaced with scalding heat a few seconds later. My vision muddied. Fleetingly, I remembered I hadn't eaten all day. Voices became garbled like someone had shoved my face under water. My body swayed, and I clawed at the sleeve of Gian's suit jacket.

"Gian," I rasped, and everything went black.

CHAPTER FOURTEEN

Gian

I paced back and forth at the foot of the bed in my childhood home. The plush tan carpet swallowed the sound of my black wingtips. This was a disaster. Evie fucking fainted in front of the entire family. She really knew how to clear out a party. Unfortunately, my mom now had it in her head that Evie was pregnant.

"I really am sorry, Gian. I didn't do it intentionally." Evie sat with her back to the headboard and her knees curled against her chest. "I don't know what happened. Your uncle's speech freaked me out, and I didn't eat all day. Then, I don't know..." She swallowed. "Did I screw everything up? I feel like a total loser."

I sat on the edge of the bed and pulled her into my arms without saying anything. I wanted to make sure she was really okay. When she swayed forward, my heart nearly burst through my fucking ribcage. I rocked her, comforting her and myself. It never failed. Every time something happened to her, a weird feeling bubbled up in my chest, compelling me to protect her from everything bad in the world. The urge was preposterous because by anyone's definition I was the big black wolf in sheep's clothing.

"What's your definition of screwed up?" I asked after a few moments.

Her shoulders slumped, and she rested her forehead against the top of my shoulder. "I heard what your mom said. She thinks you're marrying me because I'm pregnant."

"I told her it wasn't true."

She lifted her head. Her eyes were glassy like she wanted to cry, but she had some color in her cheeks again, which was better than nothing. "Does she believe you?"

"She will eventually." I wiped my hand over my lips. "She won't have any choice when our engagement ends and you're not showing."

She stared at me for a second, and then the corner of her lips started twitching.

"What?"

Laughter burst from her lips, her back shaking beneath my fingers. "This is really funny if you think about it."

I lifted an eyebrow. "How so?"

"She. Thinks. I'm. Pregnant," she said between bouts of laughter.

"Yeah, so?"

"Of all the secrets we're hiding, she comes up with a pregnancy to explain my behavior and our sudden engagement. It couldn't be further from the truth. You've never touched me. Hell, you don't even like me."

"Oh, Evie, that's where you're wrong." I traced a line from her mid-calf to her upper thigh. Her legs would be the death of me. When she came out of her room wearing this little shift dress that stopped mid-thigh, I wanted to send her back to her room to change. "I like you enough to make this situation dangerous for both of us."

Her eyes flared. "What? I thought—"

A knock on the door interrupted her, and I fleetingly wondered whether it would be a bad thing to lock the bedroom door and rip that dress over her head. What I wouldn't give to feel her melt beneath my fingertips and drink in her moans like a glass of Chianti Classico. I climbed off the bed, removing myself from the temptation to do exactly that.

"Come in," I said, looking at anything other than the beautiful woman sitting on my childhood bed.

Carmela cracked open the door. "I wanted to check on Evie. How are you feeling?"

"Better. Thanks for asking." Evie stretched out her legs and crossed her ankles. "I don't know what happened. I didn't eat much today, and I've been training really hard. I'm so embarrassed. Your family probably thinks I'm crazy."

"Pregnant, not crazy." Carmela laughed. "You don't have anything you want to tell me, do you?"

"Oh my God, no." Evie waved her hands in the air. "Please tell me you don't believe that."

Carmela's lips thinned. "I don't think you're pregnant, but I do think you two are hiding something."

"Carmela, don't start with that again," I warned.

Carmela held up her hand. "I have no intention of getting into that right now. I know neither of you will tell me anything. And besides, Dominick is waiting for you. He wants to talk to you before he takes off."

"Yeah, yeah." I nodded. "I'll be back in a couple of minutes."

I exited the room without looking back.

When I got downstairs, I said, "Hey, Dominick. What's going on?" I patted him on the shoulder with one hand and shook his hand with the other.

"I have some stuff to take care of. I trust everything is okay with your girl?"

I shoved my hands into my pockets. "Yeah. I think she was a little overwhelmed."

"She seems like a nice girl. But let's be frank here: she's not one of us. She'll never be one of us. If today showed us anything, it's that she'll never fit in. She'll be a liability from today until the day she dies."

I forced my face to remain a blank mask despite the anger surging through me. Losing my temper or lashing out at Dominick wouldn't help Evie or me. "When have I ever done anything to jeopardize the family or you? I wouldn't bring someone into this family who I didn't trust. Who I didn't think would be an asset."

"I know, I know, but have you thought this through? From what I heard, she wants to be an actress on Broadway. With any luck, she'll reach some level of notoriety. Then you know what happens?" He lifted his hands, his ruby ring glinting off the overhead light of the chandelier. "People will start looking at you. That will inevitability lead people back to the family and me. I know you don't want that, and I sure as hell don't need any light shining on us. We're finally gaining some ground now that the FBI and those jackoffs at the Department of Homeland Security are focused on terrorism instead of us."

Staring at the floor, I pinched the bridge of my nose. "What are you saying? You want me to end the engagement?"

"Gianluca, I promoted you because you have a knack for making difficult decisions, not because your dad wanted it. You'll figure out what to do." He squeezed my shoulder. "I heard she's seen some stuff."

My head snapped up. "Who told you that?"

He scratched the side of his face. "It doesn't matter who told me. What I don't understand is why you didn't mention it."

Fucking Carlo. I knew I couldn't trust him. With soldiers like him, I didn't need enemies. I had to convince Dominick to assign him to some other unsuspecting capo. "Since when have you wanted to micromanage every detail? You don't need to worry about Evangeline. Ya' gotta know, I have this under control."

Dominick pinned me with his dark stare. Then, he lifted his chin. "All right. I'll let you take care of this for now, but know that the day might come when you need to make a tough call. Until then, I need to know you'll make the *right* choice. You'll protect this thing of ours."

I bowed my head. "Yeah, you know I will."

He slapped me on the shoulder. "Good. You're better than some of those other young turks."

I flinched. Young turks was what he called the younger, less traditional generation of Mafiosi. The older guys looked down on us. They believed we were more inclined to break the old rules. In my mind, it was a direct slight.

"Yeah. Yeah. I need to get back to Evie."

CHAPTER FIFTEEN

Evangeline

I stared at Gian from the corner of my eye as he navigated the Sunday evening traffic. He hadn't said much of anything since he spoke with his uncle. At dinner, he answered every inquiry with as little information as possible, and he pushed us out the door the minute I finished my dessert.

"Dinner was wonderful. Your mom's a good cook. I can't believe how much food she made. She could've fed the entire neighborhood." I toyed the folds of my dress. "I kind of feel guilty that she did all that when we're just…you know."

"Don't worry about it. She likes to entertain," he answered, glancing in the rearview mirror.

"Yeah, I guess. What did your uncle want?"

He frowned, his fingers tapping impatiently against the center console. "Nothing you need to worry about."

"He probably thinks I'm an idiot. I can't believe I fainted." I squared my shoulders. "For the record, tonight was the first time that happened, so you don't need to worry about bringing me in public."

He glanced over his shoulder. "Uh-huh."

"Gian, what's the matter? Are you mad at me? Did I ruin everything?" I cataloged my conversations at dinner. "Did I say something stupid? Your family hated me, didn't they?"

My shoulders drooped under the weight of the self-created disasters infecting my life. Gian's dad had said exactly five words to me all night—"It's nice to meet you."

Dinner conversation wasn't much better. His uncle's early departure set the tone of the celebration. Clearly, he found me wanting, and everyone else agreed with his assessment. Everyone bowed and scraped around him like he was some sort of king. The instant that thought floated through my mind, the pieces of the puzzle clicked together, refusing to be buried under layers of excuses any longer.

Dominick wasn't merely Gian's uncle—he was the head of the Trassato crime family. The same one people whispered about in hushed murmurs with an equal measure of awe and disgust. While Gian and Carmela had never confirmed or denied anything, the writing was on the wall.

Panic wrapped around my ribcage like a tourniquet. A gust of air whooshed out of my lungs. Needles of fear pricked at my skin like thousands of poison-tipped arrows. The thudding of my heart drowned out the sound of the radio.

Holy shit.

No.

No.

No.

This isn't real.

Trembling, I covered my mouth with my hand.

"Evie, are you listening to me?" Gian's voice snapped me out of the ocean of tragedy I'd been drowning in.

"What?" I rotated toward him. One hand white-knuckled the steering wheel while the other clawed at his hair. His eyes glittered with menace. His lips were pinched. "What's wrong?"

"Open the fucking glove box and hand me the gun."

My stomach twisted into a knot. "The gun? What do you need a—"

His body bristling with violence, he slammed his hand against the dash, and I flinched. "Dammit! Don't question me. Just do what I ask for once."

Unable to get my hands to cooperate, I fumbled with the latch on the glove box.

"Make this stop," I pleaded to no one in particular.

A car hit our bumper. A loud crash echoed through my ears, and my neck whipped forward, then backward, slamming against the headrest.

Gian shoved my head down and flipped open the glove box. The shiny metal of the gun blurred through the air like a shooting star. I pinched my eyes shut. My muscles tensed, anticipating. Dreading. Fearing.

Bang.

The rear driver's side window shattered. Glass showered the top of my head.

111

Bang.

Engines revved, and my heart escalated right along with it.

Bang.

Tires squealed.

A loud, piercing noise echoed through the car, and it took me a second to realize I was screaming. I slapped a hand over my mouth, not wanting to call attention to myself. With my head braced against my thighs, I stared blankly out the window, peering at the smattering of stars playing peek-a-boo with the heavily clouded night sky.

The car whipped around the corner, and my butt slid across the seat. My shoulder bumped into the leather-upholstered door. The second I lifted my head, Gian sideswiped a parked car. The side mirror exploded into tiny shards of glass. They glittered like diamond dust in the moonlight.

"Stay down!" he yelled, shoving my head down again.

"What's going on?" I asked, my heart hammering hard enough to split open my ribcage.

"Exactly what you think." He tossed his phone in my lap. "Call Tony. He's in my favorites."

The phone slipped out of my hand and fell to the floorboard. Blindly searching, my hand scoured the rubber floor mat. The seatbelt bit into my flesh with every twist and turn. Finally, the tips of my fingers brushed against the solid rectangle. I lifted it, slid my finger across the screen and called Tony.

One ring.

Two rings.

"What's up?"

"It's Evie." My voice sounded like I had swallowed a cup of acid.

The car hopped up on the curb, and we narrowly missed a stop sign. My teeth clacked together, grazing the tip of my tongue when Gian yanked the steering wheel to the right and off the sidewalk. I clutched the side panel on the door, the coppery taste of blood hitting my tongue.

"Evie? Evie? Are you still there?"

"Yeah. Somebody shot at us and crashed into Gian's car."

"What the fuck?" he yelled. "Where are you guys?"

"Tell him to meet us at my house in twenty minutes," Gian said, his gaze zigzagging between the road in front of us and the rear view mirror.

"Did you hear what he said, Tony?"

"Yeah. Yeah. I'm on it." When the line went dead, I dropped the phone into my lap. A warm liquid trickled down my hand. Transfixed, I stared at the blood dripping from my fingers. It looked like ink in the dim light of the car.

Gian's hand swept over the top of my hair. "I think we lost them. You can sit up now."

I didn't move. I couldn't. I stared sightlessly at my hand, my breaths choppy and my mind blank. Tears dripped from my chin, and I realized I was crying.

"Are you okay? Are you hurt?"

I jerked my head rather than answering because there was no simple answer. My mind buzzed with too many jumbled emotions to communicate.

A few minutes later, we pulled into the two car

garage on the garden level of Gian's home, and I finally sat up. I blinked, cataloguing every fear and pain. My body ached, and nausea and uncertainty clawed at me, spreading through me like a slow drip IV.

The passenger door opened, and I still didn't move.

"Come on, sweetheart. We're safe now." Gian circled one arm around my shoulder and the other under my knees. I buried my face in his neck, inhaling his scent like it was the antidote for everything that ailed me.

CHAPTER SIXTEEN

Gian

Still humming with adrenaline and my thoughts shifting like chess pieces, I carried Evie into my home. I didn't know where to start. As much as I loved to believe otherwise, tonight wasn't a random act of violence. Someone had targeted me. Or Evie. I couldn't rule anything out at this point.

Sure, the Trassato family had enemies, which by extension were my enemies. We'd been battling for territory with the Russian Mafia for years as they flexed their muscle and crept out of Brighton Beach. They were big into heroin distribution, and for the most part, I stayed away from the drug trafficking business, which led me to believe they'd target the other capos before me. It didn't make sense.

"Hey." Tony stood at the base of the stairs. "Are you both okay?"

"Yeah," I replied. "My car is fucked up, but we're both fine."

"Put me down. I can walk," Evie mumbled into my chest.

She looked up at me, her eyes wide and imploring, her cheeks rose-stained, and her hand a bloody fucking mess. "Tony, I can't talk now. I'll be back in a few minutes." I jogged up the steps, ignoring Evie's request. I didn't want to put her down. I'd been in more than my fair share of dangerous situations, and I stayed calm and clearheaded. Tonight was different. They'd put Evie in harm's way.

The miserable fuckers who had the audacity to come after my girl would pay. I'd make sure of it. Nobody fucked with my family or me without consequences. Nobody. Evie may not be my real fiancée, but nobody knew that, and if I let this slide, no man would ever take me seriously.

Evie lifted her head. "Where are we going?"

I opened my bedroom door went into the bathroom, setting Evie on the counter. "You're staying in my room tonight."

"N-n-no," she stuttered. "I'm not comfortable with that." When she moved to get off the counter, I wedged my hips between her legs, blocking her escape.

"You don't have a choice. Tony has already commented on the fact that you sleep in the guest bedroom."

"So what?" She raised her eyebrows. "You said you trusted Tony. Did you change your mind? What am I missing?"

I brushed a tangled strand of her fiery hair away from her face. "This isn't about trust. It's about his oath. If he finds out I lied about us, he can't protect me, and I wouldn't ask him to either. His primary duty is to the family, not me." Darkness flickered across her face, and she closed her eyes for a beat. "And if tonight demonstrated anything, it's that we don't have any room to make mistakes."

"I know." She swallowed, anxiety creasing her forehead. "I feel like I'm dangling from the cliff and nobody is going to catch me."

Turning on the faucet, I picked up her hand and held it under the water. "I will," I said, watching the pink-hued water swirl down the drain. "We're in this together."

Dominick's warning about choosing the family over Evie looped through my head, making my gut churn with more than a little dread. I blew out a breath and shoved the unsettling emotion back into a vault in the recesses of my mind. I wouldn't let it come to a choice between the family and Evie. I'd find a way out of this mess. I dragged her into this situation, and I would get her out.

I shut off the water and patted her hand with a white washcloth. "It's not too bad." I rotated her wrist and inspected her palm. "You have a couple of cuts, but nothing that warrants stitches." I pulled a stack of bandages from my top drawer and covered the larger cuts.

"Thank you." She pressed a closed-lipped kiss to my lips, lingering longer than was prudent, given I was ready to pounce at the slightest encouragement. I tasted the lemon sorbet my mom served for dessert on her lips. All too soon, she pulled back, a weak smile picking up the corners of her mouth.

Studying her face, I trailed my hand down her side, along her hip, down the miles of silky skin on her leg. Her flesh pebbled beneath the pads of my fingers, and her pupils swelled. A tsunami of desperation and need hit me in the dead center of my chest.

I wanted to spend the night getting lost in this woman. I wanted to kiss her. Taste her. Adore her. I wanted to put the past and the future in a sealed box and pretend it didn't exist for a few hours.

I should walk out this door right now, but the longer I looked at her, the more my logic crumbled. I leaned forward, my lips only a whisper away from hers. My brain cells scrambled.

I smelled a hint of jasmine. I saw the tiny gold flecks in her otherwise dark irises. I counted the sprinkle of freckles on her nose. She had seven. It was my new favorite number.

Fuck Tony. He could wait.

"Evie," I groaned, unable to resist any longer. She was the forbidden fruit, and I needed another taste of her brand of sin.

I let my lips glide across hers. Once. Twice.

Her eyes drifted closed, and a faint hum slipped through her full lips. "Gian, what the hell are we doing?"

"I don't know." And I didn't. This was madness. From the first minute I glimpsed her from across the bar, I'd lost my fucking mind. I made dumb decisions, tempted fate, shamed my family, and stomped on my honor. Sadly, none of that mattered when I got within a hundred feet of this girl.

My arms wrapped around her waist, pulling her

flush against me. She trembled, and it had the same effect on me as tossing a match on gasoline. I felt alive for the first time in days. Maybe longer.

Our mouths fused together, and for the life of me, I didn't know which one of us was the aggressor. My tongue dove in and out of her mouth. Tasting. Teasing. Savoring. My hands were everywhere, and it wasn't enough. I explored every swell, curve, and indention. She was warm, soft, inviting, and every touch went to my head like a shot of whiskey. At that moment, I'd swear on my uncle's pinky ring that I'd never get enough of this woman. Her body. Her long, toned legs. Her waist so tiny I could span the circumference with two hands.

I shoved her dress around her waist, and her fingers sunk into my shoulders, indecipherable, breathless sounds rolling from her mouth.

"We're forgetting," I murmured, finally answering her question.

She tugged at the front of my shirt, pulling it from the waistband of my pants. Her hands skirted underneath. Each measured stroke left me panting with desire. I rocked against her, acutely aware of every centimeter of fabric between us. Regrettably, the friction did nothing to quench the ache building inside of me. I wedged my hand between our bodies, toying with the top edge of her lace panties. Her muscles bunched beneath the pads of my fingers.

Shuddering, she sucked in a gust of air, color blooming on her cheeks. The soft, dreamlike look on her face unhinged me more than I already was.

"Wait."

"Wait?" I echoed, my fingers inching lower. They had a mind of their own.

She grabbed my wrist, her eyes dark and questioning, and I couldn't have looked away if I wanted to. I watched a million and one expressions float across her face. I couldn't remember ever being so caught up in someone before.

"We shouldn't do this right now." She blew out a puff of air. "I don't think it's a good idea."

With a sigh, I leaned my forehead against hers. "No? Because I think it's a great idea. Come to think of it, I don't believe I've had a better idea in a long time." I slid my hand lower, cupping her between her legs. "I'll make you feel good."

She arched her pelvis against my hand a fraction of an inch and whimpered. "We both know this shouldn't happen. Don't make this hard."

Chuckling, I dragged my nose along her throat up to her mouth. "It's already hard."

"We need to stop." Her words were a velvety purr against my lips, and a jolt of desire zipped down my spine.

"Give me a reason to stop."

Her teeth grazed my lower lip. "I'll give you two."

"Uh-huh." I glided my finger through her folds. She was so wet, it would be criminal for me to walk away.

"Tony's waiting for you." Her pulse fluttered like butterfly wings against the ivory skin of her neck.

"Tony can go fuck himself."

With her chin tucked against her chest, she stared at me through the veil of her gold-tipped lashes. "This will complicate everything."

"I like complications." I hooked a finger inside the knot of my tie and loosened it. "Complications make life interesting."

"No. Not tonight. Tonight…" She licked her lips, and I barely held back a groan. "Everything is too charged. Neither of us is thinking clearly." When I held up my hand, she shook her head, ignoring the gesture. "I'm not thinking clearly. I'm still wound up from what happened tonight, and I don't want to make a decision I'll regret."

Nodding, I mentally pulled my shit together and took a step back. "You're right." She was, but that didn't mean the urge to press myself against her again and claim her mouth had magically disappeared. Physical awareness still buzzed through me, crackling and snapping. "Go to sleep. You've had a hard day. We'll talk tomorrow."

Her shoulders fell, and she stared at me for a second then smiled faintly. "All right. Tomorrow." She jumped off the counter and darted past me like she didn't trust me not to stop her.

By the time I changed out of my suit, she was in my bed, curled on her side, with her back facing me and the sheet tucked around her neck like she couldn't stomach revealing an inch of skin. With a resigned sigh, I opened the door and went to find Tony.

A few minutes later, I located him in my study. He sat behind my desk, twirling a glass of amber liquid.

"Feel free to make yourself at home."

"Oh shit, Gian." He jumped out of his seat and waved a hand toward the two leather club chairs. One held my briefcase and the other had my jacket draped over the back. "I didn't want to touch your stuff."

My eyes narrowed, and I leaned against the doorjamb. "Uh-huh."

He took a deep drink of his whiskey and set the glass on my desk. A loud clunk echoed through the quiet room. "So what happened tonight?"

"I think Evie's told you the gist of it. A car rammed us, and someone took a few shots at us. A window is shattered, and the back of my car is fucked up. That's it."

I bridged the distance between the desk and me. I scanned the surface to see if Tony had riffled through my papers. He wouldn't find anything. My father had taught me better than that, and tonight had opened my eyes to one cold, hard fact: I couldn't trust anyone, including Tony. A few days ago, I would have sworn he had my back. Now, I wasn't so sure.

He'd accepted my promotion without complaint even though both he and Carlo had more experience than me. Sal hadn't blinked an eye either, but that was different. He was two years younger than me, so he didn't care that I had leap-frogged over a few guys. However, I couldn't take anything at face value. Not anymore.

Tony rocked back on his heels. "Do you think it was random?"

"I don't know." I picked up a pen from my desk

and clicked the top a few times.

"It could've been. Have you told Dominick?"

"No, and I'm not sure I will."

His brows pinched together. "He'd want to know. You're a capo and his nephew. He wouldn't like someone fucking with you."

I tossed the pen on top of a stack of papers. "What can he do?"

"Well, if it was the Russians—"

"What the fuck would the Russians want with me? I don't push their shit. I don't have anything to with them."

"Exactly, and that pisses them the fuck off. You kicked one of their guys out of your club last week, and Sal roughed him a bit."

"What?" I growled. "Why didn't somebody tell me about that? You need to keep me in the loop, otherwise I look like a dumb ass."

Tony shrugged. "It wasn't too bad. He took a swing at Sal and grazed his chin. Sal landed a few good punches, but the guy didn't end up in the hospital or anything."

I studied at him, unblinking until the silence became uncomfortable. He jammed his hands into his pockets and rolled his neck in a circle. I stared down my nose at him.

"Don't keep things from me ever again. I want to know everything. Everything. If I find out you're hiding shit from me, I'll beat you to a bloody pulp. Your face won't be recognizable when I'm done with you. Got it?"

His lips tightened, and his muscles crawled up his shoulders. He vibrated with indignation.

"Whatever you want."

I kept my face neutral. "Great. Now get the fuck out of my house. I want to go to bed."

He drained the last sip of whiskey and took a couple of steps toward the door then paused. "By the way, what window was shattered?"

"The rear driver's side. Why?"

He rubbed his hand over his mouth. "Just wondering. It's probably nothing."

CHAPTER SEVENTEEN

Evangeline

I didn't know what woke me. It was still dark outside, and the full moon cast a silvery glow mixed with lengthy shadows over the room. If I squinted, I could make out the slanted roofline and streamlined edges of Gian's dresser across the room.

A soft breeze from the ceiling fan wafted across my exposed flesh, raising tiny goose bumps on my arms. My heart thumped in slow, steady beats. I squeezed my injured hands, testing for pain. Other than a slight twinge, it seemed fine.

I flipped to my side, and my breath splintered mid-exhalation. Gian lay on his side, facing me. His thick, midnight-colored eyelashes looked like dark fans beneath his eyes. Without question, they were the kind that motivated women around the world to buy mascara and fake lashes.

Dark stubble covered the lower half of his face. His lips were parted, yet they still managed to curl up at the corners. The white sheet rode low on his hips, exposing his gold-dusted skin, the mouthwatering contours of his chest, and the sharp angles of his stomach.

When he was awake, his lips were wickedly sinful, his eyes were mischievous, and his jaw hard and unforgiving. Right then, I didn't see any of those things. I saw a gentle, boyish beauty that took me off guard. It made him authentic and approachable, and liked it.

Without thinking, I traced the inside of his arm from the bulge of his bicep to his wrist. As strange as it sounded, I loved the inside of an arm. It was one of my favorite parts of a man's body. Smooth and pale, the skin there was untouched by the harshness of the sun and life. The bluish veins peeking through the skin reminded me we were all vulnerable and real no matter how tough or impervious we pretended to be in front of others.

His eyes popped open, and then his brows slammed together. I yanked my hand back so fast I was surprised it didn't hit me in the gut. "Is something wrong?"

"No." I flopped onto my back and folded my arms over my chest. "I woke up, and I couldn't fall back to sleep. Actually, I haven't tried. I rolled over and saw you next to me, and honestly, it surprised me. I didn't realize you were planning to sleep in the bed with me."

"Where did you think I was going to sleep? I told you Tony commented on our living arrangement. I couldn't exactly sleep in a guest bedroom. That would've defeated the whole purpose of putting you in here in the first place."

"That fuzzy rug on floor or maybe one of those chairs in the corner. All of them look appealing. Soft even. Hell, you could slide those chairs together and toss that rug over it." I squeezed my lips together to suppress a snicker. The sheepskin rug at the foot of the bed couldn't have been more than four or five feet long and three feet wide, and the black leather-tufted chairs didn't have arms. He'd roll off in a matter of minutes.

He raised his head, surveying his room. "Not happening. I'm good here. Besides, I hate that rug. It looks like there's a dead animal on the floor."

I giggled. "I think that's the point. Why did you buy it if you hated it?"

He dropped his head back on the pillow. "I let Carmela decorate the place, which was a major miscalculation on my part."

"You don't like it?" I leaned forward to brush his dark hair from his eyes but froze halfway and let my hand drop to the bed.

"No. It's fine. I hated the process," he grumbled. "The more opinions I offered, the more options she gave me. She dragged shopping bags into my house every night with sticky notes outlining the pros and cons of every piece. Boxes showed up on my doorstep every day. She demanded we meet every morning to discuss her selections. After a week, I couldn't stand it anymore, so I handed her a wad of cash told her to buy whatever she liked."

I patted his shoulder. Being with him like this felt so natural. Too natural. It was easy to forget we were enemies with a common goal, not friends. I pushed the thought aside.

"How cute. She manipulated you."

"No." A hundred mega-watt grin spread across his face, and my heart clenched. "My sister tortured me with discussions of texture, color trends, and the advantages of warm or cool tones."

"Sounds like Carmela. I can see you holding up dainty fabric swatches making nonsensical comments," I said between fits of laughter that quickly increased in volume when I saw the look on his face. Carmela wanted to be an interior designer. She enrolled in a few online classes last fall—though, nothing came of it. While she claimed she didn't have time, I didn't believe her. She'd been stuck in a rut since her fiancé died, and she couldn't bring herself to move forward.

"Stop laughing at me."

I buried my face in the pillow, my limbs trembling. It smelled like fresh, clean laundry and Gian. "I can't help it." My words were muffled.

"Oh, really?" His hands curved around my ribcage, and he tickled me.

"Oh my God." I kicked my legs, squirming, wiggling, and twisting until I escaped his hold and flipped onto my back. My hair covered my face, and the t-shirt I found in his dresser had shifted up my waist, revealing a good slice of my stomach.

He pushed my hair away from my face. His body hovered over mine, his topaz-colored eyes glittering with some unknown emotion. "Do you have a brother or a sister?"

I raked my teeth over my lower lip. "A younger brother who I haven't seen in years."

"Where is he?" he asked, his fingers still playing

with my hair.

"He joined the Army right after he graduated from high school, and he never has much time to talk. The four years before he left, he spent the summers at some camp on the East Coast, and I spent the summers dancing with my mom. Needless to say, we've gradually grown apart."

He nodded. "What about your parents? Are you close?"

"Nah, not really." I glanced to the side, feeling exposed under his heat of his stare. "My dad didn't live in Nebraska with us. He visited us on occasion until I turned five, when he disappeared entirely."

"What happened to him?"

"Who knows? My parents never married. I don't share his last name. I'm pretty sure I could walk right by him on the street and I wouldn't have a clue. He'd come around for birthdays and apparently with enough frequency to get my mom pregnant again, then one birthday he didn't show up, and my mom never offered an explanation." I rolled my eyes. God, she could be so stubborn. Thinking about her gave me a headache. "Even now, she won't say anything about him other than he belongs in the past. As you can imagine, we've never gotten along very well."

"Why's that?"

"Maybe we're too alike. She moved to New York when she was eighteen to dance professionally. When she didn't land any role worth a damn, she took jobs dancing in clubs in the tristate area to survive. She got pregnant, and she moved home. Needless to say, she wasn't very happy about me following in her footsteps." I cleared my throat, my impending failure clogging my throat like a ten car pileup. "I guess she was right. She failed, and it looks like I'm going to fail too."

Gian braced himself above me with one hand while the other brushed down my cheek to my collarbone. "I see."

"What do you see?"

His eyelids heavy, he halved the space between us. His mouth idled close enough that I felt his balmy exhalations as they ghosted across my lips. If I focused hard enough, I could make out every sooty blade of his lashes and every honeyed starburst in his irises.

I splayed my unsteady hands on his bare chest, and they prickled with the contradictory urge to push him away or slip my arm around his neck and pull him closer. I closed my eyes and counted the powerful thumps of his heart against my palm because the look on his face was too hard to process. It stripped me bare. It made me crave bad things.

Push him away.

Push him away.

Maybe I would have heeded my unvoiced pleas if only he weren't so close that his spicy, intoxicating scent filled my lungs. His hand skated down my side with a feather-soft touch, and goose bumps peppered my skin. Without warning, his mouth dragged down my neck to my shoulder, pausing for a beat, then skimming across my collarbone. I angled my head to the side inviting his touch, undeterred by the fact that somewhere in the back of my mind, buried beneath the fog of desire, I wondered how much I'd regret this tomorrow when the shroud of darkness lifted.

"A beautiful woman who has lost confidence in herself. A beautiful woman who will succeed if she pushes aside her fears and tries again. A woman too fucking perfect to be real." His voice was deep and smoky next to my ear, and it ruffled the strands of my hair.

My breasts tightened in response. Heat inched up my face, and my eyes opened, powerless to shut him out any longer. Powerless to resist him. Powerless to deny myself despite knowing this was the king of all bad ideas. Though my surrender would surely result in heartbreak, I was starting to think he might be worth the risk.

"You think so?" My voice was husky. Too husky for my own good. Passion burned in his eyes, flickering like a flame in the wind. "I know so. It's so clear, I can't believe you don't see it."

I slid my hand up his chest and around his neck like I promised myself I wouldn't. I felt the chaotic drum of his pulse under the pads of my fingers and the warmth of his skin. We stared at each other, both of us caught in a miasma of lust and desire. If I tilted my head up a little bit, I'd eliminate any suggestion of space between us, and my lips would collide with his.

"*Ti penso sempre*," he muttered along with a few other soft words I didn't understand. Maybe I didn't want to understand. It'd make the moment real rather than dreamlike, and I liked the castles-in-the-air feel of being with him. Being in his bed. Being in his line of sight.

I arched my pelvis into him, reveling in the solid yet satiny feel of him. Cupping the side of my face, he rubbed his thumb over my lips, hesitating for a second. I nipped him lightly. Playfully. Daringly.

"You're going to be the death of me," he mumbled, and his lips crashed against mine. Taking. Seeking. Tempting.

Lost in the wickedness of his kiss, desire swirled inside of me. I clawed at his boxers, finally shoving them down his legs with the tips of my toes. He ripped my t-shirt over my head, his hands tangling in my hair in the frenzy to be skin-on-skin.

He slid my lace boyshorts down my legs, and a warning light flashed in my brain, begging me to stop and consider repercussions. Casual sex wasn't my thing. Some people enjoyed the meaningless release and didn't have problems erasing it from their memory and conscience. I wasn't built that way. I had a hard time not getting caught up in the significance of being raw and vulnerable with someone.

As quickly as the reflection took root, my mind backtracked. A small part of me delighted in the idea of grabbing hold of the moment and seeing where this led if only to wipe away the stain of Kevin and our failed engagement and replace it with something new. Something for me. Something to reclaim my life.

I can do this. It won't mean anything if I don't let it.

With that little pep talk, the tug of war inside my mind faded. I wanted him. I needed him, if only for a few blinding moments of pleasure.

Sensing my capitulation, his finger slid through my folds, testing and teasing. His free hand cupped one breast then the other. I couldn't look away from his face. His pupils were dilated with a golden rim that gleamed in the dim light. He flicked his tongue along his top lip like he wanted nothing more than to devour me whole.

A short, needy moan erupted from my lips, and any tiny lingering reservations cartwheeling through my mind came to an abrupt cease-fire. My hands moved up and down the muscles of his arms, and they rippled, bulged, and flexed like a sculpture that had come to life. I yanked on the roots of his coarse, wavy hair, not too hard, but not with much caution either. His lips smashed against mine for another kiss that seemed to last forever, yet not long enough to satisfy my simmering lust.

I tasted the mint of his toothpaste. I tasted desire. Best of all, I tasted him.

His talented fingers forged ahead, driving me crazy with every stroke and slide and flick. Tension magnified inside of me at a disquieting velocity. My limbs tingled. My chest heaved. My lips parted.

"I'm really close," I muttered with disbelief, mostly to myself.

He pulled his hand away. "I know."

"No. Don't stop," I whined in a way that would have made me cringe under normal circumstances. Not now. Not when I was five seconds from getting what I wanted.

"Jesus, sweetheart," he groaned. "Nothing could make me stop. I've been thinking about this round-the-clock since the minute you walked into my club."

He roughly nudged my knees apart and wedged his pelvis between my trembling legs. His hands clamped around my hips, pressing his thick erection against my sex in an unspoken petition for entry. A current of electricity circulated though me, raising the fine hairs on my forearms, and I shuddered.

Gripping his shaft in one hand, he moved inside me an inch. I blinked in shock.

Oh my God. No words.

One more inch and our synchronized groans meshed into one. One more inch, and I stopped cold.

"Wait." My hands scraped down the sculpted planes of his chest. "Condom."

His gaze raked up my body until it collided with mine. His mouth ticked up at the corners. Without a word, he leaned over, grabbed a foil square from the top drawer of his nightstand, ripped it open with his teeth, and rolled it down his erection.

His body blanketed mine again, and he brushed a kiss across my lips. "Better?"

"Yeah. Now fuck me before I change my mind." My voice came out throaty and unrecognizable, not only in tone, but in every way possible. Those words didn't belong to me. I had never uttered anything remotely similar in my entire life.

He threw his head back and laughed, and his corded neck muscles stood out in sharp relief. "You're a bossy thing."

He guided himself inside of me in one breath-robbing thrust. He paused for a second. Then, moved in and out in experimental jousts that ignited little spasms of mind-numbing bliss deep inside my core.

I rolled my hips.

"Shit," he said, his voice thick and shaky with desire. "If you keep doing that, this won't last long."

"I don't care." I rolled my hips again, and this time, I dug my nails into his back, hunting for the release that already shimmered exasperatingly close.

Like a mind reader, he anchored his hands around my hips, positioning me so that each flex of his pelvis rubbed me in a way that had me mumbling senseless words and winding me tighter and tighter. Every molecule inside of me reached for him. Craved him. Within mere minutes, an orgasm split through me, my inner muscles clamping down in frenzied pleasure.

A scream tumbled from my swollen lips. My heart pounded like I had danced for hours, and the spasms kept going and going like I had all the time in the world.

Gian thrust hard and fast. With the bed frame creaking and the headboard tapping against the wall, he lost control. His lips were pulled back over his teeth, and damp strands of his hair clung to his forehead. His eyelids dropped to half-mast, and he swelled inside of me. A whisper of a groan split his lips, and he exploded.

When the haze of lust faded, he rolled off me. I pried open my eyelids and looked at him. He was stretched out on the bed with one arm propped behind his head, his chest heaving and his brow dotted with perspiration. He caught my gaze and slotted his fingers through mine without saying anything.

Lying there next to him, sated and content for the first time since I hurt my ankle was unreal. I felt like I had stepped into an alternative universe where black was white and white was black. While none of our problems were resolved and the animosity between us would unquestionably return, for right now, in this silver of time, my heart was free, and my head was clear. Amusement still toying with the corners of my lips, my eyes drifted closed, and my heart rate evened out.

"By the way, don't think I didn't notice the way you mangled my toothpaste."

"Huh?" My eyes popped open, and I looked at him. "Mangled your toothpaste. What the hell are you talking about?"

He poked the side of my ribs with our interlaced hands. "You squeezed the middle instead of rolling up the end."

I blinked. "So?"

"Who does that?"

I raised my eyebrows. "Apparently, me."

"Yeah, well, that needs to stop." He clucked at me. "That's the kind of stuff that will ruin our fake engagement."

"Thanks for the tip. I'll lodge a complaint about your dictatorial ways with Carmela to lay the groundwork for our impending breakup."

He snorted. "Carmela has to take my side. She's my twin. Twins trump friends."

I grinned. "Yeah, we'll see about that."

CHAPTER EIGHTEEN

Evangeline

My eyes blinked open, and I felt nearly as tired as I did when I finally fell asleep last night. With a heavy sigh, I rolled onto my side. Big red numbers on the alarm clock screamed at me.

9:18.

Crap.

Double crap.

I had booked time in the dance studio at ten. I'd be late even if I managed to get ready and out the door in the next fifteen minutes. I jumped out of bed, and cold air hit my naked form like a brick wall. A rush of uncomfortable memories taunted me. Jeered at me.

My stomach bottomed out. Flames licked at my cheeks. My knees wobbled, and even supposing I wanted to pretend like last night didn't happen, my first step shattered the illusion. I was deliciously sore in all the wrong…or right places. I couldn't decide which. My sleepy brain scrambled for a way

138

to rationalize what had happened between us.

Don't think about it. Don't think about him. It doesn't matter.

The clock ticking, I yanked a t-shirt over my head and ran out of the room. Ten minutes later, I was dressed with my dance bag slung over my shoulder and rushing toward the front door. I skidded to a halt when I noticed Gian sitting at the long walnut kitchen table, scrolling through his phone.

My heart stopped for a second then lurched into gear, beating double time, fueled by my already frazzled nerves. I'd counted on not seeing him for a day or two, or at worst until tonight. He was normally long gone by this time of day. Now that I thought about it, though, I'd seen him more in the last three days than the entire previous week.

"Where's Tony?" I kept my voice monotone all while silently begging my face not to blush.

It wasn't like I'd never hooked up with a guy and had to face him the next day, but it happened infrequently enough that I felt decidedly awkward. I didn't know where to put my hands. I didn't know where to look, so my gaze bounced everywhere other than on him. I licked my lips. I fidgeted from one leg to the other. More than a little annoyed with myself, I froze like a deer caught in headlights. Was there anything more pathetic than the way I was acting? Because right then, I felt like an enormous loser who couldn't handle a simple hookup with sophisticated indifference.

Gian looked at me over the rim of his blue coffee mug, one brow cocked, his ever-smirking lips mocking my discomfort. "He had some personal business today, so I gave him the day off."

"Well, then..." I tugged on the cornflower blue infinity scarf that felt more like a noose around my neck the longer he looked at me. "I guess I'll catch a cab. See you later."

He stood, the metal legs of his chair scraping across the ebony-stained hardwood floors. "Where are you going?"

"Dancing." At his blank look, I continued. "I booked some private time in a dance studio to practice and get in shape. I'll be back in a couple of hours."

"Ah, right. I don't know how I forgot." He snagged his phone from the table and stuffed it in the back pocket of his dark jeans. "I'll give you a ride."

"You don't have to do that. I'm fine taking a cab." I flipped my hand toward him. "I'm sure you have better stuff to do. Don't you have to work or something like that?"

"Nope. It's Monday. The club isn't open." He edged closer to me, his heavy footfalls ringing in my ears. "Besides, I don't want you wandering around by yourself. It's not a good idea after what happened last night."

My brows scrunched together, and my heart did this weird fluttery thing inside my chest. For a fleeting second, I thought he meant what happened between us. Then I remembered the drive home, and my shoulders uncoiled with relief. I didn't want to jump right into a conversation about the meaning of last night. It'd muddle my thoughts and tear my attention away from dancing, and I needed to remain focused on my career regardless of what happened in my personal life.

"Yeah, okay. You're probably right," I agreed despite the anxiety clawing at my chest. What other choice did I have? "Do you have any idea what happened? Was it random or…?" I didn't know how to finish my sentence.

"I'm working on it."

"Okay."

I didn't understand Gian's world. He never talked to me about the risks of what he did. I assumed he and his family were into some bad stuff and somehow connected to the mafia, and other than that, I didn't know shit. I was running blind, and I couldn't exactly use mafia movies or books to give me the down low on what not to do. As much as it irked me to rely on another man after Kevin, I had to trust Gian.

***

Twenty minutes later, I stood in the dance studio in a pair of black capri leggings and a cotton cropped black top that hung off one shoulder. I moved from leg holds to lunges and every other stretch in my warmup routine, doing my best to ignore Gian's presence. It seemed nearly impossible. My gaze tangled with his every time his feet shuffled over the hardwood floor or his finger pressed against the screen of his phone. Every movement, breath, or shared glance reminded me of last night, and I couldn't afford to be distracted.

Sighing, I stuffed my earbuds into my ears and started moving through a dance I had choreographed last week.

Pas de bourrée.

Grand jeté.

Fouetté

Every noise, thought, and twinge of pain faded away. I loved dancing. It was a part of me. I loved flowing from one move to the other, my body straining, muscles flexing and merging with the music. I loved the way the bass rumbled through me, making me feel alive. Even if I couldn't do it professionally, I knew I could never stop dancing. It was imprinted on my soul. Without it, I'd be lost.

Two hours passed like twenty minutes. Sweat misted my forehead. While my legs felt a little too much like jelly for my liking, my ankle didn't hurt nearly as much as last week. In fact, I hardly noticed it once I got into the routine.

CHAPTER NINETEEN

Gian

I punched out text after text, calling in favors, threatening people if necessary, because I needed to figure out who was behind the attempt on my life last night. The car that rammed us was a black Cadillac Escalade with dark tinted windows. Unfortunately, it didn't have a front license plate, and I never got a look at the back.

I had Tony making inquiries about a car in the shop with similar characteristics. Unless the car was stolen or the owner was a *stunade*, I didn't expect him to find anything. Sal was spending the day poking around Brighton Beach to see what the Russians were up to, and I'd been avoiding Dominick's underboss, Nico DeAngelo, like the plague. Apparently, the attempt on my life had wormed its way up to Dominick, and Nico had demanded to see me sometime today.

Right now, Nico or "Crazy Nico" as everyone called him, was the crown prince in the Trassato family. Dominick loved the bastard, but by most accounts, everyone else considered him a loose cannon with an unhealthy penchant for murder and torture. Before Dominick promoted him to underboss at the age of thirty-four, Nico had carried out more than three dozen mob hits, and all of them involved systematically dismembering the targets like a seasoned meat butcher.

I gripped the phone tightly in my hand, and I reread the coded messages for the third time. Since so much of our day-to-day activities skirted the law, we had our own vernacular. The consequence of someone reading plainly worded texts would be catastrophic.

Nico: The country club has a steak special. Do you want to meet for dinner?

The country club was code for Carmine's, a restaurant owned by another capo. We used the back room of the restaurant for meetings because Dominick had it swept for listening devices on a daily basis.

Me: Can't today.

Nico: I heard what the dogs did to your car. I want to talk to you about cleaning it.

We used dogs as a general term to discuss an enemy.

Me: Did Red tell you?

Nico: Doesn't matter.

Fucking Tony. I was going to rip his fucking head off and shit down his throat. I had serious doubts about whether I should trust him anymore. I thought Carlo wanted to take me down, but now I saw enemies everywhere.

Me: I'm busy today.

Nico: Don't eat alone.

Eating alone meant being greedy. What a miserable cocksucker. No one accused me of being greedy. I bent over backward for Dominick. He got a taste of all my business, including the legit shit. He was my fucking uncle. I wouldn't screw him over despite the fact that he was an asshole.

Me: Fuck off.

Nico: You need to report your latest scores today to finalize your handicap for the tournament.

Reporting my latest scores meant reporting shit to Nico and Dominick. Essentially, he pulled the trump card. I couldn't deny Dominick's direct orders without serious ramifications.

Dread curling around my chest, my options circled through my mind like a record player stuck on repeat. A little over a week ago, I was on top of the world. How fast things changed. Now every part of my life was on the verge of imploding.

After a few minutes of deliberation, I sent Nico a quick text.

Me: I'll meet you at the country club for dinner tonight.

I didn't have a choice. He mentioned *him*, and all bets were off. As much as his speech and our conversation last night pissed me the fuck off, I couldn't defy Dominick.

Out of the corner of my eye, I caught a blur of black in the wall of mirrors. My irritation faded the second my gaze landed on Evie. Her body dipped to the side, and she spun in a circle with one leg raised high in the air. *Marone,* the way her long, toned legs moved seamlessly from one move to the next made my cock twitch.

I remembered the way her skin felt like silk under my fingers. The way her long legs hugged my waist when I moved inside of her. The not so quiet moans she made as she came undone.

My phone beeped repeatedly—only, I no longer gave a shit. I silenced it and stuffed it in my pocket. When ten minutes became an hour, I slid down the wall to get comfortable. Engrossed didn't begin to describe what I felt while I watched her float from one move to the other. I wished the music flowed from the overhead speakers, not her earbuds. I wanted to hear what she heard, feel what she felt, and somehow be part of her secret world.

Finally, she stopped moving, and as selfish as it sounded, I hated that she didn't acknowledge me.

She'd managed to forget I was here with her, and it stung because I couldn't take my eyes off her.

She yanked her earbuds from her ears and draped the wire around her shoulders. Chest heaving, she closed her eyes and moved her head in a circle, first one direction and then the other.

I cleared my throat, and she froze, keeping her eyes squeezed shut for a fraction longer than necessary.

She turned her back to me and snagged her sweater from the barre mounted to the wall. "You didn't have to stick around. I'm sure you were bored out of your mind."

"Far from it." Needing to touch her, I crossed the room, wrapped my hands around her waist, and pulled her back flush against my chest. I drew circles on the exposed skin of her belly, loving the way her muscles jumped under my fingers. "You're incredibly talented. I can see why you don't want to give up your dream. There's no way you won't get another role soon."

"Hah." A forced laugh burst from her lips, and she twisted out of my hold. "It's not that easy. It's been a year, and people in the industry have already forgotten about me, and in the unlikely event that they haven't, my injury and lengthy absence will linger in the back of their minds."

"I don't know." I rubbed my fingers across my lips. "You might be surprised."

"Maybe. Maybe not." She pulled her sweater over her head and grabbed her dance bag from the hardwood floor. "I guess I'll find out soon enough."

I followed her out of the room. "Why's that?"

"There's an audition I'm going to at the end of next month." She paused mid-step. "That is, if you're okay with it."

My shoulders tensed. "Of course you can go to an audition. Why do you think I'd stop you?"

"I had my doubts." She shrugged. "You gotta admit you have me on a pretty short leash."

I ground my teeth together, biting back the response on the tip of my tongue.

"Wait, Miss Jeffers," called a woman with caramel colored skin, high cheekbones, and nearly black hair.

Evie lifted a hand in greeting. "Oh. Hi, Jenna. I didn't realize you'd be here today."

"I tried to run the credit card number you called in last week, and it didn't work."

"Really?" Evie twisted the hem of her sweater and a blush stained her cheeks. "I don't understand why that happened. Maybe you could try to run it again?" She shoved her hand into her open bag and pulled out a black wallet. "What were the last four digits of the card I gave you?"

Jenna's fingers rapped over the keyboard. "Nine. Eight. Eight. Three."

Evie unzipped her wallet and pulled out a silver credit card. "Huh." She tipped her head to the ceiling, and then her eyes flared. "Shit. I forgot to pay the bill," she mumbled under her breath.

I pulled out my wallet and tossed a credit card on the counter. "Put it on here."

"No." Evie slapped her hand on top of mine, waving her head. "You can't pay for my stuff. I won't let you."

148

Grinning at Jenna, I dislodged Evie's hand from mine. "Isn't my fiancée cute? She hates it when I pay for things; however, I insist. By the way, you can keep my card on file and charge me weekly for all her studio time."

"Perfect." Jenna snatched the credit card from my hand. "Thank you," she held up the card and squinted at the name, "Mr. Trassato." Her voice hitched, and her hand trembled like she recognized the name.

"Why are you doing this?" Evie hissed.

"Don't make it into a big deal."

She planted her hands on her hips. "It's fifty dollars an hour."

"So?" I raised my brows. "What's your point?"

"That's two hundred and fifty dollars for last week and another hundred for today."

"I'm not worried. I can afford it."

Her gaze flitted to the side, and her teeth grazed her plump lower lip. My breath stuttered inside my chest…just a little. If I didn't think she'd slap me across the face, I wouldn't hesitate to steal another kiss right now. She looked so damn sexy, and I hadn't gotten nearly enough of her last night. There were so many things I'd been dreaming about doing to her, and now that I'd crossed the line, I didn't give a fuck about the consequences. Provided that we both understood that it wouldn't become permanent, no one would get hurt.

"I'll pay you back as soon as I get back on my feet. I swear."

I tucked a wayward strand of her fiery hair behind her ear and pressed a kiss to the top of her head. "That's not happening, sweetheart. I take care of what's mine. Get used to it."

"I can't accept this. I'm paying you back as soon as I have the money, *with* interest."

Jenna slid the credit card across the shiny black counter, and I stuffed it back into my wallet.

"Someone booked your usual time for tomorrow, but this time is open the following day."

"What?" Evie said. "I reserved that time for the entire month."

"I let them have the time because your credit card didn't go through—"

"Unbook it," I barked.

"I can give her an hour later in the evening after the last dance class. Maybe 9 to 10. That's the best I can do. How does that sound?"

"No. That won't work."

Evie tugged on my sleeve. "It's not a big deal, Gian. I'll take the later time. If you can't take me, I'm sure Tony will or I can take a cab."

"No, Evie, it is a big deal." I pulled a couple of hundreds out of my wallet and slapped them on the counter. "My fiancée booked that hour, and you're going to honor her appointment. I'd hate for this to negatively impact your business. Do you understand what I'm saying, or do I need to spell it out for you?"

Jenna eyed the money for a few seconds, and her shoulders drooped. "I assume you'll be here at the same time tomorrow, Miss Jeffers?"

"Yes."

I hooked my arm around Evie's waist and ushered her out of the studio and into my car. Thank

God, I had more than one, or I'd have had to get a rental.

"By the way," I said, pulling away from the curb and merging into steady stream of yellow cabs. "I won't accept your money." I cranked up the volume on the radio, signaling the end of the conversation.

"You don't have a choice." Lowering the volume, she giggled with such an enchanting combination of sassiness and vulnerability I was relatively certain something inside of me had splintered wide open.

"No, Evangeline," I growled. I unclipped my sunglasses from my shirt and slid them on my face. "You're not."

"We'll see." She tugged on her ponytail on top of her head, and her long flame-colored hair spilled over her shoulders. Rays of sunlight danced across her face and around her head, accentuating the golden highlights in her messy locks and the ivory perfection of her skin. I had to forcibly train my gaze back on the road. Shit. This woman tugged on all of my heartstrings without trying.

"Are you hungry?" I asked, purposely changing the subject.

"A little. Although, it has to be something low-calorie and carb-free. Your mom's meal killed my diet last night." She waved her hand in a tight circle. "Don't get me wrong. I loved every bite, but I can't eat like that every day. Not if I want to get back in shape and get a real shot in another musical."

"You sing?"

She chuckled. "I sing. I dance. I can even act. I wouldn't think about auditioning for a Broadway musical if I didn't."

"Huh?" I tilted my head to the side. "I thought you danced and recited a couple of lines here and there."

"When's the last time you went to a Broadway musical?"

I drummed my fingers on the steering wheel. "Five or six years ago. It's…" I cleared my throat. "It's not my thing. I tend to fall asleep." *To avoid stabbing myself in the eyes,* I silently added.

Her eyes widened, and she punched me lightly on the shoulder. "Are you serious?"

"Yeah," I admitted. I'd much rather watch an action movie than a live production with people singing and dancing. Honestly, it gave me a big fat headache. I left at intermission the last time I went, swearing I'd never go back. "Don't think about dragging me to one to prove me wrong."

"What happens if I get the part I'm auditioning for? You'll have to go if only to play the doting fiancé."

"If you get a part in that play, how many months do you practice before the opening night?"

"A month. Maybe two depending on the budget."

"Our arrangement will probably be over by then." The second the words left my mouth, my insides wrenched painfully.

Evie stilled, looking at me like I had wounded her, and then she smiled, except it looked brittle. "Okay, then, I guess you're safe from being tortured by me."

"Lucky me."

For some reason, I didn't feel lucky at all. I felt vacant. I wanted to be there to see her debut. I wanted to fill her dressing room with so many flowers you could smell them from down the hall. I forced the image out of my head. "So lunch? What do you feel like?"

CHAPTER TWENTY

Evangeline

I didn't know what to do with myself. For the first time in over a week, I was blessedly by myself. No Tony. No Gian. No one. Gian met a friend of his for dinner. He didn't elaborate, and I didn't ask any questions. On his way out the door, he handed me a stack of takeout menus and told me he'd be home late and not to wait up.

I had roamed the floors of his home, peeking in rooms, opening cabinets, looking for nothing in particular. Maybe I wanted to know more about Gian. Maybe it soothed the anxiety building in my chest. For days, I had wanted time to decompress without anyone looking at me and judging me. Now that I had time alone, I hated it. I couldn't stop thinking about last night and this afternoon. What they meant. What I wanted them to mean, if anything.

Lunch and every moment afterward felt too good to be true. He opened my car door. He entertained me with stories of Carmela and him when they were kids. He held my hand while we strolled aimlessly through his neighborhood in search of the perfect dessert. We ended up in a cute Italian deli, and he ordered so many confections they blanketed the tiny bistro table.

When I finally got around to bringing up what happened between us last night, he brushed my concerns aside, claiming we didn't need to make a big deal out of it. He warned me not to complicate things. He told me we had plenty of time to figure it out. I ignored all of my doubts and continued pretending.

Pretending Gian cared for me. Pretending we were happily engaged. Pretending Gian didn't have ties to the criminal world. Pretending everything would be fine.

Except now that he had left me alone for the first time in days, I couldn't stop the tidal wave of thoughts from circling like vultures. Could I continue to crawl into his bed and pretend it didn't matter? Could I handle being with him when we didn't have a future?

Sadly, my current circumstance bore an eerie resemblance to what happened with Kevin. He swooped into my life and took over every detail, all the while chasing his dreams even as I forgot about mine. As much as I wanted to believe I wouldn't put Gian first and let my prospects crumble, my fortitude wavered in the past, and it could again.

My exploration of Gian's house at an end, I selected a cold-pressed juice from the refrigerator, an apple, and a paring knife from the kitchen. I flipped on the television and meticulously carved the apple into tiny wedges and popped them into my mouth one by one.

I flipped aimlessly through the channels, not really watching anything in particular. Instead, I stared blankly at the flickering screen, questioning everything and everyone without a single available confidant on speed dial. I'd systematically burned through every relationship I'd made since moving to New York.

After I hurt my ankle, I gradually stopped reaching out my theater friends. Being around them was too hard. With every passing accomplishment that belonged to them and not me, jealousy and regret multiplied until I couldn't stand it. When I stopped returning their phone calls, they got the hint and followed suit.

I still had Carmela and Kevin, so I pushed on, filling my time with meaningless wedding details and helping Carmela get over the death of her fiancé. Now, I had no one. Gian didn't count. If everything worked to plan, he'd be out of my life by the end of the summer.

When I realized I'd paused on an infomercial on skin care for a good half an hour, I turned off the television. My eyes heavy, I slumped against the arm of the sofa. I draped one hand over my face, and the other hand dangled above the floor, still clutching the stupid knife.

Like everything else, going to bed involved a choice. I didn't know if I should go to the guest bedroom or Gian's bedroom. The weak part of me wanted to avoid the choice altogether and fall asleep here. It'd be easier, but taking the easy path over the last year landed me in this mess in the first place. I pulled the gray throw blanket over my legs, promising myself I'd make a choice soon.

As my eyes drifted closed, the loud crash of exploding glass from somewhere near the entry ricocheted through the house. My heart skittered to a stop. The air whooshed out of my lungs in a half-scream and half-exhalation. I scrambled to my feet then fell onto all fours, tripping over the throw blanket tangled around my legs.

With my eyes wide and my blood chugging like a freight train, I scrutinized every shadowed corner of the dimly lit room. Coming to my knees, I grabbed the discarded paring knife, gripping it so tightly my knuckles whitened. My jagged breaths echoed through room, competing for attention with the hysterical drum of my heart.

I waited…

Listening for a creak of the hardwood floors, a bang of a kicked in door, or more shattered glass. I stayed that way, with one arm raised prepared to slash at anything in my vicinity, my eyes wildly searching and scanning for anyone or anything.

I heard nothing except the steady tick tock of the clock over the fireplace mantel and the constant whirr of the furnace. After I had managed to compose myself, I pushed to my feet and tiptoed to the foyer where the stairs were located.

With my back pressed against the wall, I stopped dead. A strong breeze blew through the glass panel inset in the upper half of the front door. Tiny silvers of glass littered the gray and white marble floor, and a rust-colored brick was perched on its side. Black letters in all caps stained one side. The low light and angle of the offending chunk of clay prevented me from making out the words.

"Oh my God," I mumbled, panic inching up my throat. I swallowed it back and sucked in what I hoped would be a calming breath. I didn't have time for a breakdown right now. I needed my phone. I needed to call Gian, and I couldn't do either unless I went upstairs.

Shivering, I sprinted up the stairs, my bare feet slapping against the cold treads. When I reached the third floor, I snagged my purse off the dresser and dumped it contents on the floor. Hands fumbling, I called up Gian's name from my list of contents.

The call went directly to voicemail. I tried two more times with identical results.

Dammit, answer your phone. Where are you?

If I lived with a different man, I'd call the police, but something told me Gian would lose his mind if I went that route. I scrolled through my contacts, pausing at Carmela's name. I hesitated, recounting our conversation last night after I fainted. While she hadn't done anything overtly rude, there was a big fat wall between us, and I didn't know if I'd ever scale it.

Sadly, she was my only option because my mom couldn't do a damn thing from halfway across the country and my brother was deployed on the other side of the world. I pressed her name and waited. Unlike Gian, she answered on the second ring.

"Hello?" she said over a steady hum of voices.

"Carmela, it's Evie." My voice warbled.

"Evie, are you okay?"

"No." I lowered my voice. "Someone threw a brick through the glass in the front door at Gian's house."

"Where's Gian?"

"I don't know." I rolled my head in a circle, mentally pushing away the icy grip of fear. "He went out with a friend, and he's not answering his phone."

She didn't respond for a beat, then, "Did you call the police?"

"No. Of course not." I frowned, dragging my free hand down the back of my neck. "Do you think I should?"

"No. No. It was probably a couple of kids playing a prank. I'll be there in a few minutes. I'm not that far away."

"Yeah, you're probably right." I leaned against the side of the dresser, trying to relax the knots in my shoulders. "Are you sure you're okay with coming here? If you're busy—"

"Jesus, Evie, I'm not leaving you there alone. I know things are weird between us now that you're…" she paused, and my heart constricted, "with Gian, but you're still my friend. My best friend."

"I miss you." It escaped my mouth without forethought, and it was the truth. Without question, I missed her, more than I ever imagined possible.

Horns honked in the background and cars revved their engines, and for a second, I wondered if she'd heard me.

"I miss you too, Evie. Sit tight, I'm already on

my way there. In fact, I'm less than two blocks away."

"Will you stay on the phone until you get here? I'm scared. I don't think anyone is around, but—"

"I wouldn't dream of hanging up. We can hang out at my house until Gian gets home. Okay?"

"Yeah." I rested my head on top of my knees. My muscles felt like limp noodles as the adrenaline leeched from my body. "That sounds perfect."

"I'm sorry if I haven't been supportive of this thing with my brother." She blew out a breath. "It came out of the blue, and I didn't know how to handle it. You're my best friend and all, and as bad as I want you to move on from Kevin, I don't like that you're doing it with my brother. I mean, you're engaged. How did that happen?"

My teeth clamped together to halt the urge to spill the truth about my relationship with Gian. At this point, a confession would only drive a bigger wedge between my best friend and me. "I don't know. I couldn't explain it if I tried. It just did."

"Yeah, I didn't expect you to." She snorted. "You gotta admit this is awkward on so many levels."

"I can't disagree with you."

"Is it weird that I'm torn between feeling protective of you and my brother? I want you to have a rebound. You deserve it. Everyone should go a little crazy after dating a piece shit like Kevin, but I don't like the idea that you're using my brother to—"

"It's not like that," I interrupted, tugging on the hem of my pants.

"Yeah, I don't want any details. Okay?" She sighed dramatically. "And honestly, my brother is the last person who needs my protection. He doesn't exactly have the best track record with women. I swear he has had a revolving door in his bedroom since he turned sixteen."

Although it wasn't anything I hadn't suspected, my stomach dropped like an elevator with a severed cord, and I kind of felt like I wanted to hurl. "Wow. That's exactly what every woman wants to hear about her fiancé." I forced out a chuckle so I didn't sound needy and pathetic. I was done being that person. "Thanks."

"My pleasure. I like to take cheap shots at him whenever possible." She laughed. "I'm walking up the steps now. Come open the door."

CHAPTER TWENTY-ONE

Gian

"Hey, Nico." I slid into a dark brown leather booth, opposite him. "How are you doing?"

"Good, good. You?" He leaned forward, resting one elbow on the table and the cutlery clattered. A chunk of dark brown hair covered one of his brows. Most women considered him attractive with his sharp, angled face and dimpled chin. To me, he looked like a smug bastard.

I shrugged one shoulder. "Other than last night, everything is great. Fucking wonderful."

He brushed a hand down the front of his charcoal suit, looking like Satan in the flesh with his vacant, icy blue eyes crawling over every inch of me. "You want to tell me what happened last night?"

A waiter placed two glasses on the table and a bottle of wine. Not my first choice of drink, but if I wanted to make it through tonight without getting in a fight, I needed something to relax me.

I draped one arm along the back of the booth. "There's not much to tell. I think you've heard what happened, and as of right now, I don't have a single thing to add. This meeting is a waste of time."

Nico's nostrils flared. "Listen here. You don't get a special pass because Dominick is your uncle. You have to play by the same rules as the rest of us, and that means reporting shit like this to me. First Tommy Calvo and now this. In case you didn't notice, this isn't the Gian show. This do 'whatever you feel like' shit has to stop. End of the fucking story."

I took a deep drink of my glass of wine and slammed it on the white linen covered table. Smirking, I squeezed my hands into fists to dial back the anger bubbling in my gut. Punching Nico in the face wouldn't get me anywhere.

"You have something you want to say to me?" he taunted.

"I didn't clip Tommy."

"Doesn't matter." He leaned forward, his face within spitting distance of mine. "You need to control the guys under you, or you will be replaced. It's as simple as that. Some of the guys didn't think you were ready to be a capo, and now I'm wondering if they were right."

I ground my teeth together. "I can handle my shit just fine. I don't need you to babysit me."

"Fine." He waved his hand. "Then start handling it, and tell me what happened last night because I don't have all fucking day to play patty cake with you."

I shot Nico a humorless smile filled with venom. "A black Escalade rammed us on the way home last night and took a few shots at us. I went down a one-way street and lost them. That's all I know. Tony and Sal are looking into it."

"So who the hell did you piss off this time?"

The furious tone of his voice hit me like a bullet to the chest. We hadn't made it to dinner, and I was fed up with his patronizing ass.

"Other than you?" I slanted forward, my lips curling up to expose my teeth. "Apparently, every fucking moron under me who thinks they have a right to my job, so if you're looking for suspects maybe you should start there."

He tugged on his blue tie and grinned like a shark. "Are you accusing me of something?"

"I don't know? Should I be?" Taunting the resident sociopath probably wasn't the best choice, but I refused to back down like a pussy. There was a fine line between showing him respect and handing him my dick wrapped with a giant glitter-covered bow.

Nico's eyes burning dangerously, he steepled his fingers together on top of the table. "Are you done with your poor-me tantrum so we can get on with business?"

"What business? I told you what I know, and I'm sure you already have a mental list of my enemies, so I'm not really sure why you summoned me here. Do you care to enlighten me?"

He leaned back. "What about your fiancée?"

"What about her?" I snapped.

His brows raised and his lips twisted into a sneer.

"Does she have any enemies?"

I snorted. "Fuck if I know. She's only lived in New York for a couple of years, so she hasn't had much time to piss people off. She does have an ex-fiancé. I can't imagine him trying to gun us down, though. He's some pansy ass artist."

"Yeah, maybe so." He glanced to the side. "Dominick has Tony digging into her past just to be sure."

"Great." I tossed my napkin on top of the table and stood up. I'd lost my appetite. For longer than I could remember, I wanted to follow in my dad's footsteps, make him proud, and lead his crew. Now, I didn't know if I'd made the right decision. This was bullshit. I'd never get rid of the shadow over my head. "Tell him to have fun with that."

"Where are you going?"

"Home to my fiancée. After last night, I'm a little reluctant to leave her home alone. I'm sure you understand."

I didn't wait for his response. I didn't need to hear anything else from him. I got the message loud and clear. Dominick didn't approve of Evie. He wanted her gone, and the thought pissed me off so much, I wanted to keep her around purely to spite his nosy ass. My family wanted me to marry a good Italian girl within our circle of associates. I always thought I would too, but the more time I spent with Evie, the more I resented the idea.

My life had been scripted from the moment I popped out of my mom's womb. I'd go to school, join the family business, marry a girl from the neighborhood, and pop out a couple of kids, hopefully boys. Then the cycle would start all over again. I never questioned it…until now.

I pulled into the garage in the basement of my home and ran up the steps to the main level.

"Evie!" I hollered, a twinge of unease raising the hairs on my forearms. When I reached my main floor, glass crunched under the soles of my shoes.

What the fuck?

"Evangeline? Where the hell are you? Are you hurt?"

I ran up the stairs, taking two steps at a time. If someone hurt her, I would find him and rip him apart limb-by-limb with my bare hands. A sickening brew of rage and fear bubbled up my throat.

When I reached the landing, she stepped into the hallway, my overnight bag tucked under her arm and Carmela trailing behind her.

"Oh, crap." She came to an abrupt halt, her hand flying to her chest. "I didn't realize you were here."

"What the hell is going on?"

She glanced at Carmela from the corner of her eye. "Someone threw a brick through the window in the front door, and—"

"I noticed. Why the hell didn't you call me?" Itching with the need to touch her, my hand edged toward her then paused mid-reach. I didn't know how to act with my sister's gaze boring into me with the force of a high-powered microscope.

Evie leaned her hip against the doorframe. "I did. More than once, actually, and it went to voicemail every single time. Luckily, your sister was in the neighborhood."

"What's your problem, Gian?" Carmela asked,

her finger pointed at the center of my chest. "There's no need to be an asshole. Evie was scared, and I was in the neighborhood. I asked her to come stay with me because I didn't want to leave her here alone, and I had no idea when you'd be home. Do you have a problem with that?"

I dragged the heel of my hand down the side of my face and blew out a weighted breath. This night kept getting worse and worse. "Evie, are you okay?" I asked, softening my tone. I wasn't mad at Evie. Far from it. I was pissed at myself. I shouldn't have left her alone, not after last night. I should have called Tony even though every day that passed my doubts of his trustworthiness multiplied.

"I think so."

She didn't sound okay. Her voice cracked on the last word, and my heart screamed with some unfamiliar emotion. An animalistic possessiveness surged through me at the thought of anyone having the nerve to hurt her, and all reasonable thoughts fled.

Without question, I had managed to turn Evie's life upside down in a matter of weeks. While I knew that made me a worthless bastard in most people's book, I couldn't let her go.

Two steps and I had her cradled in my arms. I buried my head in her hair, inhaling the faint scent of jasmine. I didn't have the luxury of feeling this way about anyone, especially Evie, but damn if I didn't give two fucks anymore.

I'd been caught up in her from the first second I saw her, and that hadn't changed. I had protected her when it went against every oath I made to the family, and I wouldn't stop now. Her soulful coffee-colored eyes made me believe she got me in a way no one else ever had, except maybe my twin. That was different though. And truthfully, Carmela and I had grown apart since Rocco died. She clammed up emotionally, and I couldn't reach her anymore. It was like a part of her died along with Rocco.

I smoothed my hand up and down Evie's back, and she sighed. "Did you see anything?"

"No." Her eyes slipped closed as she shifted her weight from one foot to the other. "I think they might've wrote something on the brick. I didn't want to touch it."

My muscles pulled tight like a rubber band ready to snap. "Good. You don't need to worry about this. I'm on top of it."

I would be, because I was nowhere near as calm as I pretended to be on the surface.

"I'm fine." She pulled away from me, and my arms hung awkwardly next to my sides. "I'm not hurt. Just a little on edge. I'm sure it was nothing."

"You're probably right," I agreed, not believing a single word out of my mouth. I glanced at Carmela. "Thanks for coming, sis."

"Not a problem. I was having dinner a couple of blocks from here."

"With who?"

"Ava."

My eyebrows lifted. "As in our cousin, Ava? I thought you couldn't stand her?"

Ava spent most of her days whining about everything in her life from her hair to her clothes to a chipped nail. Even when she wasn't whining, she annoyed the fuck out of me. Everything she said came out in this nasally voice that made me want to stick a knife in her eye.

"If you haven't noticed, you have successfully monopolized my best friend, so unless I want to sit around eating ice cream, I have to compromise."

"It sounds like torture to me, but it's your life."

She playfully slapped me on the side of my head. "Don't be a jerk. Ava is charming in her own way."

"Keep telling yourself that."

"Ugh." Carmela flipped her long, dark hair over her shoulder. "Well, now that you're home, I going to take off. I have to be up early tomorrow."

Evie pulled my sister into a one armed hug. "Thanks, Carmela. I owe you."

"Don't worry about it." She toyed with the button of her jacket. "This is what friends are for. Let me know if you need anything."

"Thanks."

Evie and I followed my sister down the stairs.

"I'll hammer a piece of plywood to the door and have someone fix it in the morning," I said.

CHAPTER TWENTY-TWO

Evangeline

"Here's the broom."

I moved through the living room, my gaze pinned to Gian's back. He held the brick in one hand and a hammer in the other.

Gian whirled around, anger and hostility vibrating from him. Truthfully, his intensity scared me a little bit. Not wanting to move any closer to him, I paused, my heart beating frantically.

He lifted his chin. "Do you know anything about the Russian mafia?"

I leaned the broom against the wall, and it slid to the floor with a loud clunk, making me flinch. "No. Why?"

"Just wondering." He flipped the front of the brick toward me, his amber eyes rife with something I couldn't put my finger on.

"Vor's Property" was written across the brick in

black letters with a five-point star bookending either side.

"What does it mean?"

"It's not important." He dropped the hammer on the entry table, the metal thumping against the white lacquered surface. "I think we're good. We can clean up the glass tomorrow."

I glanced at the plywood covering the glass panel on the top half of the door and then the glass littering the floor. "Are you sure? It will only take me a minute."

"Yes. I don't want to think about this any more tonight. I had a shitty night, and that was *before* I got home."

I scoured his face, searching for clues, only I didn't see any. I saw hunger mixed with a whole lot of uncertainty. "What's wrong?"

Gian pressed his fingers to my lips. "Not now."

His fingers slotted through mine, and he guided me wordlessly up the stairs. I followed, more than a little anxious from the volatile energy zipping around us like a storm on the horizon. With every thump of our footsteps on the stairs, my anxiety soared higher and higher. He bypassed the second floor, leading me straight to his bedroom. Images of last night freeze-framed inside my brain.

"Do you really think it's a good idea for me to sleep—?"

His mouth crashed against mine, kissing me single-mindedly and with enough passion to set me ablaze. His hands snaked around my hips, hauling me tightly against him. He guided me backward until my thighs bumped into the side of the mattress.

I broke our kiss. His throat bobbed heavily, and he looked at me through hooded lids, his eyes generating enough power to light up the Brooklyn Bridge.

"What are you doing to me?" I whispered, more to myself than him because I was powerless to deny him anything from the moment I met him.

His fingers curled around the hem of my camisole, and he yanked it over my head.

"Cute." He tugged on the baby pink bow at the heart of my black lace bralette, his thumbs brushing across my nipples, soft and gentle. His barely-there touches elicited sparks of pleasure in my core. I glanced up, and my belly somersaulted when I saw the look on his face.

Lust. Desire. Passion.

I gasped for breath. It was official. I was a mistake magnet. Put a bad choice in my path, and I gravitated toward it like I'd discovered a unicorn standing next to a pot of gold under a friggin' rainbow.

"Look at me," he whispered, and like a dummy on strings, I met his stare again. His eyes gleamed in the moonlight streaming in from the overhead skylight. He buried his hands in my hair, and a faint twinge of pain nipped at my scalp. "I don't want your mind anywhere else except on me."

He lowered me to the bed. "Take off your pants," he ordered, loosening his tie and pulling it over his head.

I shimmied my tight yoga pants and panties down my legs, stopping only to gape at him when he shrugged out of his jacket and tossed it on the floor. Next went his shirt. With every button he flicked open, he revealed another inch of his golden skin. My heart drummed faster and faster, and the air seemed to thicken, cocooning us in our own world.

"You look fucking beautiful sprawled out on my bed with pink cheeks, parted lips, and your heavy eyes."

"You don't look so bad yourself."

His pants pooled on the floor, and his belt buckle jingled. I barely blinked twice, and his body had already covered mine. He pulled my nipple into his mouth, sucking, licking, and grazing the sensitive bud.

His tongue leisurely flicked over my nipple, and I arched my back. The chilly breeze from the fan wafted over my skin. Less than a second later, his hot mouth pressed against the top of my breast, sucking hard. Lifting his head, he grinned at the little red mark dotting my pale skin.

"Nice," he mumbled.

I didn't object, because a little part of me liked the idea of him branding me as his if only temporarily.

His hand snaked between our bodies, his fingers moving with confidence over my already slick flesh. He found my opening, sank one finger deep inside of me, and I shuddered, my inner walls tightening in an entreaty for more.

Gian swore under his breath, and I could smell a hint of wine on his breath. He withdrew his finger and guided the broad head of his penis into place.

173

His lambent gaze collided with mine. "Can't wait," he said, his voice a wicked growl.

With one violent flex of his hips, he surged into me. I stiffened, my breath quickening. My fists knotted in the duvet cover beneath me.

"I've got you, sweetheart." The rumbling timbre of his voice ignited a full body shiver that sunk deep into my bones.

He pulled back and then slid in again a fraction, rocking against me, moving deeper little by little with every micro-thrust until he was exactly where I needed him to be. My hands curled into the rope-like muscles lining his spine. The headboard banged against the wall. Sweat glistened on his brow. His hair stuck up, and his teeth were clamped together. Our moans morphed into one heady sound.

Every stray thought evaporated, and I could only think about him and the way he felt inside of me. My entire body sang with a pleasure so devastatingly perfect I feared I'd spontaneously combust.

I panted, desperate for the release building with every second. His name tumbled from my lips along with a hundred other disjointed thoughts, each one more lurid in my mind than in expression.

I slid my hands up his back to his neck, pulling his lips against mine, needing to taste him, needing to be connected in every way possible. I gasped when our lips separated, and he nipped my bottom lip. I bucked beneath him, my nails digging into his scalp. I was close. So close. I felt him everywhere.

My legs shuddered. My hands tingled. My skin prickled. My toes curled. Before I could break down every spine-tingling sensation, I shattered into a million pieces. My eyes pinching closed, I rode the waves of pleasure speeding through me until my muscles unwound bit-by-bit.

Seconds later, Gian collapsed on me, the course smatterings of hair on his chest rubbing against my nipples and his hips surging into me with enough force that I slid up the bed with every thrust. He grunted out my full name as he came, the four syllables echoing off the vaulted ceiling like a benediction.

My senses came back to me piecemeal, as if I were awakening from a long, drug-induced sleep.

I felt him inside of me. I felt the heavy weight of his body over mine, the pounding of his heart against my chest, the sheen of sweat coating our bodies. And I felt content. Better than content. I was *happy*.

The second the thought took root, regret reared its ugly head, creeping into the fissures of my already wounded heart. As fast as the emotion materialized, I mentally beat it back with a stick. I was living in the moment tonight and for the foreseeable future because all my plotting and planning hadn't got me anywhere noteworthy.

I ruffled my fingers through his hair, and he groaned, rolling off me. When he opened his mouth to say something, I pressed my fingers to his lips and shook my head. I didn't want to talk. I didn't want to hear his thoughts. I didn't want to think. I curled my body around his, sliding my leg up over his, and pretended fate was on my side and everything would work out the way it was meant to.

CHAPTER TWENTY-THREE

Gian

A sharp *thud* sounded at the door to my office at my club. I slammed my laptop closed and rubbed a hand down the side of my face. It'd been a week since the brick incident and that ridiculous car chase on the way home from my engagement party, and I still didn't have a single fucking lead. I didn't know if the two incidents were connected. I didn't know the players or their motivations. While the strain of not knowing what was going on was annoying at first, it had grown to the point where it felt like a goddamn monkey I couldn't get off my back.

"Come in."

Nico strutted into my office like he owned the place, with his dark hair slicked back and some dumbass double-breasted pinstriped suit that made him look like a 1920s gangster. What a fool. He slid into the chair in front of my desk and hooked his ankle on the opposite knee.

He called earlier wanting to discuss some shit. I assumed it had to do with crap happening in my life, so I agreed. I was desperate. Sal had torn Brighton Beach apart looking for clues and called in half a dozen favors that led absolutely nowhere. And Tony…well, he hadn't found out anything about the black SUV either, which wasn't unexpected. Rumor had it, he spent most of his time digging into Evie's background rather than the stuff I asked him to do. I didn't understand what Dominick expected to find. She was raised on a fucking cornfield in Nebraska. What could be so sinister about that?

"How's it going?"

I waved my hand at the door. "Shut the fucking door."

He glanced over his shoulder. "I'm waiting for Carlo. He's meeting us here."

"Carlo? What the fuck do we need with him?"

"He has information you might want to hear."

Carlo was a lazy, entitled prick. I couldn't imagine he had much to add to the conversation. On the off chance he did, he should have brought it to *my* attention, not Nico's. I was his capo. He had no right to go around me.

"Does he need to hold your hand while he talks to me now? Is that why he brought you into this?"

Nico braced his elbows on the desk, his gold and onyx cufflinks glinting in the overhead lights. "He brought me in as a witness."

"A witness." I stabbed my hand in my hair. "I can't wait. This is going to be good."

His lips thinned. "You'll want to hear what he has to say."

Heaving a sigh, I leaned back in my chair. "Yeah, I bet."

"Your lack of respect is getting old."

"You know I'm right. Carlo is a lazy piece of shit. That's exactly why Dominick promoted me and not him."

Nico shot me a warning look. "Doesn't matter. You need to inspire the loyalty of the people under you or you're not doing your job, and you can kiss your new role goodbye. You'll be *broken*."

My eyes narrowed. "Are you threatening me?"

He shrugged. "Just calling it how I see it."

"Hey, man." Carlo sauntered into my office three minutes later, his hands shoved deep into his pants pockets and a shiny bluish silver tie around neck that clashed with his ruddy nose.

I tipped up my chin, staring at him, my face blank, emotionless, but I felt a helluva a lot of something.

Rage. Anger. Frustration. Hate.

All of it roared through me with the force of a hurricane. I clutched the arms of my chair so I didn't wrap my hands around his scrawny neck and strangle the life out of his worthless ass.

Nico waved at the chair next to him. "Have a seat, Carlo."

Carlo sidled up to the chair with a shit-eating grin on his face. I had to do something about him because he'd made it clear there was only room for one of us in the Trassato family. He wanted my job, and he'd do anything do get it, including making an unholy alliance with Nico, the only other person in this family that wouldn't mind if I got clipped.

"Let's get on with this. I have another meeting." I stood, trying to establish the upper hand and take control of the meeting. If Carlo had something to say, he'd do it on my terms, not his or Nico's. "Carlo, Nico told me you have some information for me."

Carlo's beady eyes shifted to the side, clearly seeking Nico's approval to speak. Nico dipped his head, giving him permission. What an ass licker.

"I heard the Russians aren't happy with you."

I swiped my fingertips along the top of my desk as I strolled alongside it. "Really? And how'd you come by this little gem of information?"

He shifted in his seat. "I was playing cards with one of the guys from Matteo's crew. He told me."

Matteo was another capo who let the Russians push drugs in his territory for a taste of the profit.

"Is that all you've got? We all know Russians are always complaining about something. This isn't new."

"Maybe you should cut a deal with them and put all this shit behind you," Nico suggested. "You don't need any more distractions. We might be able to get the boss on board if we get some money out of it."

"No." I slammed my open palm on the desk. "My dad refused to work with them, and I won't either. They're like bloodsucking leeches. They never stop pushing, and they're completely untrustworthy. Their promises aren't worth the air that comes out of their mouths."

The Russians were amoral bastards. Unlike us, they didn't have any problems taking out anyone. No one was sacred. Not cops, not prosecutors, and journalists could kiss their collective asses goodbye if the Russians didn't like them. In fact, I wouldn't put it past one of those fuckers to shoot someone simply to see if his gun was well lubricated.

Nico sat in front of me like a king on a throne. Judging. Weighing. Watching.

"They're going to keep pushing because you're young and untested. They see you as the weak link. Maybe you could give them something and they'll back off." When I started to shake my head, he held up his hand, indicating he wasn't finished. "It's good business, Gian. We don't want a war with the Russians. We already spent the last year fighting the DiTonnos because of the bullshit that went down with Rocco."

My stomach lurched. I hated thinking about Rocco. It gutted me to see how my sister had become a shell of her former self after he died. Sure, she still gave me shit and acted like she was fine, but she was my twin. I could sense she was still torn apart by his death.

"You think they were behind the car chase, not only the brick." I knew they had something to do with the brick. The word *Vor* was a term used by the Russian mafia that meant "Thief-in-Law."

"It makes sense," Carlo said, a reptilian grin cutting across his face like he actually had more than two brain cells in his head.

What I wouldn't give to wipe that fucking smile off his face...

"I wasn't asking for your opinion," I sneered at Carlo.

Carlo's shoulders stiffened, and he raised his eyebrows like a condescending fuck. He stood up to leave, stopping only to rap his knuckles against the top of the desk. "Fine. Whatever you want, Gian. Let me know if you need anything."

I glared at his retreating back as his cocky ass strutted out the door. If Nico weren't in the room, I'd seriously consider pumping a couple of bullets through his knees solely for shits and grins.

Nico stood and the wooden legs of the chair scraped across the tiled floor. "How's the fiancée?"

I gritted my teeth. I didn't want him sticking his nose in my personal life. He had already inserted his opinion into every decision I made as a capo. "Perfect. Couldn't be better."

It was the truth. Evie slept in my bed every night. She shared a cup of coffee with me every morning. Nothing about what we were doing felt fake, and my sorry ass couldn't get enough of her. Her graceful movements consumed me. I couldn't be in the same room with her without wanting to get lost in her. Her taste. Her sweet, flawless skin. Her mile-long legs. The list of things I liked about her grew every day, which was novel for me.

"Good. Good." He strummed his fingers against his thigh. "Tony dug up some stuff on her ex."

"Oh?" My gut soured.

"Yeah. Turns out he was hooking up with some slut with connections to the Russian mafia when your girl broke things off with him."

"*Was* hooking up? As in they're done?"

"Yep." He cupped his chin between his index finger and his thumb. "She didn't stick around for more than a week after your girl walked."

My thoughts were deafening as the implications whirled inside my head. Dread throbbed inside me. It could be a coincidence. I couldn't wrap my head around any other scenario that made sense because what went on between her ex and that woman happened before I entered the picture.

I pushed back my shoulders, standing taller, my arms locked behind my back. "Yeah, well, let me worry about my fiancée and her ex."

Nico open his mouth for a second like he didn't have any intention of letting this go, but he closed it without saying anything. Seconds ticked by, the pumping of music from the club giving life to the testosterone filling my office.

"I know for a fact your uncle won't pull Tony off this. You know how he is when he gets his mind set on something, and right now that something is Evie." He rubbed his fingers along his jaw to emphasize the reference to Dominick. "Let me be straight with you. He doesn't like the way this looks, and I can't say I disagree. Something stinks."

My hands trembled with fury, and I stuffed them into my pockets. "I wouldn't expect anything else. You gotta do what's best for the family."

CHAPTER TWENTY-FOUR

Evangeline

"Hello, Mrs. Trassato." I leaned my hip against the doorframe. "Gian's not here. He's working late tonight."

"Call me Helena." She squeezed my arm, the corners of her eyes crinkling. "And I didn't come to see Gianluca."

I blinked. "Oh. Okay."

She tilted her head to the side, her stiff dark hair brushing the collar of her pale pink blouse. "Are you going to invite me in, or are you busy?"

"Right. Sorry." I shook my head. "Gian didn't tell me you were planning to stop by today. So, um, yeah…" Heat climbed up my face. I sounded like an absolute idiot. I wouldn't be surprised if she called Gian the minute she left to tell him all the reasons she didn't think we were a good fit. Not that it mattered. Gian and I weren't really…anything.

A heart-clenching wave of panic thundered through me, and the thoughts I'd fought to keep at bay rushed forward like vomit. I'd done my best to beat back my feelings for him, but I wasn't deluded enough to think I'd succeeded.

She cleared her throat, and I realized I'd been hopelessly trapped in a mental quagmire of my making.

"Sorry, it's been a long day," I mumbled and opened the door wider.

She dropped a stack of magazines on top of the black coffee table and perched on the edge of the gray sectional. "I didn't tell him I planned to stop by."

My mind whirled through hundreds of reasons why she'd want to talk to me alone, and none of them were good. "Did I do something wrong? Because I'm really sorry about ruining the engagement party. I don't know what happened. It wasn't like me at all. I never faint." I'd met Kevin's family a hundred and one times, and I never felt close to this level of anxiety.

Mrs. Trassato stared at me with a condescending look. Clearly, I hadn't impressed her one bit. "Sit down. I want you to look at these so I know what kind of things you like. We really need to get a jump on the wedding plans if you want to walk down the aisle without advertising to the whole family that you're pregnant."

"Wait." I held up my hand. "I am not pregnant."

Her brows scrunched together. "You're not?"

"God, no." A nervous giggle bubbled from my lips. "I hadn't eaten a thing that day, and my nerves got the best of me. That's it." Doubt flashed across her face. "I promise. There's no reason for me to lie about it."

Her amber eyes, so like Gian's and Carmela's, seared through me, scooping up my secrets. "Well then, I apologize for jumping to conclusions. It's just that everything seemed so sudden. I've heard a little bit about your relationship with your ex from Carmela, and then suddenly Gian announced that you're engaged. When you fainted at the engagement party, I thought I'd put the pieces of the puzzle together. I guess I was wrong."

At a loss for words, I picked up the top magazine and thumbed through the glossy pages. She had earmarked pages and slapped sticky notes here and there. I couldn't focus long enough to take in any of her comments.

"So do you have any ideas in mind for the wedding, or you planning to reuse some of the ideas from the one planned with your ex?"

I winced. She didn't need a knife to cut me. Her words were more than capable of doing the job.

"Um…Gian and I aren't rushing into anything."

"You're not." She raised her eyebrows. "You're engaged and living in his home. That seems pretty rushed, but maybe that's just me. I grew up in a strict Catholic family. I never dated anyone except my husband. I always thought Gian would marry a nice Italian girl with a similar upbringing. I guess it wasn't meant to be."

My eyes bulged. *Wow. Direct hit.* Gian's mom certainly didn't pull her punches. If only the floor would open up and I could disappear into oblivion.

"I'm sorry I'm a disappointment."

"Well." She stood and brushed imaginary dirt from her tailored pants. "I still don't see an engagement ring, and you're not pregnant, so I guess there's still hope that my son will come to his senses and see you for what you are."

My back straightened like someone had shoved a steel rod down my spine. As much as I wanted to play nice with Gian's mother, I refused to be insulted. I didn't do anything wrong. Without a doubt, *I* was the victim in all of this. When I stormed in Gian's office that night, I only wanted my purse. Instead, I became a witness to a crime and snagged a fiancé who tied me in knots in both good and bad ways.

"What exactly are you implying?"

She lowered her eyes, which I hoped meant she regretted her harsh words a little.

"While Carmela only has good things to say about you, I'm having a hard time stomaching your arrival in my son's life. I'm sure you're a nice girl, and under other circumstances, I'd be happy to have you in our life, but I don't understand how you could go from being engaged to one man to being engaged to my son in the blink of an eye. Gian needs someone who's strong and will stand by him no matter what, and all the evidence suggests you're fickle."

All the anger drained from system, and my shoulders slumped. I couldn't blame this woman for her misgivings. If I were in her shoes, I wouldn't be able to overlook the circumstances either. "I-I…" My tongue thickened with the confession itching to roll off my tongue. I wanted to reassure her, but Gian obviously hadn't confided in her for a reason.

I peeked at her from the corner of my eye, and I saw a woman ready to fight for her family. Ready to defend them no matter the cost, and I respected her. I didn't think my mom would fight for me when push came to shove. My family orbited around each other, never connecting, and always keeping each other at arms' length. In the last few years, we behaved like acquaintances who checked in on each other every couple of weeks more out of obligation than love.

"It's not real."

The declaration echoed unnaturally through the room.

"What?" Her voice was a hoarse rasp.

"Our engagement isn't real," I repeated.

A mask of equal parts horror and relief slipped over her face. "Do you care to explain?"

"No." I gnawed on my lower lip. "I don't think it's a good idea. Just know that I won't do anything to hurt your son or your family. I'll leave when he tells me I can, and I won't cause any waves. I won't tell anyone what happened or why. Ever."

She pressed a hand to her chest, her face as white as a sheet of paper. "Oh my God. What did he do? Who else knows?"

Coming to my feet, I grabbed one of her hands. "No one, and I'd like to keep it that way. I don't want something to happen to Gian because he helped me." The words tasted like ash on my lips, and my stomach heaved. "I couldn't live with myself if something happened to him. Carmela is my best friend, and Gian, means a lot to me too. I will do anything in my power to keep them safe. I promise. Okay?"

She nodded, her eyes glassy and her lower lip wobbling. "Thank you."

"No. Thank *you,* for everything, but mostly for being the mother of two of my favorite people."

She wrapped her arms around me, pulling me flush against her. "Let me know if you need anything."

I swallowed. "Please don't tell Gian I told you anything. He wanted me to keep it secret."

"I won't." She stepped back, a slight frown on her face. "I'm glad I came here today and not only because you told me the truth. You're a good person, Evangeline. I'm sorry I said those things to you."

"Thanks." My voice cracked.

She picked up the stack of magazines and tucked them under her arm. "Call me if you need anything. I can be a formidable opponent when necessary, and you have an ally in me."

I didn't doubt it.

She raised her eyebrows. "These men think they can handle the world and keep us in the dark all the time, but we're far from the wilting flowers they think we are."

CHAPTER TWENTY-FIVE

Gian

I moved through the darkened hallway outside of my bedroom. It was well after two in the morning. The silent hum of the ceiling fan indicated Evie hadn't waited up for me. With the exception of a text telling me she finished dancing at her studio, I hadn't heard from her all day.

I paused at the foot of the bed, taking in her shadowed form. My gut twisted in knots every time I saw her. Something about her made it impossible for me to look anywhere other than at her when she was in the same room as me.

For five days, I hadn't asked Evie a single question about her ex or that woman. And for five fucking days, I hadn't heard another word from Nico or Dominick about it. I went to work. I made deals. I dodged Angela at every turn, which meant I needed to fire her ass soon because she couldn't get it through her head that I didn't want anything to do with her. When I ran out of distractions, I organized a high-stakes card game for this weekend. As pathetic as it sounded, nothing erased the lingering doubts about Evie and her ex.

"Hey," she rasped, flipping onto her back, and my heart banged against my ribcage. "You're home late."

"Yeah." I kicked off my black leather shoes. "Some things came up. I couldn't get away."

She switched on the lamp next to the bed, flooding the room with yellow light. "There's leftovers in the fridge if you're hungry."

Choking on a laugh, I unbuttoned my suit jacket and tossed it on the top of the dresser. "You cooked?" My mom would have a heart attack if she found out how little Evie actually knew about cooking. She burned half of the things she tried to prepare, and the other half tasted like she opened a can and warmed it up in the microwave.

"No. I ordered takeout. I think I'm done pretending I can cook. I don't think I'm fooling anyone."

I unbuckled my belt and shoved my pants to the ground, her eyes tracking every movement. She flashed me my favorite smile—the one that felt as if it was custom-made for me—when she noticed I caught her gawking.

"No. You're not, but my mom is dying to come over and give you a crash course."

Her smile slipped. "I'll pass. I don't think that's a good idea, considering…" she plucked at the edge of the sheet, "well, everything. I don't want her to get invested in something that's not permanent. It doesn't seem right, especially with your dad so sick."

A pang of unease constricted my throat. I didn't have a fucking clue how we were going to make this work. "You're probably right." I blew out a sigh laced with more than a little regret. "I'm going to take a quick shower. You should go back to sleep."

Evie curled her arms around her torso, making her dancer's frame look small and delicate. "Okay," she said, her voice soft and uncertain.

Although my gut clenched and I wanted to take back my words, I didn't. I couldn't. I had no clue what to say. I retreated to the bathroom, closing the door behind me, putting up a physical barrier to match the emotional one that never seemed to disappear between us.

A bright light flickered on the bathroom counter, reflecting off the mirror that ran the length of the far wall. I glanced at Evie's phone, and a text from her ex-fiancé lit up the screen. I knew I shouldn't read it. I should trust her, but I couldn't stop myself. I needed to know what he wanted, especially if I didn't want to hear it secondhand from Nico or that piece of shit Carlo.

I swiped her screen and pulled up her recent texts. She really needed to put a passcode on her phone; however, I wouldn't lobby her to do that any time in the near future.

Kevin: *We weren't done talking. Why you'd leave today without letting me explain?*

Evie: We don't have anything else to talk about. Stop contacting me. I don't want to work things out.

Kevin: Because of Carmela's brother. You can't trust him.

Evie: It's none of your business.

Kevin: Are you dating him?

Evie: I already told you we're friends. He's helping me out. That's all you need to know.

Kevin: He's going to ruin your life. You need to get away from him.

Evie: You lost the right to tell me what to do when I caught you fucking your so-called protégé.

Kevin: I know I screwed up, but please let me explain what happened with Ana. I owe you that. We both deserve closure.

Evie: Fine. What time?

Kevin: Be at my studio at noon. We'll have lunch.

I sucked in a deep breath, anger simmering inside me, black dots spotting my vision. I couldn't think straight. I'd let her run around the city for weeks unaccompanied. I gave her freedom. I gave her my trust on a fucking platter, and she repaid me by sneaking around with her ex. Then she crawled in my bed at night like nothing happened. Like she didn't owe me anything. Like I didn't have a right to know she'd been talking to that asshole again.

I stormed out the bathroom, flinging open the door with enough force that it banged against the doorstop with loud bang.

"What the fuck is this?" I held up her phone, flashing the screen toward her.

She scrambled out of the bed, her eyes wide, her ponytail seesawing. She held her hands up in surrender, slinking backward until she collided with the wall. "It's not a big deal. I wasn't trying to hide anything from you. You don't have any right to be mad."

"Are you saying I should be happy that you go running when your ex snaps his fingers?"

She toyed the hem of her emerald green nightie. "I can explain."

I stalked closer to her, my hand squeezing tighter and tighter around her phone with every step. "Then start talking."

Evie lowered her lashes. She looked so prim, so innocent and easily broken, my heart tripped inside my chest.

"He's been hounding me to talk to him for more than a week, and I keep ignoring him. He was waiting for me when I came out of the dance studio today."

"You could've kept walking. You don't owe him a damn thing. *He* cheated on *you*, not the other way around."

"I know, but he held up that juice I like so much, and I didn't want to be mean to him."

"He got you bottle of juice. A fucking bottle of *juice* and you invite him back into your life like nothing happened?" I slammed my hands against the wall next to her head, caging her between my arms. The screen of her phone cracked, and I tossed it on top of the bed. "Are you going to pack your bags and move back in with him now that he's no longer fucking that woman? This was a fun detour, but now you're ready to hop beds again. You don't like to waste time do you?"

Evie blinked and crystal-like tears squeezed from the corners of her eyes. Regret swelled inside my chest, but the distrust and adrenaline surging through me prevented me from backing down. I wouldn't tolerate being played by her or anyone else.

"How do you know he's not with her anymore?" she whispered, her dark eyes like pools of ink.

I leaned my hips into hers, and like someone had flipped a switch, I burned for her. It pissed me off as much as it excited me. "It's my job to know!" I yelled.

Sighing, she wiped her hand down the side of her face. "Look, I'd be lying if I said I didn't want to hear his side of the story. But I swear, that's it. I don't have any intention of getting back together with him. Ever. I won't get caught up in his bullshit lies again. I've closed the door on that part of my life."

"Then why the games?"

She licked her lips, drawing every ounce of my attention to her perfect cupid's bow. I bit back a groan. Her lips were stunning. Not too full to overshadow the delicate symmetry of her face, yet plump enough that they gave me all kinds of lewd ideas. They reminded me of that pink saltwater taffy shit I couldn't get enough of as a kid.

She curled her hand around the front of my shirt like she couldn't decide if she wanted to push me away or pull me closer. "I don't know what you mean by games."

I ran my nose along her swan-like neck, breathing her in, searing her jasmine scent into my soul. "You told him we were friends." I grazed the shell of her ear with my teeth. "Friends. Friends who fuck. Friends who share a bed every night. Friends passing time until somebody better comes along. Is that what you think we are? Is that it?"

"No." She raised her chin. "Actually, you know what? I don't have any clue what we are. You've never bothered to explain anything. As a matter of fact, you've flat out refused to discuss what any of this means on more than one occasion. Should I take a leap of faith and assume I'm more than I'm a convenient fuck? Because from where I'm standing, you haven't given me any indication that I mean anything to you."

"Convenient?" I laughed darkly. "There's nothing about you that's convenient. If my only goal was blowing off steam, I'd have plenty of options at the club who don't come with a million and one complications. And you can bet your sweet ass they wouldn't be best friends with my sister."

"Then tell me what this is, Gian, because I'm tired of pretending. I need to know if you feel anything. I can't keep doing this when I feel so…"

My shoulders tensed. Her unfinished thought hung in the air, creating a noxious cocktail of expectation and apprehension. When it was evident she didn't intend to continue, I decided to show her rather than tell her what I felt. Words held too much power, and I didn't think either one of us was ready to chisel our feelings in stone. We had too many hurdles to get over first.

I cupped her face, drowning in the familiar pull of her chocolate eyes. "I know. I know."

Dropping my hands to her waist, I claimed her mouth. Her breath caught, and her back arched. I loved the way she melted into me every damn time I touched her. It was exhilarating. Intoxicating. Addictive.

A yelp tumbled from her mouth when I lifted her up in the air, cradling her in my arms. Her fingers clawed at my shoulders, clinging to me as I set her on the top of the dresser.

I unknotted my tie and yanked on one end, the sound cutting through the air like a knife. The silky material dangled from my calloused fingertips.

"Do you trust me?"

She stared at me, her eyes simmering with lust and a hundred unspoken emotions. Uneven breaths puffed from her mouth, and my attention dropped to her breasts, searching and finding her pebbled nipples beneath her flimsy nightie.

Fucking beautiful.

"Yes."

I wrapped the tie around her eyes, knotting it at the back of her head. Her body coiled like a spring and a giant stream of air whooshed out of her lungs.

"What are you doing?" she rasped, her chin angling to the side, and her pink-tipped fingers clutching the square edge of the dresser.

"Shh." One of my hands wound around her slim neck, not applying any pressure. I just wanted to establish I was in control and I would protect her. I pressed a finger to her lips. "Relax. I'm not going to hurt you."

I slid one strap of her nightie down her shoulder then the other. The silky material pooled around her waist, exposing her tight rose-colored buds. I cupped them in my hands, strumming my thumbs over the sensitive tips.

"I can't."

I dragged her panties down her mile-long legs, the petal-soft hush of lace against skin ringing my ears. Nothing had ever sounded so damn arousing.

"You can."

I kissed and caressed every inch of her skin, and the tension gradually unfurled from her limbs. She bit her lower lip, and a ragged moan escaped her, and just like that, I knew I had her. She wouldn't object. My fingers dipped between her legs, smearing her wetness around her clit, bringing her to the brink, again and again.

"Please, Gian."

Her body arched like a pagan sacrifice. Her chest rose and fell in harmonized spurts. Her sunset-colored locks danced along her collarbone. Her pink lips were parted, and I couldn't hold back for another second.

Groaning, I shoved my boxer briefs down my hips, and dragged the head of my cock through her folds. She pawed at me, kissing my face, my chest, my neck, and any body part within striking distance.

With one hard thrust of my hips, I shoved inside her. She was warm, wet, and perfect for me. I stalled momentarily to commit the feeling to memory, and her head drooped like it was too much work to keep it aloft. The tail of my tie drifted over her shoulder, dangling like a pendulum of a grandfather clock.

I pulled her forehead flush against mine, rocking against her. The urgency inside my chest swelled, crawling up my throat. I needed to be deeper, claiming everything she'd give me and more.

My heart thundered as I moved faster and harder inside of her like this moment was all we'd ever have. Like someone could snatch her away any second and I'd be left with nothing except regrets and memories.

Every time I thrust, she arched her pelvis to meet me. The dresser pounded against the drywall.

My lungs strained, my thighs burned, and sweat trickled down my back.

Little whimpers and mewls hummed low in her throat, and I leaned forward confiscating them with my mouth, not wanting any part of her to go unsampled. Pleasure built inside of me, hijacking my body and my thoughts.

Her mouth parted, her thighs trembled, and she clenched around me so tight I thought I'd found heaven.

Our actions choreographed, our heartbeats synchronized, and her body bowed and shuddered against mine. When the last twinge of pleasure rippled through her, Evie dropped her head to my shoulder, and I let go. Silence punctuated by our quickened breaths filled the air.

After a few beats, I removed the blindfold from her eyes, still deep inside of her. Her eyes fluttered, blinking away the darkness, and adjusting to the weak lighting of the room. Her hair was tangled, her eyes were glazed, her lips were bee-stung. I'd never seen anyone look more beautiful in my life. Possessiveness coiled around me like a snake, and I struggled to suck in a breath.

"You're mine. Not your ex's or any other man's. Do you understand?" I choked out, too many emotions to name swelling inside of me.

She trailed her fingers down my chest. "And that makes you mine."

I didn't object, because it was true. She owned me. "You're not meeting your ex tomorrow."

"I know. I'll text him tomorr—"

"It's no longer your concern." I scraped the hair away from her face so I could absorb every detail. "I'll talk to him."

Her breath hitched.

"What's wrong?"

"You're not going to hurt him or…?"

"Or what?"

"Do what guys like you do when you want someone to disappear."

I cocked an eyebrow. "Guys like me?"

"I know that you're involved—"

I covered her mouth. "Don't say it, Evie. The less you know for sure, the better."

She nodded, and I dropped my hand.

"Answer one question."

I groaned. "What do you want to know?"

"Why did you choose this life?"

Shit. I didn't want to go there with Evie. "Honestly, I've never given it much thought. It's in my blood. My dad, my uncle, my grandfather. No one escapes it, and honestly, I didn't want to."

Her brows pinched together, and twin lines dented the skin over the bridge of her nose. "Why not?"

"It's hard to explain."

"Try."

Groaning inwardly, I scrambled for and explanation an outsider would understand. "When I was a kid, my dad's power mesmerized me. He could double or triple park his car, and nobody would do anything. People gave our family shit for free. We were treated like royalty everywhere we went. I didn't see the ugly side until much later, and by then, it was too late. Once you're in, you're in for life. Death is the only way out."

She opened her mouth, and I pressed a finger to her lips. "That's all you need to know. Okay?"

"Okay." She swallowed. "So what are you going to do to Kevin?"

"I'm going to talk to him until he understands my point of view."

"That's it?"

"Sweetheart, you don't need to worry about it. He's not going to disappear."

CHAPTER TWENTY-SIX

Evangeline

Ring.

I flipped over my phone, and a thread of panic wove through my gut. It was my mom, and other than Kevin, she was the last person I wanted to talk to right now. I'd successfully avoided her since I moved in with Gian, but she wouldn't let it continue much longer.

Ring.

"Hi, Mom."

"Well, thank God, I was beginning to think you were dead."

I slumped against the kitchen counter, the sharp edge digging into my lower back. "Not dead, just busy."

"So how are things going?"

"Good. Good." I traced the rim of my coffee mug. "I started dancing again."

"Really? How is your ankle holding up?"

I glanced out the window above the kitchen sink. The sun had started to come up, and it was an impressive mixture of reds and oranges competing for attention with the crowded skyline. Sometimes I missed the sunrises and sunsets of my hometown. They stretched as far as I could see, uninterrupted by buildings and smog. They were swirls of color, dancing above the swaying cornfields.

I swiped a hand down the side of my face. "It hasn't been bothering me much at all. During the first couple of minutes of my routine, it feels a little tight, but other than that, it's good as new, and my physical therapist released me from rehab yesterday. I guess taking the year off wasn't such a bad thing after all."

Gian padded into the kitchen, sidling up next me and opening an upper cabinet for a mug. My mom's words blurred together, and all I could see and hear was him.

A lopsided grin spilt his face when he caught me staring at him. "Who are you talking to?"

I cupped my hand over the lower half of my phone. "My mom."

He lifted the carafe and poured coffee into his mug. "Is that a good or a bad thing?"

I shrugged. "A little of both, but I couldn't avoid her forever, or she might hop on a plane and come looking for me."

His hands framed the sides of my face, and he studied me carefully. "You look stressed."

"I haven't told her I moved in with you." I swallowed. "She thinks I'm living with Carmela."

"Ah." He kissed the top of my head. "You don't have to say anything."

My mom's shrill voice echoed through the phone, drawing my attention back to her.

"Evangeline, are you listening to me? Did you hear a word of what I said?"

I pulled my hand away from the speaker and grabbed my cup of coffee off the counter. "No. Sorry. The reception sucks here."

She blew out a breath that conveyed her frustration better than words ever could. "I said your dad contacted me yesterday."

"What?" My heart lurched into my throat, and the mug slipped from my hands, exploding on the hardwood.

I stared at the blue shards mixed with liquid on the floor for several breaths. I didn't know how to respond. He had disappeared from our life so long ago, I barely thought about him anymore. He seemed more like a myth than a real person.

"I talked to your dad," she repeated.

"He called you? Why? I don't get it. He hasn't bothered with any of us in over a decade." She didn't answer me. "Hello, Mom? Are you still there?"

"He calls now and then. Not regularly, but he hasn't disappeared."

I lifted my head, and my eyes met Gian's. His brows were scrunched together, and his mouth was pressed into a tight line. "Are you okay?" he mouthed.

I nodded, and he crouched down to pick up the broken shards of ceramic.

"Why didn't you tell me you still talked to him?"

She sighed. "I don't know. It didn't seem important."

Anger and frustration bubbled inside my chest. "What the fuck, Mom? That makes no sense. Of course, it's important. He's my dad. What are you hiding?"

"Look, Evangeline, I can't get into this over the phone. He couldn't be a part of our lives. That's the end of the story."

"Seriously? *That's* your explanation for lying to me about my father for the majority of my life?"

"It's what he wanted."

"Great. Just fucking great." I slashed my hand through the air, nearly hitting Gian in the chest. He snagged my wrist, and his strong arms curled around me, pulling me against his chest. I melted into his embrace, my heartbeat slowing fractionally and my legs weak. Like a vampire, I drank in his warmth, and I breathed in his unequaled scent.

He pressed his lips to my forehead. "I'm here."

"I can't talk about this right now, Mom. I'll call you later."

"Wait," my mom said, her voice high-pitched.

"What?"

"He wants to meet with you."

"Why the hell would he care about seeing me now? He hasn't made any effort to see me for years."

"He checks in on you from time to time to make sure you're doing okay."

"In New York?"

"Yes. He lives near the city."

"Great. My father stalks me rather than talking to me. That's exactly what every girl wants to hear."

"Evieee…" She drew out my name. "I know this sounds strange—"

"Strange doesn't begin to describe what you're telling me. None of this makes sense. You kind of blindsided me here."

"I know. I know. He's got it into his head that you're hanging around the wrong kind of people. He wouldn't go into the details, so I can't really offer you any more than that."

"All right," I said absently. "I don't know where to go with that. I've known Carmela the entire time I lived here."

"Maybe he's talking about something else. Maybe he's overacting. I don't have a clue. Just put a little thought into moving home. Okay? I think you'd be safer here with me. We could expand the dance studio, offer more classes, maybe summer camps."

"I have an audition in a couple of weeks, and if it doesn't go well, I'll start thinking about my next move, but I can't promise anything. Even if I can't make this work, it doesn't mean I'll move back to Nebraska."

"Okay," she said after a long moment of silence. "I'm sorry for pushing. I'm just worried about you. I've tried to give you space for the past few weeks so you can sort out your breakup and your future without interference. If you're not ready, I'll let it go for the time being. I understand."

"Thanks, Mom. I'll call you next week." I disconnected the call, feeling way too tired for a person who woke up an hour ago. I buried my face in Gian's shirt.

"Talk to me," he said. "What happened?"

I closed my eyes momentarily. "I can't. Not yet."

He frowned. "Why not?"

"Because…" I struggled to find adequate words to explain the emotions swirling in my gut with the force of a Cat-5 hurricane. "I don't know where to start, but here it goes. Apparently, my dad never really dropped out of the picture, which means my mom spent the majority of my life lying to me. He lives in the New York area and keeps tabs on me. Oh, and he wants to meet with me because I'm hanging around bad people."

I spun out of his hold and snagged my dance bag from the table. "I have to get going. I'm late, and I have less than two weeks to prepare for this audition."

"Wait." He clamped his hand around my wrist.

Sucking in a deep breath, I closed my eyes for a second. My life was a complete and total mess. I couldn't fathom how far I'd fallen. How I had managed to make a string of bad decisions, and now my life was a virtual house of cards ready to collapse at any given second.

"I didn't mean to lash out at you, but just when I'm getting my life in order, someone lobs another bomb in my direction. I can't handle much more. I want it all to go away until I can get my head in the right place. My ankle. The implosion of my career. Kevin. My dad." I sucked in a breath. "You."

The second the word left my lips, I regretted it. He took two steps backward, his eyes carefully trained anywhere besides on me, his nostrils flaring, and his lips twisted. My stomach bottomed out. A hollow ache burrowed beneath my breastbone, and I wanted to kick my own ass. I didn't want to fight with him. He meant too much to me. Somehow, he'd snuck into my life, and now I couldn't picture living without him.

"Unbelievable." He laughed, only it wasn't kind. It was brittle. Dark. "I'm on the list of things you want to disappear. The same fucking list as your piece of shit ex?"

He grabbed his car keys off the countertop and stuffed them into his pocket. "After last night, I thought we had moved past this." When I reached for him, he dodged my hand. "No. Fuck it. I can't talk to you right now. We're both late. I have a shitload of work today, *and* I have to deal with Kevin."

"Gian, I didn't mean it." I cupped his face with my hands, desperate for him to look at me and see what was inside of my heart. "You're right. You're not on that list. Not even close. You're the only thing good to come out of the last year. I'm being an idiot. I am an idiot."

I untucked his shirt, and my hands dove underneath the starchy material, seeking out the now familiar connection that drew us together. My hands explored the hard planes of his chest, and I peppered his pursed lips with kisses, whispering apologies.

"Gian, I'm sorry. I feel like an ass. What can I do to—?"

Groaning, he dipped his head, and his lips

fastened onto the side of my neck, sucking hard on my skin. Without a doubt, I knew he'd left a mark, and I didn't care. He licked a line along my collarbone, and the hair lifted on my arms. I arched my pelvis into him as his hands drifted up my ribcage, only stopping to cup my breasts. He pinched my nipples hard through my leotard, his teeth nipping my ear. Lust licked at my nerve endings.

"Sweetheart, you taste so good."

"Mmm," I hummed, rubbing my hand down his hard length.

With a sharp grunt, he thrust his hips against me. His hardness rubbed against my lower stomach. On fire and burning for him, I yanked on his belt buckle.

"Evie, we need to stop. We're going to be late." He dropped his hands to my hips and forced a few inches of space between us. "You matter to me. I meant it when I said it last night, and I mean it now. We're in this together, so stop throwing shit in my face and questioning everything. Take a deep breath and enjoy the ride."

"For how long?"

"For as long as we want. There aren't any rules."

"I like that." Somewhere deep inside of my heart, the bitterness eating me up for the last month or so withered and died. "Do you mind giving me a ride to the studio?"

He brushed a kiss across my lips then knitted our fingers together. "C'mon. Let's get going."

CHAPTER TWENTY-SEVEN

Gian

I opened the door to Kevin's art studio, not bothering to knock. The dumb fucker needed to keep his doors locked, but it worked to my advantage, so I didn't give a shit. My black leather loafers clacked over the gray polished concrete floors. I spun in a circle, taking in the floor to ceiling canvases that dotted the white walls.

I definitely wasn't a fan of his work. The paintings looked like the bacteria I studied under a microscope in high school biology with a few arteries bisecting the blobs.

"Evangeline, come on back. I'm setting up our lunch." He sounded chipper. Hopeful even, and it made my temper run hotter than before.

I paused at the entrance to the back room of Kevin's studio. It resembled a small single-room apartment with a mini kitchen on the right side and a futon on the left side. A long rectangular table that could seat six to eight people divided the room in half.

"I ordered your favorites," Kevin said, his back to me.

I leaned against the doorframe and jammed my hands in my pockets. Every cell inside of me buzzed with the urge to slam his face into the food on the table. "How thoughtful of you. I didn't realize you knew what I liked to eat."

Kevin whirled around. "What the hell are you doing here? Where's Evie?"

I closed the door and flipped the lock, not wanting any interruptions. "Evie sends her regards." I strode forward until I stood within punching distance of him. "She won't be meeting you today or any other day."

"So you're the infamous Gianluca Trassato." His eyes narrowed, raking up and down me. "I recognize you from the club a month or so ago. She wanted to get back at me, so she left with you, only I didn't think it'd go anywhere."

"I guess you were wrong, but it's probably not the first time…or the last."

He folded his arms across his chest. "Say what you came here to say, and leave."

"Stop contacting my girl."

"She's not your girl. She's mine. She's going to marry me." He raised his eyebrows, a smirk on his pretty boy face. "It might not happen tomorrow, but it will happen."

I grabbed the collar of his pansy-ass tight t-shirt and jerked him within a few inches of my face. I inhaled deeply, trying to calm the feral pounding of bloodlust inside of me. "Listen, jackass, if I hear you tried to contact my fiancée again, I'll cut your dick off and shove it down your throat. She's mine, and I'm not the kind of man to turn the other cheek when another man comes sniffing around his property. Got it?"

"Get your fucking hands off me, you lunatic. You're not the only one with connections. I know people who'd be happy to make you disappear."

Rage coiled inside of me, and I smashed my fist into his nose. A sickening crack echoed through the room. He dropped to his knees, cupping his face. Blood oozed between his fingers, and he howled like a fucking baby.

"Get up." I flashed the gun strapped to the holster inside of my suit jacket. "Get the fuck up before I end you."

He crab-walked backward, stopping only when his head hit the wall. He scrambled to his feet. "Get out of here, or I'll call the cops."

I pulled a chair to the center of the room. "Sit. You're not calling anyone until we're finished talking, and I have a hunch you won't be so keyed up to contact the police when we're done here."

His eyes darted around the room, finally landing on the exit door. I ripped my gun from my holster and aimed it at him and then at the chair. "Sit."

"No fucking way."

I pulled a silencer from my pocket and screwed it on the end of my gun. "We can do this the easy way or—" I pulled the trigger, and the drywall exploded, showering his sissy man bun with white powder "—

the hard way. It's up to you. Keep in mind that I'm not opposed to carving a few parting gifts into your face."

His eyes widened, and he shook his head. I wouldn't be surprised if this guy pissed his pants. I stomped forward, grabbing his hair.

"What the hell?" he screamed.

I dragged his ass across the room and practically threw him in the chair, pulled a plastic cable tie out of my pocket, and secured it around his wrists. "Are you ready to talk?"

"Talk about what? I get it. You don't want me to contact Evie. What more do we have to discuss?"

This fucking prick wouldn't quit. I whipped the butt of my gun across his face. "I want to know everything about Ana Ivanka."

He blinked. "Ana?"

"Yes. How did you meet her?"

"I don't understand what this has to do with Evie."

"Answer the fucking question," I growled through clenched teeth. Despite my earlier threat, I didn't have all day to toy with this piece of shit. "You don't need to understand."

He swallowed. "Ana and I were introduced by a mutual friend. She wanted to raise her profile in the art community."

"Who's the mutual friend?" He started to shake his head. "Stop right there before you piss me off even more. If you want me to leave you in one piece, I need to know everything, including Ana's ties to the Russian mob."

Kevin sagged against slats of the blond wood

chair, quietly fuming as he realized his chance to avoid coming clean had slipped through his fingers. A vicious satisfaction surged through me.

"About six months ago, an acquaintance invited me to a high-stakes poker tournament. I played. I won around a hundred grand, and I was hooked. Three months later, my luck turned, and I lost a shit ton of money."

"How much?"

"Five hundred grand."

I whistled. What a dumbass. This was how it always happened. It was the oldest trick in the book. You roped in a pretentious asshole who recently started making good money. You propped up his ego with a few wins. You showed him your power and made him think he was part of something important. Then you went in for the sucker punch. Bam, he was in debt up to his greedy eyeballs, and you took him for a ride.

"Let me guess. You didn't have the money to repay the debt."

"No. I wholesaled a bunch of my paintings. I raised two hundred grand, and I tossed him another hundred grand from my savings. Needless to say, he wasn't satisfied."

I frowned. "Who?"

His faced paled, and he cleared his throat. "Alimzhan Trincher."

"Alix? You went to a poker game organized by *Alix Trincher*?"

Alix was a sociopath. On the street, they called him Bloody Alix, partly because of his red hair and partly because he'd left a sizeable path of blood and death in his wake when he rose to power.

"I didn't realize who he was at the time. If I did..." his Adam's apple bobbed in his throat, "I would have stayed far away from the whole thing."

"So Alix asked you to help Ana Ivanka."

"Yeah." He closed his eyes briefly and jerked his head up and down. "He showed up here one day with Ana, wanting me to teach her everything I knew and get her a couple of gallery showings featuring her work. If I succeeded, he agreed to forgive the rest of my debt."

I snorted.

His shoulders tensed. "What?"

"There had to be more."

"No. He hasn't been back. He hasn't asked for anything else."

"So that's it. You started mentoring her, which led to fucking her, and Evie caught you in the act."

"Pretty much." His voice sounded strangled. "I didn't mean to hurt Evie, but Ana..." his gaze went distant, "she screwed with my head. She was always touching me and brushing against me. She'd show up here wearing next to nothing. It was like Alix sent her to me to make me cheat on Evie and ruin my life. I mean, there's only so much a man can take. Right?"

My spine stiffened. "What do you mean?"

"I don't know," he whined like the man-child he was. I had no clue what Evie saw in him. "I never cheated on Evie with anyone else."

I lifted my eyebrows. "Do I have sucker written across my forehead?"

"No. You're right. I wasn't a choirboy by any

stretch of the imagination. I've had protégées hit on me. Granted, I've crossed the line a time or two, but it never went too far if you know what I mean. Ana was different, though. She wouldn't take no for an answer. She'd strip naked and ask me to demonstrate a painting technique on her body. She'd drag me into closets at parties and stick her hand down my pants while Evie was in the other room. She was everywhere, and I couldn't get away from her. Every time it happened, I promised myself I wouldn't do it again—only, she was like a shot of heroin. I was hooked, and I couldn't stop."

"Where's Ana now?"

"I don't know. She disappeared after that night we ran into you guys at that club. She disconnected her phone and vacated her apartment."

"Did you ask Alix?"

He groaned. "Yeah, and he won't tell me shit. He said we both did our jobs, and my debt was forgiven."

"That's it?"

"He said he'd end me if I ever turned up at one of his poker tournaments, again."

"Has Ana's artwork showed up in another gallery, or is she working with another artist?"

"No." He shifted in the seat. "That's the strange part. The day after we ran into you and Evie in the bar, she went radio silent. A few days later, someone broke into my studio. They took all her work and stuffed it into the dumpster out back."

I frowned. That didn't make sense unless Ana's appearance didn't have anything to do with being mentored. "Was Ana talented?"

He grinned. "In bed, yes. As an artist, not so much. Don't get me wrong; she wasn't awful, but under different circumstances, I would've never agreed to mentor her. It was clear she'd taken some painting lessons, and with the right exposure, she could've made some money. That's it."

Impatience stirring in my gut, I pressed the gun to the side of his head. "Is there anything else you're not telling me?"

"No. I swear." His voice quivered. I flipped open the pocket knife on my keychain and cut the cable tie around his wrists. He scrambled to his feet. "Is that it?"

"Yeah." I stuffed my gun in the holster. "Unless you contact Evie or tell someone I paid you a visit."

His shoulders slumped with defeat. "I won't tell anyone."

His ripped jeans and white t-shirt were crumpled and blood stained. The bun at the back his head had come undone. One of his eyes had swelled shut, and I didn't feel an ounce of remorse. He made his own bed, and he'd never win Evie back. He had his chance, and he pissed it away by getting involved with the soul-sucking Russians.

"Good, because if you fuck with Evie or me or even whisper either of our names, I won't hesitate to kill ya."

CHAPTER TWENTY-EIGHT

Gian

Evie kicked, dipped, and twirled, or whatever a dancer did, and wisps of sunset red hair floated around her face. She didn't have on any makeup. Her eyes were dreamy. A soft melody poured from her lips. It was hauntingly beautiful, and I couldn't look away.

She was like a cold beer on a sweltering day. I never thought I'd find myself so wrapped up in one woman, yet it was true. I didn't want anyone else, and I was pretty damn sure my feelings wouldn't change anytime soon, if ever.

After a long, drawn-out note, she froze in place.

I clapped my hands together, showing my appreciation. I may have confessed that musicals bored me to death, but if Evie was on stage, I was positive my opinion would do a one-eighty.

She whirled around, her hand pressed to the

217

center of her chest. "Oh my God, you scared the shit out of me. What are you doing here?"

"I missed you."

She cocked her head to the side. "You missed me?"

"Yeah, do you have a problem with that?"

"No. I'm surprised. That's all."

I closed the door to the dance studio and moved through the tiny room. With every step, her dark eyes drank in my soul, and with it, every coherent thought in my brain fled.

"You're going to nail this audition. You know that, right?"

A rose-colored blush spread up her neck to her cheeks. "You don't know that. You hate the theater, remember?"

I trailed my hand down the side of her face. "A blind person could see how good you are."

Frowning, she caught my hand and held it up between us. "What's this?"

The knuckles of my right hand were red, swollen, and cracked. I shrugged. "Kevin and I had a little bit of a disagreement. He thought you were two were going to get back together, and I persuaded him otherwise."

Her face paled. "What happened?"

"Don't worry about it. We're on the same page now. He won't be bothering you anymore."

"Gian…" She studied my face, her eyebrows drawn together. "What did you do to him?"

"Nothing permanent. He'll be okay in a couple of days." I pressed my lips against hers. "I don't want to talk about him."

Being alone with her anywhere was like lighting the fuse on a stick of dynamite. Her smell, her soft voice, her skin, they all made my self-control vanish like it had never existed in the first place.

"Then what do you want to talk about?" she mumbled against my lips.

"I don't want to talk." My voice sounded rough as I traced her lips with the tip of my tongue. Her body trembled against mine, and I snapped.

I attacked her mouth, drinking her in and devouring her. Our kiss was so much more than a kiss. Her fingers dove into my hair, pulling me closer, demanding more. I backed her into the mirrored wall, mapping her with my hands.

Her ass, her thighs, her breasts—nothing was off limits.

I groaned into her neck. "This little black leotard will be the death of me. It's like a chastity belt."

She chuckled and locked one leg around my waist, pressing her slight curves into me. I was hard and so fucking ready to explode. She made me feel like a fifteen-year-old kid groping my girlfriend under the gym bleachers.

Tugging a fistful of her hair, I pulled her head to the side. I kissed, bit, sucked, and licked every square inch of visible skin. Need and desire vibrated from her pores. I inhaled the sweet scent of her sweat, and I wanted more. I yanked on the elastic scooped neck of her top and pulled her nipple into my mouth. Goose bumps erupted on her arms, and a whimper slipped from her damp and swollen lips.

A knock on the door echoed through the room "Evangeline, your time is up. The next session starts in five minutes."

"Talk about bad timing." I buried my face in the curve her neck, my heart booming beneath my ribcage. It was becoming pretty damn clear I'd never get enough of Evie. She was under my skin, in my blood and well on the way to burrowing a permanent home in my heart. "Do you want to go to lunch or find a more private place to finish what we were doing?"

She pushed her hair out her eyes, a dazed look on her flushed face, her chest rising and falling. "I vote for a more private place. Do you have to go back to work soon?"

"You know what? I think I can spare enough time to do both."

She picked up her bag. "Then what are we waiting for?"

I draped my arm around her shoulder and tugged her against my side. "Have I ever told you how much I love a girl who knows what she wants?"

CHAPTER TWENTY-NINE

Evangeline

Tendrils of steam floated in the air above my soup. I lifted my spoon and blew across the deep red broth. I poured it into my mouth, and the taste of fresh tomatoes mixed with earthy vegetables exploded on my tongue.

When I came home today, Gian had surprised me with dinner. He'd set the table, complete with flickering candles and placemats. I glanced at Gian across the table. He hadn't taken a bite of anything.

"The soup is great. Did you cook all this yourself, or did you call your mom for help?"

He lifted the glass of ruby-colored wine to his lips and took a sip. "I might or might not have had Carmela walk me through the steps over the phone."

"Either way, I'm impressed. You didn't have to do all this."

"It wasn't a big deal. I wanted to cook for you. I couldn't stand the thought eating takeout again or, worse, eating another can of that soup you have stocked in the pantry like you're preparing for the end of the world." He mock shivered.

The past couple of weeks had slipped by with me in a dreamlike state. I couldn't remember the last time I'd been so happy or hopeful. The only way it could improve would be for me to land a part in the production I was auditioning for next week.

In the last week or so, I had buried all the recurrent doubts about my relationship with Gian and convinced myself I was finally on the right path. I told myself it wasn't too soon to feel this strongly about someone else, and nothing mattered except the way we felt about each other.

Apart from a few minor hiccups, days ran seamlessly from one to the next. I danced and danced until my feet ached, and I practiced lines from the play until I could recite them in my sleep. Even on the nights Gian worked late, he always came home in time to crawl into bed with me.

Sometimes we talked until the early hours of the morning about anything and everything. Our childhood. Dancing. Food. Our families. Our goals. Our dreams. Even though we were still in the early phases of our relationship, I honestly felt as if I knew him better than anyone in the world.

Other times, we couldn't keep our hands off each other. We'd stumble to the bed or any horizontal surface, exploring, kissing, moaning, and laughing. While I knew this moment of perfection couldn't continue indefinitely, I refused to worry about the future. I'd wasted enough of my life worrying, fretting, and planning, and nothing had worked out like I expected. Maybe that wasn't such a bad thing, or at least that's what I was starting to believe.

"Hey. It's not that terrible, and it's organic."

"Exactly. Organic and tasteless."

I took a few more bites of my soup. "So what's the plan for tonight?"

"I have to work tonight. I won't be home until late."

I rested my spoon against the side of my bowl. "What's late?"

"I don't know. Three. Maybe four in the morning."

"Why?"

"There's a special event at the club, and I need to be there to supervise."

I lifted my napkin and wiped the corners of my mouth. "I'm sorry. I didn't mean to keep you from doing your job. Are you going to get in trouble?"

"No. My dad and I own the club together." Gian tensed, and his jaw flexed. "When he got sick, I took over, and as you can imagine, the day-to-day management is not high on his list of priorities anymore."

My stomach lurched at the mention of his dad. We'd stopped by to visit every morning before Gian dropped me off at the dance studio. I never knew what to do while Gian holed up in his dad's room for a good hour. I tried to make myself useful by doing any dishes or starting a load of laundry, except domestic things were never my strong suit, and I secretly wondered if his family wished I stayed away.

Admittedly, the tension between Mrs. Trasatto and me had lessened significantly since my confession, and sometimes, it seemed as if she liked me. She hugged me and kissed both of my cheeks every morning like I was really going to be her daughter-in-law someday. Like she would be happy to have me as a member of her family. An ache bloomed inside my gut, and I rubbed my breastbone, pushing away the thought.

Stay in the present.

"I'm so sorry, Gian."

"No need to apologize." He sucked in a deep breath, ridding himself of the sorrow visible in the tense set of his shoulders. "You've been wonderful to my family and me over the last few weeks. My mom can't stop singing your praises. By the way, that's a big deal because she's normally pretty stingy with her compliments."

Some of the tautness lessened in my limbs, and I chuckled, trying to lighten the mood. "Are you sure about that? Because I thought she was going have a heart attack when I tried to reheat some of her marinara sauce in the microwave."

He laughed, and his golden eyes looked like twin pools of warm honey. My cheeks heated. "She got over it quickly when she saw how perfectly you folded her laundry."

I snorted. "I guess all those summers slaving away at the local department store weren't in vain after all."

He leaned over and kissed me, loitering there for a few beats. "I need to take off. Call me if you need anything. Do whatever you want as long as it doesn't include the dishes. I'll clean up when I get home."

I looped my arms around his neck and inhaled his intoxicating scent. Like every time I touched him, my anxieties melted away like they never existed in the first place. Gian wanted me. I felt safe with him, both physically and mentally.

I was quickly coming to the conclusion that I wanted to be part of his life as long as he'd let me. Sure, I had tried to keep my feelings for him under wraps—though, I'm pretty sure I lost that battle before I started fighting. As treacherous as it sounded, I liked his arms around me at night. I liked the way my heart doubled in size when he flashed me one of his covert smiles. I liked nearly everything about him.

CHAPTER THIRTY

Gian

I stalked the perimeter of the VIP room of my club. The only way to get in here tonight was if you had over a three-million-dollar net worth, you passed our background check, and you knew the secret password.

Tony and Sal had set up six round tables. One table was dedicated to blackjack, and the remaining five were reserved for high-stakes poker. Piles of red, blue, and white chips sat in front of every player, only because the games started less than an hour ago, and the winner and losers weren't evident yet. Cigar smoke curled into my nose, burning my lungs. I hated the sickly sweet scent infinitely more than cigarette smoke.

I paused at one table to watch the new dealer. The cards waterfalled through his fingers, his attention remaining fixed on the players at his table. While he was damned good at his job, I still didn't trust him. You could never be too careful. There were too many people and organizations, both criminal and legitimate, clamoring to infiltrate the Trassato family and take us down.

Angela slid into the lap of the man directly in front of me, rubbing herself against him like a cat. "You look like you need a good luck charm," she practically purred.

Tony and Sal had staffed the event tonight, and the minute I heard her voice, I regretted my decision to delegate the details. Everything from her blonde hair and overly plump lips grated on my last fucking nerve. I couldn't remember why I hired her in the first place. She was a gorgeous in an overly groomed way, except nothing about her appealed to me anymore. The entire week she had followed me around like a lost puppy making suggestive comments. By mid-week, I decided to fire her, but I couldn't pull the trigger until after tonight.

"Angela," I snapped, "let the man play his fucking game. You're here to serve drinks, not give lap dances."

Her red-stained lips hinged open.

"Aw, she's not bothering me," the nearly bald man muttered, running his hand up the inside of her bare, overly tanned thigh.

"You're here to play poker," I said. "Either do it or get the fuck out."

"Fine. Fine." He held up his hands. "I'm playing."

I pointed at Angela then to the far corner of the room. "Follow me."

Angela scooted off his lap, her heavily made-up eyes narrowed into slits. She huffed and stomped across the floor on her sky-high heels.

"What was that about?" she hissed.

The pungent smell of alcohol wafted across my face.

Fucking hell.

I didn't allow my employees to drink during working hours. There was too much at stake, especially tonight.

"You're here to serve drinks to my guests, not yourself."

She swayed on her feet, and I knew the alcohol I smelled on her breath wasn't the result of a few sips. I had invested a lot of money into this game. She'd fuck up the entire night if I didn't get her out of here. She curled her pointy fingernails around the lapel of my jacket, and I wasn't sure if she wanted my attention or if she needed help standing.

"I only want to make sure they have a good time." She pushed out her lower lip into a practiced pout. "Isn't that what you want?"

"Great. Serve them drinks, flirt a little, but stay the hell out of the players' laps."

"Wait. I know what this is about." She flipped her hair over her shoulder, a predatory smirk on her face. "You're jealous. You've been ignoring me for weeks, pretending you weren't interested, and now you can't stand the thought of me touching another man. You still want me."

"You're drunk. Do me a favor. Take a thirty-minute break, drink lots of water, and don't touch another sip of alcohol for the rest of the damn night."

She leaned forward, her breasts brushing against

my chest. "You can have me. All you have to do is say the word. It'll be our little secret. Nobody has to know. Not Tony, not Sal. And that fiancée you keep hidden away…" She clumsily snapped her fingers a few times. "What's her name again? I heard the guys talking about her."

"She's none of your business. Don't mention her ever again," I growled.

She pushed up onto her tiptoes, brushing her lips against my neck. A shiver of disgust rushed down my spine.

"What your fiancée doesn't know won't hurt her. We'll have a good time. Do you want to go somewhere private for a do-over? You won't regret it. I promise."

If Angela thought I'd lay a finger on her drunk ass, she was thicker than I suspected. I gritted my teeth and the edges of my vision blurred, pulsing in time with my escalating anger.

Anger at myself for entertaining hooking up with her to get Evie out of my head. Anger at her for misreading every blatant dismissal I tossed in her direction. Anger that I didn't fire her earlier in the week.

While I would never lay a hand on a woman, right now she was tempting me to do exactly that. "Go into my fucking office. I'll meet you there in twenty minutes. We need to talk."

Grinning like an idiot, she took a few micro-steps backward. "Right now? Are you sure you don't want me to work?"

I flicked my wrist. "I'll grab one of the other bartenders. You're done for the night."

CHAPTER THIRTY-ONE

Evangeline

"Did you get a hold of him?" Carmela's voice echoed through the speaker of the car I'd borrowed from Gian's garage.

"No." I flipped on my blinker. "He's not answering my phone calls either, but I'm pulling up in front of the club."

Carmela heaved out a breath. "Thanks so much for doing this. I would've gone, but I don't want to leave his side, and my mom needs me. I can't leave her alone."

I turned off the ignition and opened the car door. "I understand, and you don't have to thank me. What's happening now?"

"He's better now. His blood pressure is down, and he's asking for Gian." Her voice quivered.

I jumped out of the car, half-walking, half-jogging. "I'll do what I can to make sure he gets there as soon as possible."

"Call me as soon as you find him. I need to talk to him, preferably before he meets with my dad."

"I will. See you soon." I disconnected the call and cut directly in front of the line curving around the side the building. My head down and my hands shoved deep in the pockets of my long cotton cardigan, I ignored the groans and taunts as I approached the bouncer at the entrance.

"Hi." I beamed. "I need to get inside to talk to my fiancé for a few minutes."

The man folded his bulky arms across his chest, his gaze raking over my less than club worthy appearance. "Wait in the line."

My eyes narrowed. "What's your name?"

"Andy," he grumbled. He opened the red velvet roped and waved two people inside.

"Well, Andy. I'm Evangeline Jeffers, Gian Trassato's fiancée, and it's really important that I speak with him right now. Something happened to his father, Antonio Trassato, and he would want to know about it."

He scanned through the names on his clipboard. "Sorry, you're not on the list. I can't bend the rules for anyone, even Mr. Trassato's fiancée."

I gritted my teeth. I didn't have time for this shit. Gian needed to add me to the list so I didn't have to stand outside like the pathetic spurned fiancée.

"If you don't trust me, you can use that walkie talkie thing clipped to the back of your belt and check. Call Gian or Tony. Either one of them will clear me to go inside."

"No can do. They can't be interrupted tonight."

"Please." I knitted my fingers together and pressed them to the center of my chest. "Just call. I promise you Gian won't be mad. Or better yet, do you know his sister Carmela? I can call her, and she'll tell you to let me inside."

"No, don't bother her." He groaned. "I'll call Gian."

With his dark eyes fixed on me, he held the black walkie-talkie to his lips. "Mr. Trassato, Evangeline Jeffers is here to see you. I told her to wait in the line, but she was insistent." He paused, his eyes widening fractionally. "Right. Of course."

He fastened the walkie-talkie to his belt and unclipped the rope. "You can go in. Gian will meet you right inside."

"Thank you for your help." I squeezed his arm, ignoring the urge to gloat. He was simply doing his job.

I stepped inside, halting briefly to let my eyes adjust to the flashing lights. The loud bass vibrated my insides. I didn't understand how Gian could work here every day. One week of working in a club would be more than enough for me.

Gian's giant strides closed the space between us in a matter of seconds, and he hooked his hands around my upper arms. "Evie, what's going on? Why are you here?"

"It's your dad. His blood pressure spiked, and your mom is worried about him. He's okay now, but he's asking for you. You weren't answering anyone's calls, so I came here."

Stunned, he stared at me, the torment in his eyes slicing through me. "Dammit," he muttered. "Do they know why?"

"Not really. Since he's in home hospice care, they won't do anything except try to make him comfortable."

"Yeah." His hands slipped from my shoulders. "That makes sense."

"I drove here, so we can leave when you're ready, unless you're too busy. I know you planned to work late tonight and everything. We could go tomorrow morning."

"No. Tony and Sal can take care of everything here." He brushed a kiss across my lips. "Wait here while I grab a few things from my office."

As he disappeared from view, I remembered Carmela's request for him to call her as soon as possible. "Shit," I mumbled, weaving through the crowd, dodging elbows, drinks, and swaying torsos.

Holding up my phone, I pushed open the door to his office. "Gian, Carmela wanted you to—" The rest of the sentence died on my lips. The sight in front of me hit me like a hard punch to my solar plexus. A very naked woman was draped over the top of his desk like something out of a porn set. Frozen with shock, I covered my mouth to stifle the horribly embarrassing sounds crawling like spiders up my throat.

Not again.

Humiliation burned the corners of my eyes. I clamped my eyes closed, trying to scrub the scene in front of me from my memory.

Inhale.

Exhale.

Inhale.

I'm okay.

My mind grappled for a response, only my mouth wouldn't cooperate. I pried open my eyes.

The woman yanked a black dress over her head that looked more like a bunch of ribbons than an actual dress. Her face resembled a red tomato, and her skin clashed with her brassy hair.

"Excuse me," she muttered her voice so soft I nearly missed it. "I need to use the bathroom." With her panties and bra balled inside of her fist, she opened a door next to Gian's desk and ducked inside.

He crossed the room, his footfalls echoing like gunshots in my head. "Calm down, Evie." He brushed his fingers down the side of my bare neck, and my muscles tensed a little more. "It's not what you're thinking."

"Let's not talk about this now. Your family is waiting for you." When I forced my hands between our bodies, trying to escape him, he squeezed me tighter. "You can take the car, and I'll call a cab." I fought back the nausea bubbling in my gut like I drank too many shots of tequila.

He pressed his lips to my forehead. "No. You're not leaving here without an explanation."

"I can't do this again, Gian. I just can't. It'll kill me." My voice sounded like I had swallowed a mouthful of gravel.

"Okaaay," he said, drawing out the word like I'd been hit on the head, and I was incapable of making sense. "Apparently, I'm a little slow on the uptake, so you're going to have to explain what you mean."

"What do you know about my ex?"

His eyes burned with fury, and his lips thinned. "Enough to know he's a spineless piece of crap."

I rubbed my hands along the sides of my thighs. "Yeah, I caught him with that woman, and I don't have any delusions she was the first. He only mentored women, and when I witnessed firsthand what that entailed, I realized it would never stop. Those women spent time alone with him, and he had power in the industry they wanted to break into. It was a recipe for cheating. It had the three As to create the perfect storm."

"The three As? What the fuck are you talking about?"

"Availability. Access. Alibi. When the three of those aligned, he cheated with immunity."

"Yeah, so, what exactly does that have to do with us?"

"You own a nightclub. A lot of the employees are women. I would never know if you cheated, because this is your world. No one would ever tell me."

He folded his arms across his chest. "Don't ever compare me to him."

"I'm not. It's just..." I swallowed, uncertainty ballooning between us.

Angela slipped out of the bathroom door, her clothes now firmly in place. She dipped her head and slipped by me, smelling of booze and cheap perfume. She paused at the door, her hand curled around the doorknob. "Well, yeah, I guess I'll get to work."

I studied the tips of my white slip on sneakers. I couldn't look at her, and I certainly didn't want to have a conversation with her. Not now. Not ever. The memory of her sprawled out on Gian's desk was embedded in my head, and it made me more than a little self-conscious. She embodied everything I didn't.

She was carefree. I was uptight.

She had curves for days. I had long, toned muscles from years of dance.

She had fake breasts that belonged on the cover of some less than honorable magazine. I had a B cup on a good day.

Yuck.

"Don't bother," Gian barked. "I asked you in here to terminate your employment. You can pick up your final check and sign the necessary paperwork tomorrow when you're sober."

She set her hands on her hips. "Are you serious?"

"What do you think? You showed up to work drunk, you draped yourself over my guests like a prostitute, you sprawled your naked ass on top of my desk. Sounds like a lot of good reasons to fire you. Get the fuck out of here, or I'll revoke my offer to pay you for the last two weeks."

"Whatever," she mumbled, slamming the door with a loud thud.

"I'm going to go," I whispered when the silence became unbearable.

Gian locked a hand around my wrist, his jaw hard and his eyes glinting. "We're not done talking about this."

"There's nothing to talk about."

"Seriously? You're going to take off without

talking to me?"

Inhale.

Exhale.

"You have more important stuff to do right now, Gian."

"Nothing is more important than you," he fired back.

He tugged me hard against him, forcing my hands to circle his neck. He smelled like cigars and whiskey. My legs pressed against his, and damn it, his closeness affected me more than I wanted to admit. He wanted to subdue me and unstitch my resistance. I sensed him willing me to look at him, and somehow, I found the self-respect to rebuff his unspoken command.

Punishing me for my defiance, he slid his hands around my waist and squeezed my ass, rocking his hard length against me. "Why would I want that woman when you do this to me?"

I didn't want to like his dominant manner, except somewhere in a deep, dark place in the back of my mind, I kind of did. Swallowing the moan on the tip of my tongue, I dug my fingers into the soft weave of his suit jacket. My fingers simultaneously longed to pull him closer and slap him across his too-smug face. I hated that he could arouse me even as betrayal and hurt churned inside of my gut like acid.

"Don't do this to me," I whimpered, revolted by the weakness in my voice. In my soul. In my heart.

"I asked her to meet me in here so I could fire her, Evie. That's it."

"You don't have to explain anything. Your father is waiting for you."

"No." His hands framed my face. "Not until you believe I didn't do anything wrong."

His lips slammed against mine, chased with a hard thrust of his tongue. All of it orchestrated to possess me, claim me, and pacify me. He tasted like a lethal concoction of anger, whiskey, and seduction. I jerked my head to the side, severing the connection.

"Stop."

He speared his hand into his hair. "Nothing happened. She was here when I got here."

I backpedaled a few steps until my thighs hit the rounded arm of his sofa. "You obviously sent her signals that you were interested."

"You'd like that, wouldn't you?" His hand trailed down the side of my neck, pausing on the front of my white collared shirt. "You'd like me to be a lying cheater exactly like your ex so you don't have to deal with what's going on between us."

"No." My voice was barely a whisper.

He tugged on the sides of my shirt and two buttons popped off, skidding across the floor by my feet. He cupped one breast, pinching and teasing my nipple. I gasped.

"Then why don't you believe me?" He flipped open the button of my baggy boyfriend jeans and shoved them, along with my panties, down my legs. I couldn't bring myself to stop him.

My fingernails sunk into the arm of the leather sofa on either side of my hips. "I want to, but I'm—"

He plunged his fingers between my thighs, stroking the sensitive flesh and effectively stopping my words mid-sentence. I arched my hips. His touch was Heaven *and* Hell. Heaven because I wanted him. Hell because I didn't think I'd ever get enough of him. His lips were everywhere, his stubble like sandpaper on my flesh, his tongue licking and exploring. All of it drove me to the brink of insanity.

"I'm scared of what I feel for you," I confessed more to myself than him.

He crouched down, a hand on each of my knees. "Why?"

"Because it's too big, and I don't want to be hurt again."

He lifted one of my legs over his shoulder. "I'm never going to hurt you, sweetheart." With his amber gaze burning into me, his tongue licked a devastating path up the inside of my thigh. "You're mine, and I protect what's mine."

His warm breath wafted over my folds, and my eyes drifted shut.

"Look at me."

Too far gone to resist, I opened my eyes, and he leaned in, dragging his tongue over my clit, teasing me, taunting me.

"Holy shit," I moaned, raking my teeth over my lower lip.

His mouth devoured me in adept movements made up of tiny probes and decadent swirls.

I bucked my hips. My legs shook. My fingers and toes tingled. My muscles bunched.

"Gian. Ah. Oh," I whimpered along with a hundred other incoherent words and syllables.

"That's it, Evie. You look so beautiful all spread

out for me," he growled, sliding one finger inside of me and then another.

Pleasure spiraled down my spine. Heat bloomed through me. His fingers moved faster. Harder. It felt so good. Too good. And then I tipped over the edge, my sex clenching around his fingers, wave after wave of pleasure spiraling through me.

He set my leg back down on the floor, the air thick with the smell of my arousal. Reluctantly, I looked at him. His hand drifted to my face. His knuckles traced the line of my jaw, and I knew what he was going to say before the words left his mouth because I felt the exact same way, and I couldn't deny it any longer.

He angled forward, pressing his lips to mine, and all my worries, expectations, and doubts faded. It didn't make sense, but I knew deep down in my bones his words were the absolute truth.

"I love you, Evie."

I wrapped my fingers around his muscular forearms, breathing in him in and shuddering with relief. "I love you too."

CHAPTER THIRTY-TWO

Gian

"Gianluca," my dad croaked.

He looked like shit. His skin was ashen rather than the usual deep olive hue. His hair had started to grow back in uneven patches, and he couldn't have weighed more than one hundred and thirty pounds. It killed me to see my once-strong father like this.

I settled into the sofa next him. "Dad, what happened tonight?"

He brought the straw of a clear plastic water bottle to his lips. "Alix Trincher and his son stopped by earlier tonight."

"What the hell? Why did you let them inside the house?"

He jammed the water bottle between the sofa arm and his leg. "I didn't want to scare your mom."

"Alix is a loose cannon. He could've shot you or Mom or Carmela, and don't get me started on his son. I've heard he's worse than the father."

"I sent your mom and sister on an errand." He dragged a hand down the side of his sunken cheek. "And honestly, I wouldn't have fought too hard if he tried to kill me. A bullet to the head is preferable to this slow death."

My stomach dropped like I swallowed a brick. "You don't mean that. Something could change." Neither of us believed my words. Barring divine intervention, which wasn't likely given my dad's long list of sins, he was going to die sooner rather than later. The fact his death was imminent didn't eliminate the feeling that someone had lodged an ice pick in my chest when I thought about never seeing him again.

He raised one eyebrow, drawing my attention to his eyes. They were dilated and cloudy from the liquid morphine he ingested regularly to keep the pain at bay. "I didn't ask you to come here to talk about my death."

Clearing my throat, I rubbed my hands down the fabric of my pants. "Then why am I here?"

"The Russians, Alix in particular, want access to your territory."

I curled my hands into fists. The fucking Russians. First they tried to kill me. Then they hurled a brick through my front door, and now they thought they were entitled to special perks for being assholes.

"Tell him to take it up with Nico," I snapped.

"He did," my dad replied. "Apparently Nico wants you to work out the details with Alix and present them to him."

"Really? And why does he think I'd be his advocate? He's been fucking with me for weeks."

He jerked his head toward me. "What do you mean?"

"I don't want to get into it. I have things under control."

He nodded absently. "Do Nico and your uncle know about this?"

"Yeah. Yeah." I slanted forward, balancing my elbows on my thighs. "Like you said, Nico thinks I should make a deal with the Russians, but I don't think it's necessary. They're pushing me because I'm new. In a couple of months, they'll back down, and everything will go back to normal."

"I don't think so." My dad shook his head, the corners of his mouth curving downward. "He said you have something of his, and he wants compensation, or he wants it back."

"What the fuck? That doesn't make sense."

"Yeah, well, he wouldn't elaborate."

I stood and rubbed the back of my neck. "So what happens now?"

He took another sip of his water. "You're meeting him tomorrow afternoon to discuss the details and see if you can work this out. You're supposed to take that fiancée of yours."

"Excuse me?"

"Take Evangeline."

"No."

Dad flinched from the sharpness of my voice. "It's non-negotiable. Apparently, she's wrapped up in this shit somehow, and if you don't show up with her in tow, we might as well go to war. Nobody wants that. We've barely recovered from that bullshit with the DiTonnos and Rocco."

Fuck! If Kevin had lied about his debt to Alix being satisfied, I'd rip him apart with my bare hands. It'd be totally like that self-centered ass to promise something that wasn't his. Something to do with Evie.

"You're keeping something from me." It was a statement, not a question.

Dammit. High as a kite and riddled with cancer, and I still couldn't get a lie past my father. He was a human lie detector.

"Nothing important, Dad."

"Don't hide shit from me, Gianluca."

I bristled under his scrutiny. "Fine. I don't know if it means anything, but Evie's ex owed Alix a half a million dollars."

"I assume he didn't pay him back or you wouldn't be mentioning this."

"As I understand it, he paid some of it back and did him a favor." I rested my chin against my chest. "He told me Alix considers the debt paid in full now."

"What does Evangeline know about this?"

My head jerked up, a nauseated feeling swirling inside my gut. I'd never asked her anything, because I didn't want her to worry about shit she couldn't control. "As far as I know, she doesn't know a thing."

"Jesus Christ, Gian." He yanked on the collar of his t-shirt like he couldn't breathe. "Tell me you asked her about this. Tell me you aren't in this relationship with her based on blind faith."

I glanced to the side, avoiding his condemning stare. I'd been living on my own for close to a decade, yet he could make me feel like a five-year-old kid caught with his hand in the cookie jar in a matter of seconds.

"You checked her out, didn't you?"

"She's not some stranger off the street. She's Carmela's friend," I answered as though it made a difference. It didn't, not to my dad.

He shot me a glare, his lips trembling with rage. "You didn't listen to a damn thing I taught you. I went to bat for you. I thought you had a good head on your shoulders. Now you're gonna make a fool out of me." He pushed to his feet, cringing with pain. He shoes clipped over the hardwood floor, each thud more ominous that the last. He flung open the door and it banged against the wood paneling.

"Helena!" he yelled, his voice cracking. "Send Evangeline in here."

My throat bulged with resentment. "Dad, back the hell off. I'm not a kid. I'll talk to her tonight and find out what she knows. You're too sick to deal with this."

"*Sta ta zee*." He grabbed a fistful of my shirt. "I can't believe you. I can't trust you when it comes to this chick, can I? She has your balls in a vise. You aren't thinking straight."

"Um, hi." Evie stepped into the room, her attention boomeranging between my dad and me. "What's going on? Is something wrong?"

My dad released my shirt, his face red and his eyes like daggers. "You could say that."

"Evie—" I slipped my hand into hers "—we

need to ask you a few questions."

"Cut the bullshit, Gian." My dad pointed a shaky finger at Evie. "Tell me everything you know about Alix Trincher."

"Alix Trincher?"

"Yes. Alix Trincher. Bloody Alix. Vor." His voice dropped to a gritty whisper. "Do any of these names ring a bell?"

Evie tipped up her chin, her flame-colored hair dancing around her shoulders. "No. Why?"

I squeezed her hand and tugged her closer to me. "Did Kevin ever mention that name?"

"Not that I remember. Is he an artist?"

My dad barked out a laugh. "No. He's a fucking psychopath who wants to meet with you and Gian tomorrow."

Her eyes widened. "Me? Why would he want to meet with me?"

"Hell if I know." My dad leaned against the wall, tiredness etched into every line of his face. "You two need to make an appearance at Carmine's at two. My brother will join you."

"He's going too?"

"Yeah. Yeah. I think you'll need someone with you. Alix is bringing his son." He pushed away from the wall. "Now, get outta here. I'm going to bed," he grumbled, exiting the room with an uneven gait.

CHAPTER THIRTY-THREE

Evangeline

I sat a table in the back corner of Carmine's, Gian on one side of me and Dominick on the other. Starched white linens covered the tables, and red drum-shaped pendant lights hung over every table. The smell of garlic, basil, and fresh bread filled the air.

Last night, Gian didn't offer much information other than we had a meeting with Alix Trincher and his son, whoever he was, and that Kevin had gotten tangled up with him. Other than the staff and us, the restaurant was deserted. Still, Gian's eyes routinely scanned the entrance behind me while his other hand periodically tucked inside his suit, fingering his gun.

Dominick hadn't said one word to me since he joined us ten minutes ago. On the off chance I had misread the blatant hints that he disapproved of me at the engagement party, I couldn't ignore it right now. I offered my hand when Gian introduced us again, and he looked at me like a piece of gum on the bottom of his shoe.

Gian tapped his fingers on the table. "So what's the plan? They should be here in the next ten minutes and you haven't said a single thing."

Dominick grunted, his dark gaze glued to the front window. "We see what they want."

"And if they push for access to our territories?"

Dominick brushed some invisible lint on his jacket. "We tell them to fuck off."

"Nico thought I should negotiate," Gian said. "See if we could come to terms that were mutually beneficial."

"I'm not going to negotiate with these animals," Dominick said, slicing his hand through the air. "They don't have anything I want."

"You should make that clear to Nico." Gian folded his arms across his chest, and his chair creaked. "Because he thinks we should bend over and take it up the ass. I'm starting to think he's lost his edge."

The bell over the front door jingled, and my muscles pulled tighter. Gian and Dominick stood, not ready to come face to face with the man known as bloody Alix, I froze in place. My heart sounded like machine gun fire in my ears. My breath became shallow, and I felt like someone had stuffed a plastic bag down my throat.

"Evangeline," a familiar coarse voice echoed through my ears.

I jumped out of my seat and whirled around, a

huge smile splitting across my face. "Kon? What are you doing here?"

My brother looked the same, yet different. I hadn't seen him in over three years. He'd lost the baby fat on his face. He was all sharp angles and high cheekbones. Dark tattoos peeked out of the cuffs of his shirt, stretching over his first knuckle. His light blond hair, so like my mom's, was longer than the last time I saw him.

His pale blue eyes roamed all over me as if he didn't believe he'd find me in one piece. "We're checking in on you." My brother stretched his arms wide. "Come here and give me a hug."

I took one step forward, and Gian grabbed the back of my shirt, yanking me against his chest.

"What the hell is going on, Evie? How do you know him?"

"This is my brother, **Konstantin. You know, the one in the Army. I told you about him, remember?**"

"He's not in the fucking Army. He's in the Russian mafia, and your father is Alix fucking Trincher," he snarled, releasing my shirt and pointing a finger across the room.

My gaze followed his finger, landing on a man hovering near the entrance. He had an arrogant sneer on his face. Deep grooves lined his forehead and the corners of his dark brown eyes. His red hair was liberally threaded with silver. His wide shoulders tapered to a slightly thickened waist.

Long-buried memories pushed to the surface. A man with bright red hair pushing me on the swing in the backyard. A thickly accented voice whispering something in my ear at bedtime. A man with my name tattooed on his forearm.

Nausea swam in my gut. My heart thumped hard, and my vision blurred. "I have no idea what you're talking about. I don't know that man." My voice sounded more hopeful than convincing.

Gian's eyes narrowed and the muscle at the corner of his jaw twitched. "Don't lie to me." His hands dug into my shoulders. "Was this the plan all along? First, you help your dad bury your ex under a mountain of debt, then you move on to me. Tell me, what's the favor your father's going to want from me? Money? Blood?"

"Get your hands off my daughter." Alix stalked forward, his nostrils flaring and his eyes burning like the pits of Hell.

Gian shoved me to this side and ripped his gun from his holster. "Back the fuck up."

I clumsily tugged on the side of Gian's suit. "No, Gian. Stop. Don't do this."

My brother lunged forward, circling his arms around Gian's waist. Everything happened in slow motion. They tumbled backward, hitting the tiled floor with a loud *oomph*.

The gun skittered across the tile, stopping near my feet. One punch turned into ten until they morphed into a mass of swinging and kicking limbs. The sound of flesh hitting flesh punctuated by grunts boomed through the otherwise silent restaurant.

A scream split my lips. My knees rattled, threatening to buckle, and I leaned into the table so I didn't fall. "Please. Please," I said so many times I lost count.

Tony materialized from the kitchen, sinking one hand into Kon's hair and the other into the back of his shirt, pulling him off Gian. Gian scrambled to his feet, blood dripping from his nose and his chest heaving. Tony wrangled Kon across the restaurant with his arms behind his back.

Kon spat a mixture of blood and saliva on the floor. "Get your fucking hands off me."

Dominick stepped forward. "Tony, let him go."

Tony's head jerked to the side. "Are you serious? He jumped Gian."

"Release him right now," he said, enunciating each word. He advanced to the front door of the restaurant and flipped the lock. "They came here to talk. We're going to hear them out. Then, they will leave, right, Alix?"

"I don't have a problem with that as long as pretty boy over there keeps his hands to himself." He raised his arms in the air, and I saw the last three letters of my name peeking out of the sleeve of his shirt.

No way. This isn't happening.

Shock rippled through me, and I couldn't look away from him. His eyes looked like my eyes. His hair resembled mine interspersed with gray. That bump on his nose was eerily similar to the one I saw every morning in the mirror. Bile burned the back of my throat, and I staggered into the chair behind me, my heart racing and my mind buzzing with a dozen contradictory emotions.

"He's my dad," I whispered, my entire body vibrating and my chest incredibly tight like I couldn't suck enough oxygen into my lungs. "I

251

haven't seen him since I was five. I didn't remember much about him. My mom called him Al when I was younger. Then, she stopped talking about him entirely after he disappeared. He was more like a ghost than a real person."

My eyes sought out Gian. His head was bowed, his face was pinched, and his shoulders drooped with something akin to defeat. "I'm so sorry, Gian. I didn't set you up. I promise. I would never hurt you or your family intentionally."

I reached out my hand, pleading without words for him to say something. Anything. I didn't know what to do. My heart squeezed with the urge to comfort him, but deep down, I knew he wouldn't welcome my touch.

Gian cursed under his breath, his eyes glazed with rage and darkness. He shook his head, clearly unable to believe what was happening. "We're all busy men. Let's get this over with. What do you want, Alix?"

CHAPTER THIRTY-FOUR

Gian

I looked everywhere except at the woman who'd stolen my heart one piece at a time. She might as well have cleaved open my ribcage and wrenched my still-beating heart out of my chest. A bitter brew of humiliation mixed with hope churned inside my gut.

Humiliation because I had fucked up. I should have made sure I knew everything about her before I invited her into my life for real. Hope because every cell inside of me wanted to believe she didn't have anything do this with this. I'd witnessed her reaction when her mom called and mentioned her dad. Her reaction wasn't fake, not entirely.

Dammit, how did this happen? How could the one woman I should stay far away from end up being my sister's best friend, and the one woman I wanted more than any other?

253

"I want to clear up something first," Alix said, his voice gruff.

I curled one hand around the top of a chair, and my knuckles whitened. "Go ahead."

"Evangeline is telling the truth. I haven't had any contact with her for nearly twenty years. As for her ex, I only screwed with him because I couldn't stand the thought of my daughter marrying that schmuck."

Evie gasped. "What? Why would you do that?"

Alix flicked his wrist. "He was a piece of shit. All I had to do was dangle a little bit of money and a piece of ass in front of him, and he took the bait. Believe me; you're better off without him. You don't want a man who can be manipulated so easily."

"You had no right." Evie's voice cracked on the last word. "I didn't ask for your help."

He shrugged. "I did it for me as much as I did it for you. I wanted you to give up your acting pipe dream and move back to Nebraska, and I didn't want anyone using you to get to me. As long as you're in New York, you're a liability. I can't protect you here."

I pinched the bridge of my nose, trying to get my rioting thoughts under control. "But you're okay using her to get what *you* want. That's why you're here, isn't it?" I sneered. He'd been playing with Evie's life behind her back. He didn't even have the guts to come out of hiding until she had something he wanted.

He flung one beefy arm wide. "The stars aligned. What can I say? While I love my daughter, that doesn't mean I'm above capitalizing on an opportunity that lands in my lap." He chuckled. "You know, I always considered her a burden. Boy, did she prove me wrong. She reeled in a member of the Trassato family. I've been trying to negotiate with your father for years, but she batted her eyes, showed a little leg, and *bam*—" he punched his fist into the air "—she secured a proposal from you in a matter of days."

I snatched my glass of wine off the table and took a huge gulp, feigning amusement. Underneath my tailored suit and lazy grin, my blood boiled, and my skin crawled. I wanted to defend Evie. At the same time, I instinctively knew that was exactly what he expected from me. He wanted me to fly off the handle and show my hand. He wanted to know if I'd fight for her, and how much I'd be willing to give up to keep her.

"As enlightening as your little speech was, let's cut to the chase. What do you want?"

"I want access to all of the Trassato controlled territories to expand my business."

While not unexpected, Alix's demand reverberated through the room with the force of a grenade.

"No," Dominick said firmly. "That's not happening."

"Then he's not marrying my daughter." Alix pointed his finger at Evie. "You. Get up. We're going."

Konstantin stomped across the room and seized Evie's arm, trying to pull her to her feet. "We need to leave."

She slapped his hand. "Are you crazy? I'm not going anywhere with you *or* that maniac."

"Get over yourself. You're engaged to a fucking capo, not an altar boy. Do you know what that means?"

I lunged at her brother, snagging him by the collar of his shirt. "You touch her again, and I'll fucking kill you."

His nose flared. "Is that a threat?"

"No." I shoved him backward. "It's a fucking promise."

Dominick's hand landed on my shoulder. "Let her go, Gian. Your engagement is over. I won't negotiate with them, and even if we did, you could never trust her. She's toxic."

"Don't touch me." I sidestepped his hold. "This isn't over."

"Like hell it isn't. You're done with her." He ripped his gun from a holster around his waist and jammed the barrel against my chest. "I'm not bending over so you can marry this *puttana*."

"Shut the fuck up. Don't talk about my fiancée like that!" I roared, my vision narrowing. I swatted the gun away from my chest and pinned Dominick against the table. He didn't fight me. He stood there with a fucking smirk on his face. "Do you understand?" I seethed, glaring at him. "Do you?"

"You think you can threaten me?" he scoffed. "You may be my nephew and godson, but that won't stop me from putting you in your place."

"Go ahead," I said through gritted teeth.

"Enough!" Evie jumped out of her chair, her eyes wide with panic and her hand clutching the sleeve of my suit. "Gian, can I talk to you alone for a second?"

I released Dominick and dragged her by the arm to the kitchen. The staff froze mid-task. "Get the fuck out of here!" I yelled.

Knives, plates, and pans clattered to the floor.

"Move!" I repeated, my eye twitching like a fucking lunatic.

Three men in white shirts and black pants scurried out the back door with their eyes glued to the floor.

"We can't be together anymore," she said, her lips quivering.

An adrenaline-laced tremble shot down my spine. "We'll find a way to make this work."

"Maybe, but at what cost, Gian? What will you have to give up? And at what point will you start resenting me? Resenting us? I can't let you do this." Her voice wavered, her gaze dancing around the room.

"Let me take care of this, sweetheart."

"What happens if you have to walk away from everything—your family, your friends your life—to be with me? Are you okay with that? Is that even possible?"

"It won't come to that."

"You don't know that. They could kill you. Your family could disown you."

I shrugged. "Some things are worth fighting for."

She wiped her hands down the sides of her thighs. "I don't want to fight."

"What do you mean?"

"I don't like what you do. I don't like what my

257

so-called family does." She sucked her lower lip into her mouth. "I don't want to be a part of that life. I want to dance, act, and sing, without worrying if someone will take a shot at me when I'm driving down the street, or worse."

My heart stuttered. "Yesterday you told me you loved me, and now, all of a sudden, you have a problem with what I do? I don't buy it. Not for a second, Evie. Don't push me away again because you're scared."

She lifted her head, looking straight at me. "Gian, take a step back and think about this. Our relationship has been a colossal disaster from the start. I never wanted this. You never wanted this. We were forced into this situation. It was supposed to be temporary until we could bow out unscathed. Now I have the chance. We both do, and we need to take it."

I captured her chin, forcing her to look at me. "That's what you want? You want to bail on us without trying?"

We locked gazes. I refused to look away first. Her eyes glistened. I bent my head, pressing my lips against hers, my grip still firm on her chin. Even though she didn't kiss me back, I couldn't stop myself from wanting her.

I tasted her salty tears, felt her sorrow. I smelled her delicate jasmine scent.

A half-gasp, half-whimper escaped her lips, and she pulled back. When she looked up at me, she swallowed, her eyebrows pinching together.

"I don't want to try. It's not worth it. We're not compatible...not for the long run. We have different goals and dreams, and now's the time to pursue mine. I have to put myself first, and that means walking away from you and this whole mess before it destroys me." Her words came out ragged and grief-stricken.

"Give me a little more time."

"No. I'm walking out the door now, and I don't want to see you again. Don't try to contact me. Don't try to find me. Just let me go. It's for the best. You know it, and I know it."

I slammed my fist into the wall next to her head. She flinched, clutching her heart.

"You're not fucking going anywhere." I punched the wall over and over. Drywall showered her head like pixie dust. My knuckles cracked open. Blood dripped from my hand. "You're mine. I won't let you go."

She covered her tear-streaked face. "I'm not yours, and you're not mine. We had fun, but it's over now. I don't want you, and you don't want me. Not really."

This isn't happening. She wouldn't give up on us so easily.

My heart squeezed. Pain sliced through me with more misery than I thought possible. My hands curled into her shoulders, and I tugged her against my chest, clawing at her like a fucking animal. "Don't lie to me."

Tony's arms closed around my waist, hauling me backward. "Let her go, Gian. It's done."

I struggled against him, kicking and yelling. "Fuck you, Tony. You don't know anything."

"This is the way it has to be," Evie whispered as

Tony dragged me out the back door of the restaurant.

The minute the door slammed behind us, Tony released me.

"Get a hold of yourself, man. You're acting like a fucking pussy."

I buried my face in my hands. My shoulders jerked up and down, and my eyes stung. I couldn't believe I was about to burst into tears for the first time in twenty years. My life was spinning out of control. Despair and rage wrapped around me like a straightjacket, and I wanted to storm back into the restaurant and kill Alix and Dominick and set the place on fire.

Instead, I walked away with every inch of me still aching for her.

CHAPTER THIRTY-FIVE

Evangeline

The moment the door closed behind me, I wanted to die. I'd torn Gian's heart out, but I might as well have torn out my own. I ruined us. I had pushed away the only person who ever wanted to fight for me.

I wanted to take back my words. I wanted to run after him and tell him I lied. Tell him I loved him. Tell him I wanted him. Only I couldn't. Not now, not ever. He had already sacrificed enough for me. I wouldn't let him sacrifice his family and honor too. While I might not like what his life entailed, I wouldn't let him throw it away for me.

Likewise, I refused to play into my father's twisted logic and hand him the Trassato territories on a silver platter so Gian could be with me, a woman who he'd only known for a couple of months. I'd rather spend the rest of my life missing him than lining Alix's pockets.

I swiped away my tears and strode out of the kitchen with my head held high. My shoes hammered against the floor like detonating bombs.

"Where are you going?" Konstantin asked.

I kept going, not meeting any of the stares searing into my flesh. "It's none of your business."

"Don't walk away from me, girl." Alix caught my arm the second I stepped over the threshold of the door.

Shivering with disgust, I broke his grip. "Gian and I are over. You'll have to find another way to get what you want."

CHAPTER THIRTY-SIX

Evangeline

One Week Later...

"Evie, you were great up there. They'd be crazy not to give you a part. I'm so proud of you. You're so much better than Mom ever was."

I spun around. "Kon, what are you doing here?"

My brother shoved his hands into the pockets of his dark jeans. A yellowing bruise circled one of his eyes, and he had a scab on his lower lip. "We need to talk."

"That's funny. I'm pretty sure we don't have anything to talk about."

I slung my dance bag over my shoulder and pushed open the door to the outside. Wind whipped my hair around my face. The smell of an impending rainstorm mixed with grease from the burger joint next door hung in the air. I pulled my hood over my head and darted down the clogged sidewalk.

Halfway down the block, Kon tugged on the back of my jacket, stopping my retreat. All pretenses of humor had disappeared from his face. "I'm not done talking to you."

I sighed. "You know what? I don't care."

"Why aren't you answering Mom's calls? She's worried about you."

I ripped my hand out of his hold. "Because I don't have anything to say to her, just like I don't have anything say to you or my sperm donor."

"Don't be like that." He frowned. "We're your family, and you need us. Especially now."

"No, I really don't. Quite honestly, if I never see any of you again, it'll be too soon."

He rolled his eyes. "Don't be so dramatic."

I curled my hands into fists, my fingernails digging into my palms. "You guys lied to me about everything."

"Come on, Evie. Don't be like this. You're making a big deal out of nothing."

"Seriously?" My voice was low and accusing. "My entire childhood was a lie. Do you have any idea how many hours I've wasted combing over every conversation and event in my head, searching for missed clues and hidden meanings?"

"We did what we had to."

Squeezing my eyes closed, I shook my head. They had dangled the truth right in front of my face my entire life, and I'd been too trusting to follow the breadcrumbs. Every time I thought about it, I felt like someone had taken a sledgehammer to my skull.

"Those summer camps on the East Coast weren't really summer camps, were they? You spent the summers with Dad. You lied about joining the Army. When I questioned Mom about our dad, you never said a word to contradict her."

My attempts to stay calm failed. Childhood memories banged around in my head, and they no longer seemed sweet. They were tainted with betrayal and lies.

I yanked on the emerald necklace Kon gave me for my sixteenth birthday and crumpled it into a ball. Its sharp angles bit into my palm, but it was better than letting it hang around my neck like a noose. "This necklace." I shoved my fist into the center of his chest, and he grunted. "It wasn't from you. It was from *him*. You didn't save all your money from shoveling snow off our neighbor's walks. He gave it to you to pass along to me. And those stupid Russian classes Mom made us take." I ground my teeth together. "Ugh. I can't even go there."

He pushed my hand away. "Get a fucking grip, Evie. Don't jump to conclusions. There are two sides to every story."

I flung my hands into the air, the chain of the necklace slipping like sand through my fingers. "Then please, by all means, tell me yours. I'm dying to hear what compelled my entire family to keep me in the dark about the fact that my sperm donor is a lying, murderous criminal."

A bolt of lightning flashed through the sky followed by a rumble of thunder. A few drops of rain slapped against the gray sidewalk.

"Don't make this into something bigger than it is. We did what we had to do to keep you safe. Mom and Dad didn't want you to get caught up in Dad's life." His lips pursed into a tight line. "It's dangerous."

"So their solution was to let me fumble around in the dark like an idiot?"

He scrubbed his hand down his face. "It kept you safe. It allowed us to do things we couldn't otherwise do."

"Like what? Bury my ex-fiancée under gambling debts so he has to mentor some woman whose sole purpose was to encourage him to cheat on me? Was that fun? Were you lurking around the corner when I caught them fucking? Did you laugh? Was it funny to watch your sister get her heart ripped out of her chest?"

"He didn't have to gamble. He didn't have to cheat. We might have manipulated things to shove him in that direction, but he could have resisted the temptation."

I stared at him. Deep down, I knew he was right—though, it didn't lessen the blow. "You didn't have to meddle in my life. You could've told me what you thought of him."

Konstantin tugged on the end of my ponytail exactly like he did when we were kids. I wanted to melt into him and let him shelter me from this like he did with so many things when we were younger. I stepped away to stifle the urge.

"You know that wouldn't have worked, and we did you a favor. You didn't really love him."

I swallowed over the lump lodged in my throat.

"Then what about Gian? Someone chased us in a car and shot at us. Someone threw a brick through Gian's door. I know Alix is behind both of those things. Don't try to deny it. All evidence to the contrary, I'm not gullible enough to believe those things were a coincidence."

He scratched the side of his neck. "We did what we had to do. It's the way things work in our world. Gian Trassato knows this. Hell, he's done worse, and that's exactly why I don't want you anywhere near him. And trust me, he hasn't let a day go by over the past week without fucking with us. You should be able to live your life untouched by all this shit. That's what Dad, Mom, and I always wanted." A hard edge of anger infused with frustration laced his words.

I stared at my shoes, lost in a daze. The people on the sidewalk wove around us. Horns honked. Music floated out of car windows. People laughed. Somewhere in the distance, a dog barked, and a woman screamed insults into her phone. None of it seemed real.

Memories of Gian assaulted my mind. The way he smiled at me like I was the only person in the world. His taste. His golden eyes. His rough laugh. The way his face crumbled when I told him he wasn't enough and that we'd never work. My head started to pound again, and my chest felt empty. So empty I might as well have been dead. I clenched my teeth together to suppress the sob on the tip of my tongue.

Over the last week, I had fallen into a deep darkness that only dancing had pulled me out of.

When I danced, I temporarily managed to convince myself I would get through this and stop missing Gian. As soon as the music stopped, I'd get caught up in the messy trap of reminiscing, and I'd promptly dissolve into another weepy fit of tears. Thank God the musical I'd auditioned for today dripped with sadness and melancholy. It suited my mood perfectly.

"Then cut the ties. Let me live my life how I see fit and make my own decisions."

"Maybe at one time that would've been possible, but not anymore," he said so quietly, I strained to hear him.

I adjusted the strap of my bag. "What's that supposed to mean?"

"Now that your connection to us is no longer a secret, you're a target. Without us, you could be killed or kidnapped for ransom by the end of the week."

Bitterness rushed though me like lava, settling in the pit of my stomach. "Great. What am I supposed to do now? Walk around with giant crosshairs on my back?"

He stepped toward me, reaching into his pocket and pulling something out. He dangled a set of keys from his index finger. "Here."

"What's this?"

"Keys to your new apartment."

I stared at the gold keys like they were a stick of dynamite. "No. I'm not taking anything from you."

I'd checked into a hotel last week, promising myself I'd find a more permanent place to live as soon as possible because the money I got pawning the engagement ring from Kevin wouldn't last for more than a couple of weeks with Manhattan prices. If I didn't land a role in this play, I'd find a job and move out of the hotel.

"It's temporary, and it will make my job a helluva lot easier. The building has a doorman and security. I wrote the address on the key chain."

"Is this a consolation prize from dear ol' Dad?" I raised my eyebrows, an indignant smirk on my face. "Whoops, sorry, long-lost daughter that I abandoned. I know I ruined your life and destroyed more than one of your relationships, but here's a place to live. This should make up for it."

"No. It's actually my apartment. I'll stay somewhere else until you get back on your feet."

I inched backward. "No." I didn't want to be indebted to anyone ever again. I needed to stand on my own two feet.

"Just take them." He shoved the keys into my pocket. "Think of it as my penance for lying to you."

"Are you going stay there with me?"

He glanced to the side. "I'll stay with Dad's family."

My stomach pitched. "He has another family?"

"A wife and two daughters. They're a good ten years older than us."

"So Mom was his *mistress*?" I asked, my mouth twisting with revulsion.

He shifted on his boot-clad feet. "Don't feel bad for Mom. She knew the score."

"His wife doesn't care that he shoves his bastard son in her face?"

"He wanted a son, and she couldn't have any more kids. They made a deal. He got his son, and she got to keep her life as long as she welcomed me into their house every summer. It worked out for everyone."

I fought back a scream of frustration. I couldn't believe this. My life was a joke that never stopped. "I guess that makes me collateral damage. A necessary evil. An unwanted complication on the road to conceiving the golden child."

"Don't think about it like that," he said, pity splashed all over his face. "Dad loves you as much as he does the rest of his kids. He just has a screwed-up way of showing it."

Fuck this. I was going to use the apartment. I saved and scraped over the last few years, trying to make my dreams comes true. My brother was right. He owed me.

"It's too late." I pulled the keys from my pocket and dangled them from my fingers. "Thanks for the place to live. I'll text you when I move out."

I took a few steps backward then paused. "Oh, and Kon?"

"Yeah?"

"Don't contact me ever again. You can slink around in the shadows and do whatever it is you do, but I never want to see you or anyone in my so-called family again. You're all dead to me, and if any of you meddle in my life again, I'll find a way to kill you myself."

CHAPTER THIRTY-SEVEN

Carmela Trassato

Two Months Later...

I stared at the man known as Bloody Alix and his son, Konstantin. My hands trembling in my lap, I kept my face a cold mask. These assholes would eat me for dinner if I showed any weakness. I couldn't believe Evie was related to these two men.

"What can you offer us?" Konstantin said, popping a powdered sugar confection into his mouth like we were discussing the weather.

I straightened my spine, refusing to give in to the urge to cower in front of them even though one well-aimed insult would expose me for what I really was—an uptight ball of anxiety waiting for a reason to tuck my tail between my legs and run out of here.

"Just Evie's happiness. She's part of your family. Isn't that enough? She loves my brother,

271

and he loves her." I lifted my hands in a plea. "Why are you standing in their way?"

"Love is for fools." Evie's dad slid his elbows along the rust-colored fabric covering the round table. "They may think they love each other now, but give it a year. The things they loved about each other will become the very things they can't stand. It will build and build until the love they shared mutates into hatred. In another year, the hatred will become indifference, and they'll wish they'd never met. I'm saving them a lifetime of bullshit. They should be thanking me for ending the farce before it's too late."

Stunned, I blinked, then a rough chuckle escaped my mouth. "You don't really believe that."

He ran his fingers through his reddish-gray hair, his eyes void of emotion.

What a soulless bastard.

"I don't give a shit about love stories. Maybe you can offer me something more tangible to convince me to reconsider."

I cleared my dry throat. "Like what?"

He leaned back in his chair, propping his thick meaty fingers behind his head. "Like unfettered access to the Trassato territories to distribute my goods. I think your brother owes me that, considering he pilfered six of my high-roller poker players this week alone. Do you have any idea how much money he's cost me?"

"I didn't come here as a representative of the Trassato family." I crossed and uncrossed my legs, trying to get comfortable. "I can't make any deals on their behalf."

Alix pushed his chair away from the table, and the wooden legs scraped across the cream-colored tile floor. "Then you're wasting my time, missy. You don't have anything I want. Send someone who has the power to bargain because I'm fucking sick of your brother's antics. I've let him play his little games, but I'm done." His eyes narrowed. "Unless…"

Alix wrapped one arm around Konstantin's shoulder and pulled him close. I couldn't make out his hushed whispers.

Konstantin folded his arms across his chest. "That's fucked up."

Alix grinned like a maniac. "Kon, don't play coy. I didn't miss the way you looked at her at the Trassatos' house, and I know how much you want to make this right for your sister. You've been in my ear nonstop about making peace with her. This would be the perfect way to give everyone a happy ending."

"Everyone except me."

Konstantin speared me with his icy glare as he drummed his tattooed hand on the table. Intricate stars, triangles, and crosses decorated his fingers like rings. Equal measures of interest and disgust curled in my gut. Since he and his dad stormed into my parents' home a couple of months ago, he'd dominated enough of my thoughts to make me more than a little uneasy.

"Get over yourself. Men like us don't have a normal life with a wife and white picket fence. We get something better: power and wealth."

He blew out a breath. "I'll do it *only* if it happens

on my terms."

Alix lifted his chin. "Fine, make it work, and I won't have any complaints."

I wiped a sweaty palm down the side of my face. "What are you talking about?

Kon stood, and he looked so much bigger than I remembered. The corners of his lips curled up, making his angular face handsome. He wore a black leather jacket with jeans and a silver-studded leather belt. At that moment, he commanded the room, even more so than his father.

He ran a tattooed finger ran down my cheek to the hard line of my jaw, and his leather jacket squeaked. With a flick of his hand, he tipped up my face. His too plump lips hovered within a hairsbreadth of my mouth. I could smell the powdered sugar on his breath. I barely suppressed a shudder while I waited for him to speak.

"I know how to make this work."

My eyes widened and hope surged through me. "How?"

"We do a trade."

"A trade?" I parroted, the two words scraping over my vocal cords like sandpaper.

"Yes." He stroked the length of my hair. "My sister for Gian's sister. How does that sound?"

My heart rate skyrocketed even as my mind refused to do the math. "What are you suggesting?"

Konstantin leaned forward, and the smell of leather and wood wrapped around me like an embrace. "You know exactly what I'm suggesting." His lips vibrated against the shell of my ear, and the weird, combustible chemistry always buzzing and crackling between us raised the fine hairs on the back of my neck. "But I'm happy to clarify. Gian gets my sister without any conditions, and we get engaged."

Shock ricocheted through my chest like a pinball machine, and I jumped out of my chair. "No. Absolutely not. I can't make that deal. I don't have that kind of power, and my family would never accept it."

Konstantin shrugged, unconcerned. "Then it looks like your brother will have to accept that he will never come within a hundred feet of my sister again, or I'll slice him into a million pieces and feed him to my dog."

I tipped my head toward the ceiling, staring at the garish red paint and brass chandelier with detached fascination. I wanted Evie and Gian to be happy. God knew I did, and I'd do most anything to make it happen. Be that as it may, I didn't know if I could spend my life tethered to Konstantin. He may have been Evie's brother, but where Evie was light, he was dark. And I was pretty sure ice water, not blood, pumped through his veins.

I groaned. "I can't."

"Is that your final answer?" Alix hissed.

"How will an engagement between your son and me benefit you?"

"Well, let's just call it a step in the right direction."

"Or it will start a war."

"I'm not worried. Your family won't go to war with me after what happened with the DiTonnos."

I closed my eyes, hoping to stave off the

landslide memories about my dead fiancé. It didn't work. Rocco's open smile and his dark eyes haunted me. My heart still ached with how much I missed him. I'd do anything to have another day with him. I'd never love anyone the way I loved him. Truthfully, I couldn't remember a day when I hadn't loved him. He was my childhood friend, my lover, and eventually my fiancé, and he'd been dead for nearly two years. Images of Rocco plaited together, making me hurt deep inside my bones. With a blinding clarity, I knew the feeling would never disappear entirely.

If Evie and Gian loved each other half as much as I loved Rocco, I couldn't let this opportunity slip through my fingers. While I might never find love again, it didn't mean I had to my condemn brother and my best friend to loveless life. Besides, it didn't matter if I committed my foreseeable future to the man next to me. My heart was dead, and it would never beat again. Not for anyone and certainly not for Konstantin Trincher.

"Fine," I rasped, dread spreading like venom through my vital organs. "I'll do it."

A smirk stretched across Alix's face, crinkling his already weatherworn face, and my stomach lurched. "It looks like we have a deal."

I fingered the engagement ring that dangled from a long chain around my neck. My mom had been begging me to take it off for over a year. She'd got it in her held that the gesture would help me move on. Well, now she had her wish, only not in the way she would have liked.

I cleared my throat. "Are you going to contact

my brother, or should I?"

Alix strummed his fingers on his thigh, his eyes holding me prisoner. "I'll send you something indicating we've removed any objections to Gian's involvement with Evangeline."

"Thank you." I exhaled. "What about me?"

"Don't worry about it." Konstantin squeezed my shoulder, and goose bumps broke out over my arms. I hated that my body reacted to him, and I sent out a silent prayer for indifference. "We'll work out the details later. I'm not in any rush."

Unable to utter a single word, I nodded. I fled the tiny Russian restaurant in Brighton Beach without looking back, my favorite black heels ticking like a countdown to the end of the world. I'd sold my soul to the devil. Thinking about my future almost made me throw up.

CHAPTER THIRTY-EIGHT

Gian

"Gian, this needs to stop."

I drained my glass of whiskey, the now familiar burn the only thing that made me feel alive these days. "I don't know what you're talking about, Carmela."

"I know what's going on. I know you're screwing with the Russians every chance you get. I know you're drinking too much. I know you're pissing people off purely because you can. You're being reckless, and that's not who you are."

I slammed my glass down, the ice rattling together. "You don't know shit."

She shut the door to my office with a definitive thud. "Contrary to what Dad and Dominick think, Mom and I do have eyes and ears. We hear the whispered conversations. We see the strained looks."

I clenched the arms of my chair. "So what?"

"In case you haven't noticed, Dad is dying sooner rather than later, and rather than making peace with his life, he's going out of his mind because he's worried about you, which means Mom is coming out of her skin."

I didn't need this shit right now. I had all the guilt and regrets I could swallow. "They don't need to worry about me. I'm fine. I'm better than fine. The club has never made so much money. I went on a date with the Amato girl like Mom asked. What more do you want from me?"

That would be the last date I went on for a long time. I could barely be civil to the woman. There was nothing wrong with her. She was attractive. She had a pleasant smile. Our families were friendly, except she wasn't *her*. I spent the entire night counting off the minutes until I could leave without offending her or her family. After sixty-three minutes, I slapped a wad of money on the table and hailed her a cab.

Carmela's lips puckered. "I want you to be happy."

"Dammit, Carmela. Leave it alone. Okay? I don't want to do this tonight." I stood and edged around my desk. "I have a meeting in ten minutes. You need to go."

She stuck her hand in her tote bag, rooting around for something. "Opening night is tomorrow."

I shuffled some papers on my desk, ignoring the dull ache in my chest. Fortunately, my sister was smart enough not to mention Evie by name. The last time she did, I came unglued. I woke up with a black eye and a hangover I wouldn't forget for years. "Great. Have fun."

She tossed a rectangular ticket on my desk paper clipped to a white envelope. "This is for you."

Hope flickered inside of my chest. "Who gave you this?"

"I bought the ticket for you. I thought you'd want to see the show."

I eyed the ticket like it was a snake primed to bite me. "Yeah, well, you were wrong. She doesn't want anything to do with me, and even if she did, it wouldn't matter."

"It matters because you love her."

I swiped the ticket and envelope from my desk and held it out to her. "Goodbye, Carmela."

She swatted it away. "Read the letter, you stubborn jerk."

"Is it from her?"

"No." She rolled her eyes. "Read it anyway. You'll like what it says."

I tossed the ticket on the chair next to Carmela and slid my finger across the seam of the envelope.

Gian,

I no longer have any objections to your involvement with our mutual acquaintance. You're free to pursue her without interference.

-A.T.

"Is this real?"

She folded her arms across her chest. "Yes."

"How did you get this?"

"Her brother and I wanted to make this right. We met to discuss our shared interest in helping you two be happy, and this letter showed up at my house a few days later."

I stuffed the letter and ticket in my pocket. "Fuck, Carmela, tell me you didn't meet him alone."

She bit the side of her lower lip, and I knew she was lying. She was my twin. I knew her gestures like the back of my hand, and biting on her lower was her tell.

"I wasn't alone. We met in public, and I'm fine and in one piece." She twirled around in a circle. "You don't need to worry about me. I'm a big girl. I can take care of myself."

"You're lying. What happened?"

"Gian, nothing bad happened. We talked. We came to an understanding, and now you need to go get your girl."

I didn't know if I had it in me to keep chasing her. I loved her, but I needed her to show me she wanted me too. Because every single time we hit a bump, her first instinct was to run away.

"I can't keep chasing her. She said I wasn't worth it. She didn't want to fight for us. She doesn't want anything to do with my life."

"Then don't chase her. Go to her show, say hello, and leave. She'll know the ball is in her court. She may do something about it, or she may not."

"Seriously, Carmela? How does that help either of us?"

"If you don't try, you'll never know."

I fingered the ticket in my pocket. Regardless of what happened between us, I couldn't deny I wanted to see her perform on a stage and talk to her one more time. If she wanted more, she needed to tell me because I was done pleading my case. I pushed her to kiss me to make her ex jealous. I pushed her into a fake engagement. I pushed her to try a real relationship. I told her I loved her, and she fled when things got complicated. I gave her what she wanted. I haven't contacted her, and I'd continue to leave her alone unless she told me otherwise.

"Fine. I'll go. I'll talk to her, but I can't promise anything other that."

She flicked me in the chest. "She won't let you go again. You'll see. By this time tomorrow, you'll be one-half of a sickeningly happy couple again."

"I'm not so sure, but thanks for setting this up. I owe you."

As she strutted toward the door, she shot me a parting grin over her shoulder. "In case you're hard up for a way to thank me, you should know I like shoes. Expensive shoes. With red soles. And four-inch heels."

"Yeah. Yeah. I get it."

CHAPTER THIRTY-NINE

Evangeline

Still on a high from finishing my first live performance in over a year, I scrubbed the stage makeup from my face. I didn't land a lead role, but I had one solo, which was more than I expected given my yearlong absence.

Laughter floated into the small dressing room I shared with a couple of other girls, along with the distinct pop of champagne bottles being opened. Friends and family members roamed the halls, congratulating loved ones.

There was so much to be thankful for tonight. My ankle didn't hurt. I hadn't missed a note. The performance went off without a hitch, and I couldn't wait to read the reviews. Judging by the applause and the electricity humming backstage, everyone expected them to be favorable.

Underneath all the excitement, I couldn't deny I

felt a thread of sadness that hadn't gone away in months. I'd moved out of Kon's apartment as soon as my agent told me I got this role, and I hadn't exchanged a single word with him since. My mom had stopped reaching out to me over a month ago. Carmela had texted a quick note to say good luck this morning, but other than the time we met for coffee so she could hand deliver my suitcase stuffed with my clothes and personal belongings, I hadn't seen her. And Gian...well, I hadn't heard a single word from him.

Although I had managed to rebuild a couple of friendships and make a few new ones, nothing filled the hole in my heart from the loss of Gian and my best friend. During my late night searches of Carmela's social media, I never found out anything about him. Not a mention. Not a picture. The thought of never seeing or hearing about him again made me sick to my stomach.

I quickly brushed away the thought. I couldn't jump down the what-if rabbit hole tonight, because it led to a shit ton of tears and swollen eyes.

Someone rapped on the already open door, and I spun around.

"Hey, Evie," John, one of my co-workers, said. "Do you need a ride to the after party?"

"Yeah. Let me finish up a few things, and I'll be out in a couple of minutes."

"Take your time. We're not leaving for a half hour or so." He took two steps backward then said, "Oh, and there's someone waiting for you at the end of the hall."

"Who?"

He shrugged. "He didn't say."

"Huh." I shoved my arms into my jacket. "Okay. Thanks."

I hoped it wasn't Kon or my dad. I wouldn't put it past Kon to show up tonight and pretend nothing had happened. As for my dad, while I didn't think he'd come here, he was a wildcard. I had no idea what he would want from me, if anything, going forward.

"Sure thing, sweetheart."

I cringed at his use of that endearment. It reminded me of Gian, and I didn't want to think about him tonight. I wanted to celebrate a successful opening and the resurrection of my career. I stepped out of the dressing room and saw *him*.

"Evangeline." Gian's smoky voice raced through me like a shot of morphine.

"Gian," his name rolled off my lips with longing, regret, and more than a little hope. "What are you doing here?"

"I couldn't miss your opening night." He handed me a bouquet of stargazer lilies. "These are for you."

"Thank you. They're beautiful." I brought them to my nose, inhaling their sweetly fragrant scent. "I hope you didn't fall asleep."

"No. I barely blinked." He chuckled, and then his eyes softened, and they looked like warm honey. He brushed his fingertips along the tip of my nose, and I swayed toward him. It'd been too long since he'd touched me. "You had pollen on your face."

"Oh." I smiled through hollow ache in my chest.

"Thanks."

We lapsed into silence, and I twirled the bouquet in my hand.

"You were beautiful out there. I couldn't take my eyes off you, and I'm pretty sure nobody else could either."

My heart squeezed. "Thanks. Does that mean I changed your mind about musicals?"

His mouth twisted into a lopsided grin. "Only if you're on the stage." He pressed a kiss to my forehead. "I better get going. Carmela said the cast is having a big party tonight to celebrate the opening."

"Yeah."

"Take care, sweetheart, and don't be a stranger. Carmela misses you. So does my mom. I think they're planning to catch one of your shows next week."

The minute he turned his back to me, my eyes blurred with tears.

Oh, shit. Why now? Why when I finally had my life together.

"Wait, Gian."

He halted mid-step, glancing at me over his shoulder. "Yeah?"

"I wanted to let you know you're worth it. You're worth everything. I didn't mean what I said that night at Carmine's, and I um…" I licked my lips, waiting, hesitating, not knowing if I should continue. Was I too late? He didn't say he missed me. He said his mom and sister missed me.

His face was blank.

"I still love you."

"You do?" His hands in his pockets, he turned to face me.

"I do." He didn't respond right away, so I kept rambling. "I didn't mean what I said that night. It was stupid and hurtful. I mean, I don't like what you do, that much is true. But I still want you in my life. I know there's chance you've moved on, and you're done with me...maybe we could still be friends?"

He sighed, and his body sagged, drawing attention to the shadows under his eyes. "Is that what you want? To be friends and nothing else?"

I dropped my arms, and the flowers brushed the side of my pants. "I'll take whatever you're offering. It's up to you. I screwed up and didn't fight for us when it counted." I pushed my hair away from my face. "For what it's worth, I really thought I was doing the right thing."

He grabbed my hand and knitted our fingers together. "And what was that?"

"I was ashamed of my family, and I felt guilty for putting you in a position where you had to choose between your family and me. I refused to let you sacrifice anything for me."

He raised his eyebrows. "So you made the choice for me?"

I dropped my gaze to the floor. "I guess so."

"Well, you chose wrong."

"I-I did?"

"I love you, Evie. I would've found a way to make things work. Your dad's demands were just that: demands. There's always room for negotiation. You walked away without giving us a chance to fix things."

"What now?"

"You tell me. The ball is in your court."

I tilted my head to the side. "It is?"

"What are you going to do, sweetheart? Are you going to fight for us, or are you going to run away again?"

I didn't have to think about it. I knew exactly what I wanted. "I want to be with you. I want to fight for us. I want a second chance, one that starts with truths instead of lies. Life instead of death. Love instead of fear."

A huge grin spread across his face. "Thank God," he murmured. Then, his lips crashed against mine.

"Just so you know," he whispered next to my ear, a few minutes later. "I won't let you go again."

"I don't want you to."

I didn't, because Gian was my present, my future. My everything.

It was strange how fate worked. When I had left his club that night with him as my fake fiancé, I was sure I'd lost everything. Little did I know, fate had handed me the key to a new life. A better life. Sure, it might not be perfect, but it was perfect for me.

EPILOGUE

Gian

Six Months Later...

The second I entered the restaurant with my arm around Evie, the air shifted. Without greeting me, the owner barked out orders. The staff shifted into motion. Patrons stirred in their seats. Hushed whispers filled the room. Some people knew of me; others recognized Evie. All eyes were on us.

Her play was an instant hit, and she'd become a Broadway star. The critics raved about her skill and her grace. Good thing she was so talented because I would have ripped out their tongues if they said anything unflattering.

The owner dipped his head. "Mr. Trassato, Miss Jeffers, so nice of both of you to visit us tonight."

I pulled Evangeline closer to me, loving the way her body fit against mine. "Only the best for my girl."

He beamed. "Follow me. I have a special table

289

on the back deck for you where you'll have all the privacy you need."

"Thank you."

Evie eyed me with more than a little suspicion. I had told her I wanted to take her out to celebrate six months of being together, which was only half true.

The minute we settled into our seats, a waiter popped open a bottle of champagne, filled our glasses, and disappeared inside, leaving us alone.

Lanterns dangled from a trellis over our heads and circled our table on the floor. Red and white rose petals were scattered over the white linen tablecloth. Soft music played in the background.

Evie leaned forward, and her emerald green dress gaped at the front, drawing my attention downward. "Hey, eyes up here," she said, snapping her fingers.

"Sorry." I chuckled. "I can't help myself. You look amazing in that dress." She did. It complimented her hair color and her skin, and I really loved the way it showed off those legs of hers.

She flung her arm in a swooping motion. "What's all this, Gian?"

I grinned, fishing my hand into the pocket of my best black suit. "Well, Evangeline, I wanted to make sure everything was perfect this time."

"This time. What do you mean?"

I pulled the white box from my pocket and dropped down onto one knee. Her hand fluttered to her chest. "Gian…what are you doing?"

"Evie, the first time we were engaged, it wasn't real, but everything about it felt right. Since you've agreed to be part of my life again, my mom, Carmela, everyone has been asking me when we're getting engaged for real." I paused, cocking my head to the side. "By the way, my mom told me you ratted us out about the first engagement not being real."

A blush stained her cheeks, and she covered her face with her hands. "I don't know what to say. Your mom can be really intimidating."

I pried them away. "I don't care about that now. I only care that I still can't refer to you as my wife to everyone and anyone who will listen."

I opened the tiny box and held the ring between my thumb and index finger. It was several bands woven together with one princess-cut diamond in the center, holding them together.

"I picked this ring for you because, to me, it symbolized our journey together. It's been twisted and taken a lot of unexpected detours, yet somehow we still ended up together. You're my soul mate and my other half, and I can't imagine anything better than spending the rest of my life with you. Evangeline Jeffers, will you make me the happiest man alive and marry me?"

"Yes. Of course." She wrapped her arms around my neck and showered my face and neck with kisses.

"Wow," I mumbled against her lips. "You're really picking a stroll down the aisle with me over a swim in the Hudson with cement boots?"

She shoved me in the shoulder. "Why do you have to bring up the dumb crap I said at a time like this?"

"Because I love you, and I love our story. It's one of a kind. Exactly like you."

Her eyes softened. "I love you too. Always."

"Forever."

Sneak Peek

KON

THE TRASSATO CRIME FAMILY, Book #2

BY LISA CARDIFF

CHAPTER ONE

Konstantin

"I need a fiancée like a need a fucking bullet in my head." I slammed the shot glass onto the burled walnut countertop.

A toxic combination of loud music and vodka swam through my veins like a drug. Instead of mellowing me out, it only made me angrier. God knew, I should drag my pathetic ass home before I did something to piss off my dad even more, yet I couldn't bring myself to move. So many things were wrong with my life, I didn't know where to start. So I engaged in my favorite pastime as of late—drinking.

No matter how much I drank tonight, I couldn't forget my sister was getting married right now, and she didn't invite one family member. Not me, not Mom, not Dad. Not even an estranged aunt or uncle.

I couldn't blame her. We'd meddled in her life behind the scenes for years. I threatened every boy in our high school who even looked in her direction.

Once she moved to New York, things weren't as simple. Her career took off, and we both had our own shit to deal with. Somehow she'd ended up engaged to a cheating, mealy-mouthed loser.

Granted, we could have handled things differently. We didn't have to set him up to fail; he would have managed that all on his own. However, I didn't regret it for a second. Better I sacrificed our relationship than have Evie waste the rest of her life on her piece of shit ex. But damn, I missed my sister. Although we hadn't spent much time together over the past few years, she'd always been in my thoughts and my heart.

I loved her. She was the one person I could always count on, and she never had a hidden agenda when we spent time together. I couldn't say that about anyone else in my life.

"We've already had this discussion. I'm done talking about it. Take the Trassato chick out a few times. Get to know her." Anatoyli shrugged. "If it works out, then great. If not, tell your dad to go fuck himself. You know he won't make you marry her. I'd be hard pressed to find anyone who despises the concept as much as your dad. He'll come around."

"Then you don't know my dad very well. He's set on this dumbass plan, and nothing's going to change his mind." I lifted my shot glass and pinned the bartender with a glare. I should have asked for the bottle when I walked in an hour ago so I didn't waste his time or mine. "Making money is the Holy Grail to my dad, and he's got it in his head that if I marry Carmela Trassato, it'll solve all of his problems."

"Fine. Roll over like a dog, and do what your dad wants. You let him win every damn time, all because you're too big of a pussy to challenge him." He rubbed a hand down the side of his face, bringing attention to the scar that ran from his temple to his eyebrow. It made him look scary as fuck, but for some reason chicks dug it.

I pulled an envelope from my back pocket and slapped it on the counter. "I should shoot your ass for talking to me like that."

"Yeah, except you won't, because without me, you'd be in the gutter somewhere licking your wounds." He twirled his drink. "I've saved your ass more times than I can count in the past few months."

"Yeah, whatever man." The bartender refilled my glass, and I chugged the clear liquid the minute he turned his back. "I haven't been that bad," I grumbled—although, my denial lacked conviction. Over the last two months, I'd started more bar fights than I could count, fucked more chicks than I could remember, and only my dad's money and connections had kept the police from throwing the book at me.

He threw his hands in the air. "You're fucking self-destructing."

"Yeah, well, that shit's behind me now." I slid the envelope toward him. "I need a favor. I need you to find Carmela Trassato and—"

His eyes narrowed. "I gotta be real honest with you. As much as I love you, I won't trade places with you if that's what you're thinking. I'm way too young to acquire a ball and chain. Don't get me wrong. I've seen some pictures of her, and she's not half bad, but I don't have a death wish. Between your dad and Dominick Trassato, I'd be a dead man walking the minute I touched her."

I tapped the envelope. "Hand deliver this to her. I can take care of the rest."

"Uh huh, and where will I find her? Because there's no way in Hell I'm going to knock on the Trassatos' door. I don't give a shit if her old man is dead. I'm not going there."

"You're going to my sister's wedding."

"Her wedding?"

"Yeah." I popped my knuckles. "It's at some old mansion outside of the city. I'll text you the address."

"No way." He wagged his head. "They'll have security everywhere."

"No one will be guarding the side entrance between 8 and 9."

He cocked one eyebrow. "And how do you know that?"

I kept my gaze steady and my lips firm. "Because I'm that good."

"Fine. I'll do it, but you owe me…again." He glanced at his phone, then scooped it up and stuffed it into the pocket of his too-tight black jeans. He looked like a stupid hipster with his tight shirt, tapered jeans, and straggly beard. "One more thing. If I end up dead, I'll haunt your miserable ass until the day you die."

"I wouldn't expect anything else." I snagged my black hoodie from the back of my chair. "And wear this so no one gets a good look at you."

ACKNOWLEDGEMENTS

I wrote the first two chapters of this book a couple of years ago, but I couldn't figure out what or who Gian would be until some great authors from The Mafia Book Club came up with the idea of a Mafia Anthology. Suddenly, Gian had a purpose, a life, and I couldn't wait to get Evie and Gian out of my brain and onto the computer screen.

Along the way, I had help from some really great people:

Kat, Christine, and Chris for weeding through this book back when it was ugly and unedited.

Felicia A. Sullivan for editing this book and giving me valuable, honest opinions.

All of my relatives. I hope you aren't offended I stole names from our family tree...Trassato, DeAngelo, Angela, Carmela, Helena, Gian, DiTonno.

Limitless Publishing for continuing to support my work.

And of course, to all the readers, bloggers, and reviewers who took the time to read this book. Your support and feedback make all the time staring at my computer screen worthwhile!

ABOUT THE AUTHOR

After spending years practicing law and running a real estate development company with her husband, Lisa decided to pursue her dream of becoming a writer and she must confess that inventing characters is so much more fun than writing contracts and legal briefs. A native of Colorado, she lives with her husband and three children in Denver. When she isn't managing the chaos of raising three children and owning her own business, she can be found reading or writing a book or tinkering in her garden.

Facebook:
https://www.facebook.com/lcardiff11

Twitter:
https://twitter.com/lcardiff_author

Website:
http://lisacardiff.com/

Goodreads:
https://www.goodreads.com/author/show/7692079.
Lisa_Cardiff

www.ingramcontent.com/pod-product-compliance
Lightning Source LLC
Chambersburg PA
CBHW031555240626
47153CB00002B/510